Joss Wood loves books, cof[...] the wild places of Souther[...] She's a wife and a mom t[...] bossed around by two cats [...] cow. After a career in local economic development and business, Joss writes full-time from her home in KwaZulu-Natal, South Africa.

https://josswoodbooks.com

𝕏 x.com/josswoodbooks

f facebook.com/josswoodbooks

instagram.com/josswoodbooks

Also by Joss Wood

Confessions of a Christmasholic

This book is dedicated to my smart and sassy, magical and marvelous, feisty and funny daughter, Tess.

As EE Cummings said, 'You are my sun, my moon, and all of my stars.'

Playlist

Butterflies - Kacey Musgraves ♥
Home for the Summer - Sara Kays ♥
Late Night Talking - Harry Styles ♥
sleeping with my friends - GAYLE ♥
July - Noah Cyrus ♥
Overkill - Holly Humberstone ♥
Risk - Gracie Abrams ♥
Dress - Charlotte Sands ♥
Don't Know - HAIM ♥
Slow It Down - Benson Boone ♥
that way - Tate McRae ♥
Gimmie! Gimmie! Gimmie! - ABBA ♥
Juno - Sabrina Carpenter ♥
Talk talk - Charli xcx ♥
invisible string - Taylor Swift ♥
What A Time - Julia Michaels, Niall Horan ♥
Angel Baby - Troye Sivan ♥
Our Way - Mark Ambor ♥
Wildest Dreams - Taylor Swift ♥
Bed Chem - Sabrina Carpenter ♥
Breakaway - Kelly Clarkson ♥
That Part - Lauren Spencer Smith ♥
This Love - Taylor Swift ♥

Chapter One

Driving her rental car away from the airport, Bea Williams wished she wasn't in a rush to get to Golly's Santorini villa near Oia. It was midday, and the sun was high in the dense blue sky, coating everything in a luminous glow. Despite summer being over, the bougainvillaea, jasmine, and potted geraniums still pulsated with colour, while the lake-smooth turquoise sea shimmered. The Greek sun created sharp contrasts between light and shadow and accentuated the contours of the cliffs and rocky outcrops of the caldera.

Mid-October, when many of the accommodation establishments closed their doors and the owners wiped the sweat from their foreheads and checked their bulging bank accounts, was her favourite time to be on the island.

The sunsets were as vibrant, the sea still warm, but the island, especially the famous, blue-roofed town of Oia, wasn't a portly man's vest bursting its buttons. In October, Oia returned to being part of a community, a place where people lived year-round, where you didn't need to fight your way through the streets because the selfie crowd needed to pose in front of the iconic views of the caldera, or because they *had* to capture the always amazing sunset.

Thank God the island was, for Santorini, relatively empty. Bea didn't know if she could contend with hoards of pushy tourists. The next two weeks were going to be busy. She was organising Golly's joint retirement and seventieth birthday bash while wrestling with a combination of writer's block, imposter syndrome and characters who wouldn't bloody talk to her.

She'd visited Santorini in every season, sometimes several times a year, sometimes to write, sometimes to relax. This island was her second home, the place where she'd banged out the first book in her *Urban Explorers* series, where she'd gathered her courage to show Golly her work, praying her acerbic godmother wouldn't strip ten layers of her skin while she critiqued her work before telling her it was unsaleable.

It *had* been unsaleable, back then, but Golly had made a series of suggestions and Bea had rewritten the book three times. A year later, her super-agent godmother sold the first three books in the series. Bea'd submitted book nine of the series a few weeks back and was currently plotting book ten. Lately, she was as insecure as she'd been as a debut author five years ago, jumpy and jittery and second-guessing herself at every turn.

She couldn't remember when she'd last lost time in front of the keyboard, stumbling out of the story bleary-eyed with cramping fingers, knowing the letters she tossed onto the screen were pure gold. The voices in her head – snatches of conversation between her characters, some in whispers, some shouted – were silent. She no longer saw short video clips of what they were doing or how they were reacting.

Writing, her solace, her joy and her escape felt like dragging stone-heavy feet through peanut butter...

Blup...

Bea cocked her head and hit the volume button to turn down Shaboozey's 'A Bar Song' blasting from the rental car's small speakers. She usually caught the bus from the airport to Oia, with just a rucksack on her back, but this trip to Golly's Folly required a large suitcase and dresses in bags. What *was* that strange noise? Not recognising it, she shrugged, lifted the volume, tapped her fingers against the steering wheel and wished for her own double shot of whisky.

As Bea's professional crisis was ratcheting up, Golly had announced her retirement and told the publishing world she was closing her literary agency. That meant Bea (and the agency's other clients) needed to find alternative representation. She'd been tossing back antacids like chocolate-covered peanuts since first hearing her godma's news.

'I've got more money than God, Bea-darling, and I want to spend it! I want to spend some time at the Hidden Beach Resort, party at Tomorrowland, and drink Ayahuasca in the Orinoco* *basin. I want to read for pleasure, Bea-darling,' if I find the time between learning Spanish and my Pilates and Bikram yoga classes. I also intend to find a lover.'*

The fact that Bea needed to look up the Hidden Beach Resort – it was a luxurious nudist colony on the Mexican Riviera – and refresh her mind about Ayahuasca – the Amazon version of psychedelic 'shrooms – was a little embarrassing. Golly was extremely eccentric, vivacious and super cool. Everything she was …

Not.

Her godmother – actually Golly was her mum's godmother but, thanks to Bea being dropped on her doorstep every holiday since she was six because her mum couldn't be arsed to have her during the summer as per her parents' custodial agreement – lived life at a thousand miles per hour.

While Bea was still trying to take in the soul-sinking news about her retirement, Golly went on to say that she wanted her seventieth birthday and retirement bash to be on the Greek island of Santorini, at her villa on the outskirts of Oia.

Golly was a stalwart of the London and New York literary and art scenes and had a vast network of contacts all over the world. She wanted everyone she worked with: editors and authors – *friends* and *foes, Bea-darling!* – to attend. It took Bea a week to whittle the thousand-plus guest list down to two fifty, with Golly kicking, shouting and pouting while they argued about whether a lover she'd

ONE BED

JOSS WOOD

One More Chapter

a division of HarperCollins*Publishers* Ltd

1 London Bridge Street

London SE1 9GF

www.harpercollins.co.uk

HarperCollins*Publishers*

Macken House, 39/40 Mayor Street Upper,

Dublin 1, D01 C9W8, Ireland

This paperback edition 2025

1

First published in Great Britain in ebook format

by HarperCollins*Publishers* 2024

Copyright © Joss Wood 2024

Joss Wood asserts the moral right to be identified

as the author of this work

A catalogue record of this book is available from the British Library

ISBN: 978-0-00-870236-6

Printed and bound in the UK using 100% Renewable Electricity by CPI Group (UK) Ltd had in her forties warranted an invitation. Or her beauty therapist or her new hairdresser.

Golly didn't see the point of holding a small party. She wanted a crowd, dammit, so she could be the belle of the ball and be painted with adulation, buoyed by blandishments. Bea thought she was being a tad optimistic believing everyone thought she was wonderful. Golly'd had numerous lovers, had broken up a marriage or two – *I didn't cheat, Bea-darling, they did*! – and was once a powerful editor in publishing before establishing the G&T Literary Agency, a play on her initials and her favourite drink. It started out small and exclusive, and stayed *very* exclusive. The agents she employed looked after the interests of many well-known and mid-list authors, but Golly repped a couple of New York Times bestsellers, a Booker Prize winner, and the publicity-shy Parker Kane, an author *Library Journal* had called 'an exceptional, exciting talent'.

Bea tuned back into her music and hit the button to drop the window open and allow the fresh, herb-scented air to stroke her cheeks and mess up her hair. It wasn't a bad way to spend a Sunday.

Golly was her anchor, her true north. She was the font of irreverent wisdom, the kick up her butt, the Doric columns holding up her world. The only person she trusted to be there for her. Bea had friends, but she kept them at arm's length, never allowing them to get too close; and thanks to her mum and her ex hooking up, Bea rarely dated. What was the point when she was terrified of being hurt and being disappointed again? But she'd allowed Golly behind her mile-high wall. Her life would be paint-dryingly boring without that tiny, cigarillo-smoking, alcohol-swilling, filter-lacking loudmouth, the person who invented the concept of giving no fucks, in her life.

Golly's house had always been where Bea escaped to when life with her dad became too overwhelming, the only place she could be a kid. Golly had scooped her up after her father died when she was sixteen, becoming her mentor, aunt, grandmother and best friend all rolled into one. And as her literary agent, Golly was the only person (apart from Reena, Golly's oldest friend) who knew that Bea was Parker Kane, the author of the surprisingly successful *Urban Explorers* series for pre-teens. Golly – confident, loud, gregarious and generous – was whom Bea strived, with little success, to be.

When she'd dropped the news of her retirement – without the gravity it deserved – Golly had asked Bea to help with two things: one easy, one bitterly hard.

'I'm combining my seventieth birthday with my retirement, and I need you to organise everything, Bea-darling. I'm saying goodbye to my old life as a literary doyenne, so I want a blowout, raise-the-roof, fuck-with-everyone's-head party. Can you organise that for me?'

With the help of an event planner, that part was easy peasy.

Her second request was more difficult.

'You also need to think about how my retirement affects you, Bea. Currently, I'm the shield between you and the world, and

you need to figure out what you are going to do. I'd like you to step out from behind your pseudonym. I can't force you to do that, but, if you still want to hide, then you need a new agent. How do we get you one without revealing who you are?'

It was a conundrum and one that made Bea's head ache. She was no closer to an answer than she was when she'd first heard Golly's news. What nobody, not even Golly, understood was that she and Parker Kane were two different entities. The Parker Kane who replied to reader's letters and bantered with her fans on social media was hip and switched-on; a little glam, a lot confident; someone cosmopolitan and creative, who knew how to use words like 'yeet' and 'sus' and 'flex' and didn't have to look them up on Urban Dictionary. Parker was on the ball, confident, funny, and smart.

Parker Kane was the protective barrier between Bea and the world, a way to shield herself from the criticisms of reviewers and readers, and the fluctuations of an industry that could, on some occasions, be brutal. Bea, the person she was away from her computer, was plagued by self-doubt, someone who found it difficult to trust herself, someone who occasionally, despite some success, often felt lost, and overwhelmed. She could blame her useless parents for her F'd-up mindset.

And she did.

Her parents couldn't have been more different, and despite racking her brain, Bea failed to comprehend how polar opposites had come together to produce a child. Lou, her mum, was loud, vain, narcissistic, selfish and ambitious.

Her dad had been, up until his death fifteen years ago, spineless, ineffectual, a classic victim who believed the world was against him.

They'd never married, nor lived together, and Bea only saw Lou a few times a year. Her father, a twig on some aristocratic branch, had lived off a family trust and royalties and was, on paper, her primary parent.

Like Bea, he'd been a children's author, but also an illustrator. He'd had little time for children, though, and hated being bothered by them. It was lucky for her – was it luck or a means of survival? – that she'd been the adult-iest child ever. Bea couldn't remember a time when she didn't feel like he was the child and she the person holding it all together. She always felt grown up, loved being praised for being a mature and responsible child and she withered under criticism.

At ten, she'd cooked their meals, at twelve she'd paid the household bills and kept an eye on her dad's finances. And the more she did for him, the more he relied on her. She'd been addicted to his infrequent validation, and all her wheels fell off when he criticised her. To avoid any censure, Bea did everything in her power to avoid making a mistake. Two decades later, she still never went anywhere without doing a week's worth of research, and never argued a point unless she had salient facts to back her up.

In her early twenties, Bea had met Gerry, and within weeks she was living with the aspiring musician and immediately became his caregiver and solver of his problems. It took her five years, numerous infidelities on his part, and the threat of physical violence for her to realise she was reliving her childhood, prepared to move mountains because he'd occasionally, usually when he wanted something, told her he loved her.

When Golly sold her *Urban Explorers* series, Bea's constant second-guessing of herself – oh, and her mum's public hook-up with Gerry, but that was another story – led her to publish under a pseudonym, hiding her true identity and avoiding the vulnerability of public criticism and scrutiny.

And yes, she knew she'd recreated her missed childhood through her books, she'd figured that much out! And yes, Parker Kane was her alter-ego, but she was someone who lived outside of her, *apart* from her. Parker was someone that Bea – who spent far too many hours on her arse mainlining coffee, and the bulk of her time alone, who constantly second-guessed herself – wasn't.

Bea rolled her shoulders, frustrated by what she was – scared, uncertain, a little lonely – and what she wasn't – brave, outspoken, confident.

She turned up the volume to maximum, hoping to drown out her thoughts. She'd start thinking about herself and her future when her two-week working holiday was over.

But she'd probs find another excuse not to confront the PK question – revisions, deadlines, plotting her next series – when she got back to London. It wasn't something she could put off forever.

Next week. She'd think about her future as Parker Kane,

a future without Golly steering her, next week. Or maybe the week after.

Blup, blup, blup…

The steering wheel started to vibrate under her hands and Bea noticed the flashing light on the dashboard. She steered the car off the road into a lay-by and switched off the engine, placing her forehead on the steering wheel as spiteful trolls excavated her brain with pickaxes. Since hearing Golly's retirement news four weeks ago, her headache was her most faithful companion, the result of far too much stress and way too little sleep.

She'd asked Golly if she'd continue to represent just her, selling it as a way for Golly to keep her hand in, to stay connected to the world of publishing. Golly'd immediately seen through her ruse, told her she was a manipulative baggage, and refused. Golly wanted to be free, to not have to worry about anyone or anything book-related, and that *'includes, Bea-darling, you!'*.

Golly'd made up her mind and there was no changing it. She was determined to enjoy the golden years of her life, vowing to fly into old age with a huge smile on her face, yelling like a banshee.

Nuts. She was nuts. Batshit crazy.

But, God, Bea loved her.

There'll be lots of drinking and lots of dancing at my party, Bea-darling! We can let our hair down and have some fun, in bed and out.

She'd rather not think about Golly's bed-based antics, and Bea wasn't a one-night-stand type of girl. Truthfully, she was more of a got-my-heart-smashed-and-now-I'm-done type of girl. She'd only had two lovers before she met Gerry, and, unfortunately, sex with her ex wasn't anything like romance novels described – it had been messy, quick and a little boring. Genuinely, she did not understand why sex sold. But it did, and many authors made gang cash by writing dark, sexy romances and erotica.

She pushed her sunglasses up into her thick, dark brown hair—Golly called it walnut brown, Bea called it boring – and opened the door to step out onto the gravel area of the lay-by. To her left was Oia, with its distinct blue-domed churches and blindingly white buildings. She had a one-eighty view of the entire caldera, the lava islands at its centre, the island of Thirasia in the distance and the sea a shade of blue she called Santorini Stunning. On the other side of the island were the famous beaches, Red Beach and Kamari, as well as her favourite, Baxedes Beach, popular amongst locals because of its seclusion, white sand and shallow waters. She hoped to have time to visit them this trip, but she had the next book to plot and a spin-off series to plan. She wanted to get that down before the revisions came in for book nine, but she was expecting, hoping, they would be light.

She also had to make sure Golly's party would be a classy success.

She'd learnt the hard way that if she didn't keep an eye on her godmother, there was every possibility this coming weekend would turn into a bacchanalian feast.

Bea placed her hands on her hips and scowled at her car.

She couldn't see any steam or smoke drifting out from underneath the bonnet, so that was a plus. Maybe. She walked around the car, the hem of her brown-and-white patterned dress swirling around her calves. She kicked the back left tyre with the toe of her flat sandal, it looked fine. But the front left tyre was not. It sagged into the gravel, looking sad and sorry for itself. Damn, she'd picked up a puncture...

And changing a tyre wasn't a life skill Bea possessed. She was a writer, someone who used words, and her arms were day-old noodles strong. Now Pip, the enterprising and practical twelve-year-old ringleader of the motley bunch of underprivileged miscreants who were the stars of Bea's books, would whip out tools and would know where to find the spare wheel.

It's in the boot, dummy...

It was the first time she'd heard his voice in a while, and she smiled. Was he back for good? God, she hoped so. 'Pipe down, squirt.'

So what was she going to do? There was nobody at the villa who could help her, so she'd have to call the rental company or get a mechanic out from Fira. Bea was about to reach for her phone, when she heard the low-pitched rumble of a deep-throated engine. Over the roof of her car, she watched a roof-and-doorless Jeep pull up to a stop behind her. A big man with aviator glasses and windblown hair sat behind the wheel. A bright blue canoe rested on the passenger seat behind him.

She watched as he climbed out of the Jeep and her

eyebrows shot up when the unfamiliar hum of attraction vibrated up and down her spine. So … *wow*. He was tall, he had the best part of a foot on her five-four and he was, holy hell, ripped. Instead of helping her to change the flat tyre, Bea was pretty sure he could just pick up her car and walk it to Golly's villa.

His loose, long-legged stride quickly covered the space between them. The breeze coming off the ocean played with his wavy hair skimming the collar of his shirt, a deep, rich shade of old gold.

His nose was long and a little hooked, and his face was all angles and planes.

Sexy in a diabolical way, the love child of Jimmy Dean and Clint Eastwood. She couldn't pull her eyes off him, partly because he was how she imagined her fictional Pip would look like when he was all grown up. If this guy had light, silver-blue eyes, like Pip, her knees might buckle. They were halfway to doing that already. She mentally urged him to remove his glasses, but they stayed on his face. *Dammit.*

Capable, masculine, a little hard, a lot streetwise. Instinctively she knew he didn't take crap, not from anyone, anywhere.

He was dressed in tailored shorts and a linen shirt, sleeves rolled back to reveal his strong forearms. He'd only buttoned three of his four shirt buttons, and, thanks to the wind, she caught glimpses of his Canada-wide chest and ridged stomach. Expensive leather flip flops covered his big, so big, feet.

Confident, charismatic and oh-so-cool…

'Do you need some help changing your flat?' he asked in a chocolate-over-rough-stone voice. His accent was American, but fairly generic. It did, however, hold a tiny hint of Southern drawl.

'Uh … that would be amazing,' she replied, not looking a gift horse, or a knowledgeable guy, in the mouth. 'What I know about cars is dangerous. I don't drive that often, I'm a take-the-Tube girl.'

He lifted his chin, silently acknowledging her babbling reply. 'I'm London born and bred,' she continued, wishing she could slap duct tape across her mouth. God, she was so bad at flirting. It was his turn to say something, *anything*.

He didn't.

'Are you on a canoeing holiday?' she asked, nodding to the canoe in the back of his Jeep. She looked at the lake-flat sea.

'That's a kayak.'

Wasn't that what she said?

'Technically, you kneel in a canoe, and use a one-sided paddle. You sit in a kayak and use a double-sided paddle,' he explained, catching her confusion.

'Oh, right.' Both activities sounded tiring and something that required a lot of energy. And upper body strength. She far preferred to lie on the beach reading a book, taking the occasional dip to cool off. She was adventure-averse, but her characters made up for her lack of skills. Pip was incredible on his skateboard and Jemima had amazing parkour skills. Hettie, her big-brained nerd,

One Bed

could pick any lock anywhere, Gus was a street fighter and Bas a fearless hacker. None of her imaginary friends were scared to wade into dangerous situations. Bea wondered how she could get them to use a kayak/canoe in an urban environment. On an underground river, on a lake? On the Serpentine?

She waited for more and when he didn't elaborate, she jumped in. *Again.* 'Did you hire it in Fira?'

He didn't answer her but nodded to her car. 'Do you want to pop the trunk?'

Pop the *trunk*? Right, he was asking her to open the boot. Bea ducked into the car, found the lever and before she could straighten up, or give him a warning, Big and Beautiful lifted the hatchback's door. Her overly full toiletry bag—only half closed because she'd grabbed the bottle of aspirin from it earlier—tumbled to the ground and burst open. A packet of anti-diarrhoea pills landed on his foot and a couple of tampons escaped their box and hit his bare toes. Cream and applicators to treat thrush completed her trifecta of embarrassment.

She hurried forward to gather her possessions and yelped as her bunny-ears vibrator fell to the gravelled road. Bea watched in horror as a big, broad hand snatched it out of thin air. Dark eyebrows rose and the side of his sexy, mobile mouth lifted in amusement. She waited for a snarky, sleazy comment, but it didn't come. Instead, he swiftly gathered her items, shoved them into her toiletry bag and handed it and the vibrator to her, his expression equanimous.

'Thank you,' Bea mumbled, flames eating her face. And thanks bunches for not being a sleazy prick.

She pushed everything into the bag so she could close the zip. Her rescuer gestured to her large suitcase and the stuffed-with-dresses clothes bag. 'I need to move these to get to the spare wheel and the tools.'

'The suitcase can sit on the road, and I'll put the clothes bag on the back seat,' Bea said. He lifted her heavy bag like it was full of cotton wool – she'd needed both hands and to bend her knees to lift it into the rental car – and placed it on the road. He draped the clothes bag over her arm and lifted the carpet in the boot. And there sat a lovely, new-looking spare.

Excellent. She'd be on the road in no time.

Bea put the clothes and toiletry bag on the back seat and returned to watch her rescuer position a jack under the car. 'Can I do anything to help?' she asked.

He looked up at her, and Bea noticed a few silver hairs at his temples, glinting in the sun. She wished she could see his eyes. 'Do you know how to change a flat?' he said.

'That would be a solid no.'

'It'll probably be quicker if I do it myself.'

In minutes he had the tyre off, the new tyre on and had tightened the bolts. He put the car back on its four wheels and Bea looked at her watch. OK, she had no idea how long it took to change a tyre, but she sensed he'd made short work of the task. She was impressed.

Gerry had found it difficult to put fuel in the car. Found it even harder to pay for it.

The spare went back into the car, along with the cross-like spanner thing and the yellow jack. He replaced the carpet and easily lifted her heavy suitcase back into the boot. 'There's space for your toiletry bag and the clothes bag now,' he told her.

She shook her head. 'No, I'll leave them where they are, I don't have far to go.' She held out her hand. 'I'm so grateful you stopped. I have so much to do today, and you saved me a lot of time.'

His hand engulfed hers and tingles shot up her arm as baby fireworks erupted on her skin. It had to be because he was so roughly handsome, so big, the most masculine man she'd ever met. And the fact that he could sort out her car with ease added another layer to her attraction. 'You're obviously good with your hands.'

When he grinned, she realised she'd spoken out aloud. 'So I've been told,' he drawled.

She blushed, and dropped her eyes, cursing her bright cheeks and the splotches blooming on her chest and neck. Well, *obviously*. He was in his mid-to-late thirties, gorgeous, and if he hadn't picked up some bedroom skills, she'd be disappointed. How would his hands feel on her skin? Would he taste as good as he looked, and could his rough-looking stubble be softer than it appeared?

Right, *definitely* time to move on. 'I'd offer to pay you, but I have no cash on me,' she told him. *Why are you reacting like this, Bea? He's waaaayyyy out of your league!*

'I wouldn't take it, so don't worry about it,' he said,

shutting the back door to her hatchback. 'I hope the rest of your trip is drama-free.'

Since she was dealing with Golly, she had zero chance of that happening, so she smiled and nodded. He strode to his Jeep, climbed in and started it up. After pulling on his seatbelt, he looked at her again, smiled and lifted his hand.

And with that, he was gone. And she'd never see him again.

Chapter Two

Gibson Caddell glanced in his rearview mirror, watching as the wind plastered her white and brown patterned dress to her shapely body. Puncture Girl was tiny, five-three or five-four, she didn't even reach his shoulder, but she was a sexy woman. A casual glance would peg her in her mid-twenties, but the fine laughter lines at the corner of her amazing eyes – were they blue or grey? – made him revise his estimate upward, putting her in her early thirties.

She disappeared from view as he rounded the corner and Gib shoved his shades into his hair to rub one eye, then the other, trying to ignore the flash of lust, the punch of want. Was that what sexual attraction felt like? It had been so long, he'd forgotten. When was the last time he had sex? Six months ago? He rolled back through his memories and realised it was closer to a year.

Fuck me.

Or, to be accurate, no fuck me. And, if anyone needed him to, he could testify that solo sex didn't make you go blind.

Dating himself was all he had time for this past year. As the CEO of Caddell International, the production company his father and uncle had established that now included a worldwide talent agency, an event company, a PR consultancy firm and a music label, he had a million balls in the air. He'd just come off a four-day conference on AI and, before that, he'd spent two weeks in company seminars, one in London, one in New York. He was peopled out.

All he wanted to do for the next two weeks was spend time on the water in the kayak, drink the odd beer and read the odd book. Binge-watch a series. Contemplate his navel.

What he didn't want to do was to talk to anybody. About *anything*.

As the new face of Caddell International, he'd stood in the limelight for the past year and had batted away questions about his love life, his past, his parents' deaths when he was sixteen, where he intended to take the company and how far. He happily answered questions about Caddell International, but ignored any about his personal life. His being an orphan (and his guilt), and whether he was in a relationship (not on the cards) had no bearing on how he did his job.

He was super sensitive – *thanks, Mom!* – to any invasion of his privacy and personal questions made him feel defensive and uneasy. And after a year of non-stop curiosity about how he lived his life, and who was in it, he was stick-a-fork-in-him *done*. He badly needed time out, and hiring the cottage on Golly's Santorini estate was his way to get the quiet he needed.

He was so burned out that even talking to Puncture Girl had been an effort. The only people he could stand to be around were Navy and Navy's dad, Hugh. But Navy had his hands full with his agency and his author clients, and Hugh, now Chairman of the Board of Caddell International, was covering for Gib as he took some much-needed time out.

Life would've been easier for him if Navy was still with the company, but both he and Hugh knew Navy would one day jump ship to follow his lifelong dream of working in the publishing industry. While Gib loved the cut and thrust, the high-octane lifestyle of running a massive international company, Navy did not. It was Hugh – smart and supportive – who'd pushed his son into following his dream, who gave Navy permission to walk away from the company that Hugh and his brother, Gib's father, established and Hugh built and grew.

Gib'd met Golly at The Ivy in London. He'd been keeping Navy company while he was waiting for Golly to arrive for their lunch meeting. She wore an aqua sheath with an acid-yellow half jacket, biker boots and carried an unlit cigarillo. Her fingers ended in inch-long, vampire-red nails and her accent was Upper West Side arty. Her attitude was pure Brooklyn street fighter.

After a drink at the bar, a G&T that was heavy on gin and light on tonic, she demanded Gib join her and Navy for lunch. He agreed, and she reminded him they'd met before, when he and his dad had stayed at her villa when he was … what? Eleven? His father's best friend was a friend of Golly's, and he and his partner had joined them for a holiday on Santorini, where they'd stayed in the villa's cottage while Gib and his dad had slept in the main house.

Memories, warm and comforting, rolled over him. It had been the best summer of his life, the best *time* of his life, six weeks of pure fun. His mom hadn't joined them, he couldn't remember why not, so he'd been free of her never-ending, intrusive conversation and he'd run wild. Without his mom's scrutiny and intensity, his father relaxed and let him *be*, and those were his best memories of his dad. The only fly in the ointment of that summer having to share a bedroom with a solemn, far-too-serious kid. A *girl*.

After that holiday, his father immersed himself in establishing Caddell and he rarely saw him. When he did, he was exhausted and stressed, and there were many nights when he never made it home at all.

That meant there had been no one to deflect the spotlight off him.

During lunch, Golly went on to quiz Navy about his literary agency. During their rapid back and forth, Gib discovered she was retiring and was sussing out literary agents for her special clients. Navy diplomatically asked her whether an author – Patrick, no Parker … Kane? – would consider signing with him when Golly retired.

'I have no idea what she intends to do, the stubborn girl!' Golly had said. 'But I have a list of recommendations.'

'Am I on that list?' Navy asked, far too eagerly. Gib'd wanted to smack the back of his cousin's head and tell him to play it cool. While Gib had the reputation of being imperturbable and nerveless, unreadable, Navy was an open book.

Golly'd narrowed her heavy, kohl-lined eyes. 'Maybe, but you are new to the game. I know the other agents, but I don't know you.'

'What can I do to change that?' Navy demanded.

Golly ummed and ahhed but trying to get an answer out of her was equivalent to stapling slime to a wall. She told Navy she'd consider him, but Gib wasn't convinced. When they moved on to discussing her retirement bash and her home on Santorini, she invited them to attend. Navy had another commitment, but the thought of a Greek island break appealed to Gib. There was no way he could recapture the halcyon days of his childhood, but if he could sharpen those memories by being back on the island, he'd consider that a win.

Unfortunately, the only time he could take for a vacation coincided with Golly's birthday bash, but he had no intention of attending. He did, however, ask for a recommendation on where he should stay on the island. Golly tipped her head to the side, smiled and insisted her cottage was his for however long he wanted it. He countered her offer by offering to hire it, and she'd eventually agreed.

By the end of that day, he had her bank account number and secured the cottage for two weeks. His paying to hire the place made it a business transaction and he didn't feel obligated to attend her retirement/birthday bash. It was this coming Saturday, and he already knew wild horses nor gun-toting aliens would drag him there.

Gib was sorry that Navy couldn't make Golly's bash, where he assumed he'd have the opportunity to meet a few of Golly's author clients. *If you come away with nothing else, Gib, make sure you get me an introduction to Parker Kane.*

Navy wanted Parker Kane, and if Gib could give his cousin and best friend what he wanted, he would. Navy had opened his life, home and heart to Gib in those horrible weeks after his folks died. Although Hugh's house was a five-bedroomed mansion, Navy rearranged his bedroom so that they could fit another double bed into his room, so that Gib wouldn't be alone at night. Navy quickly became his best friend and brother, and Gib was still grateful he didn't have any issues about sharing his father, or his extensive group of friends, with him.

Gib pushed his hand through his hair and checked his satnav, realising he was almost at Golly Trent's villa. The cottage he'd rented was, according to the pictures Golly sent him, a small, one-bedroomed guesthouse set in the olive grove behind the villa. It looked fine to him, he didn't need anything luxurious.

The island wasn't big, he had this hire car to get to the many beaches so he could kayak and swim, a rare treat. The sun was shining, the air was rich, fragrant and warm, and he was looking forward to his break, to being by himself, desperately needing some time to wind down. The only other thing he'd like was sex...

But unless he paid for it – something he wasn't prepared to do – sex required some sort of interaction and he was too, excuse the pun, fucking tired to summon up the energy.

Gib gripped the wheel and kept his eyes on the road. It had been a while – too long. But as the new CEO of what Fortune called *'one of the most exciting privately owned companies in the world'* work had been crazy and, after fourteen-hour days, he only had enough energy to go for a run or to the gym, eat and then pass out face down on his California King, whether it was in his apartment in New York, the company flat in London or his home in Nashville.

They said there was more to life than work. Maybe one day he'd figure out what that was.

As Bea turned off the road to Golly's Folly, her shoulders dropped and the tension in her neck eased. She'd been coming to this island since she was a little girl, and the air always tasted sweeter here, the load on her back lighter and her lungs looser. It didn't hurt that the house was surrounded by riotous swathes of multi-coloured bougainvillaea. Golly's mini-estate, like the island, was a testament to tranquillity, a place where the world slowed down.

But Bea wouldn't be able to enjoy the slow pace because she had so much to do to ensure Golly's party was a success. Yet, now that she was here, the task didn't seem as overwhelming. She ran through her mental checklist for the next few hours. She had a guy from Fira coming later to string the lights across the courtyard in preparation for the party on Saturday night. Or was that tomorrow? She needed to check. But sitting down with the event planner, Cassie, was imperative because she needed to check whether Golly had sabotaged any of their plans.

Bea'd come into the party planning process later than she'd liked – deadlines for copy edits for book eight meant she'd missed the first two meetings with Cassie – but listened in horror to Golly's idea of how to entertain her guests. Because Golly had more money than God and morally dodgy taste, Bea had quickly vetoed her suggestions of nude girls mud wrestling and a pie-eating contest. Bea also nixed the naked trapeze artists and the male strippers. She would not have the weekend marred by tacky decorations, badly behaved guests or less than brilliant service. Golly was over the top and a free spirit, but she still deserved a classy event.

If Golly wanted to end her fifty-year career with a bang, then it would be a classy bang, dammit!

'Actually, stepping into my new life with a bang would be the perfect transition, Bea-darling.'

But Golly had managed to talk her into having appropriately clad fire-eaters at the party, as well as belly dancers. Exhausted, Bea had agreed. They'd serve coffee and hot croissants at five in the morning and the party would end, officially, at sunrise. And Golly, and more than a few of her guests, would be there 'til the end. A few of Golly's close friends would then spend the next week on Santorini recovering, lying on the beach and exploring.

Bea lifted her water bottle to her lips, gagging at the car-warm temperature of its contents. It was noon, but she had no doubt Golly would be onto her third G&T by now. When in Greece, daytime drinking became morning drinking, and sometimes it was simply carry-on-from-the-night-before drinking. Golly's liver was indestructible. Bea wondered if they'd had any last-minute RSVPs. And if her mum would rock up. She hadn't been invited, but Lou wouldn't let a pesky detail like that stop her. God, Bea hoped her mother had something, or someone, better to do.

Lou's hooking up with Gerry after he and Bea had split was, and always would be, unforgivable. Telling the world about it in her wildly popular, frequently salacious, weekly tabloid newspaper column was worse. What on earth had Bea done in her previous life to rate such crappy parents?

Dropping her window open, Bea waited for her first view of the house, with its many windows and intricate wrought-iron balconies. The style of the house was Spanish-adjacent, with a touch of English Victoriana, and had nothing in common with the blindingly white Cycladic architecture on the rest of the island. The roof of the double-storey mansion was laid with terracotta tiles, perfectly complementing the warm stone building below. A sculpture fountain, a twin to the one in the courtyard, sat in the middle of the circular driveway. Guests were expected to park on the gravel area to the side of the house. Being the first visitor here, she'd nab the spot under the branches of the old olive tree and keep the rental car in the shade. She swung left and frowned when she saw the yellow Jeep parked in her usual spot.

What the hell was the guy who fixed her puncture doing here? And, more importantly, who was he? The villa only had five bedrooms: Golly had one room, and Reena, Golly's oldest friend, the other. The Farrow twins, Jack and Jacqui – she rolled her eyes, what were their parents thinking? – were old friends of Golly's, and her favourite interior decorator and art dealer. They would use bedrooms three and four. The last room was allocated to Cassie and her wife. As event manager and caterer, they needed to be on-site.

And Bea'd called dibs on the one-bedroom guest cottage. It was where she always stayed when she was on the island, it was her bolthole and her refuge.

Of course, the kayaker could simply be visiting, but who was he here to see?

Bea parked, switched off the ignition and released her seatbelt. Leaving her bag and phone behind, she exited the car and slammed the door. Pushing her hand into her hair, she hit a snag. Grimacing, she ducked down to look in the side mirror and sighed. Yep, her hair definitely needed a brush. Admittedly, she looked a lot better than she usually did – she normally had the corpse-at-a-computer look nailed – but she'd never be as glamorous as Golly, as impeccably stylish as her mother or as hipster cool as Gerry.

At her best, she was pretty, but more girl-next-door than gorgeous.

And, damn, she had mascara dots under her eyes, and she desperately needed some lipstick. And how was it that the freckles on her nose and cheeks seemed darker and denser in the few hours since she left London? Did they sense the Greek sun and decide to pop out for some superstrength Vitamin D?

'*Bea-darling*!'

Bea stood up so fast she spun around and wobbled. She placed her hand on the roof of her hatchback, resting it there until the ground settled under her feet, and grinned at the sight of Golly and her oldest friend Reena hurrying towards her. Unsurprisingly, Golly had a cigarillo in one hand and a large, icy G&T in the other. Her hair was newly dyed, a shade Bea could only call bordello pink.

'What the hell took you so long, Bea-darling?' Golly demanded, in her thirty-a-day rasp.

'I'm here! Finally!'

She flung her arms around Golly, placed her cheek against hers and rocked her from side to side while Golly patted her back with one hand and held her G&T steady with the other. Cigarillo smoke and Chanel No 5; it was the smell of Bea's childhood, of safety, of *home*.

'It's so bloody lovely to see you, Bea-darling.'

Bea smiled. She'd last seen Golly ten days ago in London and had spoken to her several times a day since, but Golly always greeted her as if they'd been separated for months, if not years. Bea stepped back from her to greet

Reena, who'd only tolerate a quick buzz on her wrinkled cheek.

Reena's steel-grey eyes were overshadowed by strong, bushy black-and-white eyebrows. Her snow-white hair was cut close to her head, mostly because she couldn't be arsed to brush her hair every day. She wore her usual outfit of a polo shirt over jodhpurs and riding boots.

Reena smelt of hay, horse and summer. 'Have you just come in from a ride?' Bea asked.

'I went to a neighbouring farm and exercised their nags for them. There's no one to ride them and they are getting fat and lazy.'

Bea helped herself to a sip of Golly's G&T, her eyes widening. There couldn't be more than a splash of tonic in her glass. 'Has the electrician arrived?' she asked, darting another look at the Jeep.

Reena answered her. 'It's Sunday, Bea. He said he'd be here either Wednesday or Thursday.'

That wasn't an issue because the lights only needed to be up by the next weekend. They had plenty of time. 'OK, not a problem.'

Golly looked at Reena, who shook her head, seemingly unmoved by her beseeching expression. 'No, *you* invited them, I had nothing to do with it. If you want lights, you tell her.'

Invited who? Tell her what? 'What have you done?' Bea asked Golly, narrowing her eyes.

Golly's eyes slithered away, a sure sign that she knew she was skating on thin ice. Then she attempted to look innocent, and Bea winced. Oh, this was going to be bad. 'I've invited some people around for a cocktail party Tuesday night … you know, just the early arrivals. I would like the lights up before then.'

Bea looked at Reena, who lifted her hands in resignation. 'Not my idea.'

Bea'd hoped for a few quiet nights to gather her energy, to soak in the calming atmosphere of the island, to pull herself towards herself. 'How many people did you invite?' she asked through gritted teeth.

Golly hummed, a sure sign she was about to lie. 'I'm not quite sure… Ten? Twenty?'

Bea knew her well enough to know the number would be, at least, double that. 'Be a dear and organise some more champagne and canapés, Bea-darling.' Golly's request was accompanied by a charming smile. 'I want to have it on the esplanade, but it would be lovely to have the lights up in the courtyard.'

Sure. Now where did she leave her wand? She could argue, but nothing she said would change Golly's mind. Bea bit the inside of her lip, thinking hard. What Golly called the esplanade was a long, open, level area a little way from the house, overlooking Oia and the caldera. A waist-high low concrete wall stopped guests from tumbling down the hill, and a vine-covered pergola stood over the outside bar, pizza oven and outdoor kitchen. The 'esplanade' had the best views of the caldera on the property. It was the perfect place for a cocktail party on a warm summer or still warm autumn evening.

Champagne was easy enough to source, but getting someone to provide canapés for forty would be tricky. Did Golly think she was a miracle worker? Honestly, she was impossible!

'I need to speak to Cass,' Bea said, pushing her hair behind her ears. She could walk to the villa and find her, but calling her was quicker. While she waited for Cass to answer, she poked two fingers at her eyes, and then pointed them at her godmother. Golly just grinned, unrepentant.

She darted a glance at the Jeep, her curiosity growing. Who was he and what was he doing here?

Cass answered and, because this wasn't the first time they'd spoken today, didn't bother with a greeting.

'What does Golly want this time?' she asked, in her always cheerful tone. Cass was a 'can do' person, and very little fazed her. Thank God, because Golly changed her mind often, and arranging her birthday/retirement weekend was like trying to wrestle a twelve-legged octopus. 'A merry-go-round? A Mexican death ritual? The merry-go-round *might* be a possibility, the death ritual difficult.'

Bea laughed. 'Neither. She's hosting a cocktail party and wants champagne and canapés on the esplanade at sunset.'

'Tonight?' Cass squeaked.

'No, Tuesday night,' Bea hastily assured her.

'Oh, that's doable,' Cass replied, sounding relieved. 'But I saw her an hour ago, why didn't she ask me then?'

Bea relayed the question to Golly.

Golly shrugged. 'I only started making calls about twenty minutes ago.'

Good God. 'Number of guests, Bea?' Cass asked, ridiculously calm.

'No idea. She mentioned twenty, but it could be a lot more.'

Cass was silent for a minute. 'Nadia can whip up a selection of simple canapés. I ordered tons of champagne on consignment, we can spare a few cases. There's enough liquor to float several battleships. If Golly can keep it to under forty, it shouldn't be a problem.'

Nadia was Cass's wife, and together they could pull purple-spotted rabbits out of hats.

'I'll tell her. And have I told you how unbelievably amazing you are and that I am going to organise a fat bonus for you when we're done?'

Cass laughed. 'I *am* amazing and I'm going to hold you to that bonus. This assignment has been a ... challenge.'

Diplomatic Cass. 'It's been a raging headache and a full-on pain in the arse!' Bea corrected her, scowling at Golly. Golly didn't even look remotely chastised.

'By the way, I've arrived at the villa, and I'll wander up to say hello later.' Bea disconnected and pointed her phone at Golly. 'Keep it to under forty guests.'

Golly blew her a kiss, not for a milli-second doubting that she'd get her way. Oh, to be that confident and assured. Bea rolled her head, trying to work the knots out of her neck. She'd wanted to spend a little time working this afternoon – if she could get the bare bones of the new series arc down she'd feel a little more in control – but now she had to help Cass prepare for Golly's spur-of-the-moment soiree.

Not being at her laptop for a few days, even for a few weeks, wouldn't stop the world from turning. She was always several weeks, sometimes months ahead of her deadline but she hated not working, taking time off. It made her feel like a slacker, like she wasn't professional and that she wasn't taking her job seriously.

She was and she did, but doubts hid in dark corners waiting to ambush her.

When would she feel like she'd made it, when would she stop feeling like a fraud? Was it at fifteen books? Twenty? Fifty? When would she feel like she wasn't some imposter calling herself a writer? Would there ever come a time when she emailed off her first draft and didn't immediately wish she hadn't, that she'd taken the time to read it over once more, and make some changes? When would she feel confident in her talent? Would she ever stop second-guessing herself?

Bea rubbed the back of her neck and pushed her hair behind her ears. It was time to get her luggage into the cottage, so she opened the back passenger door and handed Reena her clothes bag and Golly her toiletry bag. She still had to ask about the owner of the Jeep and why he was here.

But first things first. 'Have you had any more RSVPs for the weekend?'

A lot of people had replied to Golly directly instead of

using the email on the invitation, and Bea knew the final count could be somewhere between 150 and 220 people.

'No idea. Reen?' Golly asked. Her glass wobbled, sloshing liquid over her hand. Golly sucked it up, leaving a bright red lipstick smudge behind.

Reena pulled Golly's phone from the pocket of her godmother's kaftan and peered at the screen. 'Nothing so far today, but we're still expecting a couple of twats to respond at the last minute.'

Reena didn't suffer fools. If she thought you were a useless waste of space, then she had no problem telling you so. Hers and Golly's friendship went back to their university days at Magdalen College, Oxford. They'd met on a march through central London in 1960 to protest against the massacre of sixty-nine unarmed South Africans at Sharpeville. The following year, they were arrested at a Ban the Bomb demonstration and sharing a cell cemented their relationship.

Reena was as much a part of Bea's life as Golly, and the only other person who knew Bea was Parker Kane. Reena was a vault, and anyway, Bea suspected she'd long ago forgotten her pseudonym. Reena wasn't a reader, unless it was *Horse and Hound* and horse-racing forms.

'Fabio Rossi sent his regrets—'

'Had an affair with him, would absolutely recommend,' Golly stated, holding Bea's overfull toiletry bag to her chest. 'Younger than me, such an amazing lay.' She smiled. 'Men love me, Bea-darling.'

God, she was a few sips off being properly pissed, and

needed food to soak up some of the alcohol. 'Lunch?' Bea asked Reena.

Reena nodded. 'Good plan. Dump your stuff in the cottage and come to the villa. Nadia's made a Mediterranean salad.'

Awesome. One of the best things about the next week was that with Nadia cooking their meals, she'd be spared Reena's kitchen experiments. Reena was addicted to hot food and everything she made had the kick of a stroppy mule. Golly had the domestic skills of a pot plant.

Bea hauled her suitcase out of the car – so heavy – and nodded at the Jeep. She had to ask, her curiosity was killing her. 'Who does that belong to?'

Golly looked at Reena and Reena at Golly, and neither of them answered. Bea frowned at her godmother. 'What's going on, Golly?'

'It's not a big deal, darling.'

Oh, *shit*.

'I just had a senior moment.'

Golly never had senior moments, she was the sharpest septuagenarian she knew. 'What have you done?' Bea asked through gritted teeth.

She'd barely finished her sentence when she saw her rescuer walking towards them from the direction of the cottage. His now unbuttoned shirt gave her tantalising glimpses of his tanned chest. Her eyes widened at his Jack Reacher body.

He slowed down as he approached them, his face unreadable. Bea managed to pull her eyes off his body onto his face and into his silver-blue-grey eyes. The dude from the Oppenheimer movie eyes, *Pip's* eyes…

Oh, God.

'We meet again,' he said, casually buttoning up his shirt. He didn't seem overly excited to see her, damn him.

'Gibson Caddell, meet Bea Williams, my goddaughter. Bea-darling, Gib is the CEO of Caddell International.'

She'd heard of Caddell International. Pretty much everyone with a pulse had.

Golly drained her glass. 'Gib and his cousin, Navy Caddell, met me for lunch at The Ivy a few weeks ago.'

Navy Caddell? Golly'd had lunch with the new shit-hot agent on the block? *What the hell?* Bea flinched. 'Why were you lunching with Navy Caddell, Golly *dear*?'

'I am looking for someone to take on Parker Kane, *Beatrice*, since the bloody woman is dragging her feet.' Golly's eyes narrowed. 'Navy only set up his literary agency a year ago but already has an impressive list of clients and has made some eyebrow-raising sales.'

Bea'd told Golly, more than once, that she wouldn't be pushed into meeting agents until she was ready. Which wasn't now, and just might be never. What the hell was Golly thinking going behind her back and vetting agents for her?

'Maybe *Parker* isn't ready to take that step and would like to make that decision herself,' Bea said through gritted teeth. 'You know she hates it when you overstep the mark, Golly.'

'Well, she needs a swift kick up her arse!'

Golly was angling for an argument, but now wasn't the time. They had company. Bea rubbed the back of her head, trying to ignore her headache. It was noon, but it felt like she'd already put in a ten-hour day. She had things to do, and an unexpected cocktail party to organise.

But Gibson Caddell's rough sexiness scrambled her brain. *Wait, hold on…*

Why had he walked from the direction of the cottage?

'What exactly did you mean by 'senior moment' just now, Golly?' Bea asked, her eyes narrowed.

'What are you accusing me of now, Bea?' Golly asked, her eyes guileless. Oh, *sod it*. When Golly sounded innocent, it usually meant she was about to drop a conversational nuclear bomb. Bea's stomach went into free fall.

'*Golly!*' Bea snapped. She wasn't in the mood for games. Not today.

'Well … I sort of promised you both the use of the cottage,' Golly airily replied. Her expression was pure whimsy, as close to '*oh shucks*' as Golly got. Bea didn't buy it. Golly was working some angle and Bea wasn't going to let her.

'I have been staying in the cottage since I was sixteen years old, Golly, and I am organising your weekend,' Bea told her, heat creeping into her voice. 'I'm sure Mr Caddell can find somewhere else to stay.'

'I've paid a lot of money to hire her cottage, so if anyone is moving out it's you,' Gib replied, sounding properly pissed off. She didn't blame him. Bloody Golly.

Golly waved her empty glass around. 'I'm sure you two

can find a solution to my faux pas. Of course, alternative accommodation would be the answer, but the island is also hosting the ginormous wedding of a stunningly wealthy Greek industrialist's daughter on Saturday. The week-long festivities started yesterday, and you might struggle to find a decent room.'

What was her point? Did Golly expect her to share her cottage? Her *one-bed* cottage? That wasn't, on any level, acceptable.

'This island can sleep roughly seventy-thousand people, Golly, I'm sure Mr Caddell can find somewhere else to stay,' Bea said through gritted teeth. She *needed* to stay at the cottage, being anywhere else was inconceivable. The cottage was where she felt most inspired, and utterly relaxed. It was her home away from home.

'*Mr* Caddell will be staying where he is,' Gib stated.

Golly ignored him. 'That's at the peak of summer, Bea, when all the hotels and rooms-to-let are available. Many have closed now the season's over.' Golly waved her hand, tipped with coffin-shaped nails. 'Now don't be so square and unaccommodating Bea-darling and Gib. You two can share the space for less than a week, the bed is big enough to sleep four, and then Bea can move into the main house. Besides, you've shared before.'

'What?' Given that Bea's love life was desert-sand dry, she definitely would've remembered sharing a bed with Gibson Cadell. He looked equally confused. 'What are you talking about, Golly?'

'Gib stayed here when he was about ten or eleven, I had a full house that summer and you two shared a room.'

Bea cocked her head to the side, as the memory of a gangly boy, with too-long hair and knobbly knees came into focus. While she'd been happy, OK, *resigned* to sharing a room with him, he'd thrown a wobbly, loudly protesting he didn't want to share with a *kid*, and worse, a *girl*. She remembered him making his dad promise he'd never tell someone – he couldn't remember the name – that he'd been forced into what he considered an *atrocity*. She'd needed to look that word up in Golly's dictionary and was hurt by the harshness of the definition.

Later, after noticing he never spent any time reading – the greatest sin in her six-year-old eyes! – Bea realised he probably didn't even know what the word meant. But most stupefying of all was that she'd modelled her beloved Pip on that long-ago boy who ran wild. The memory of him must've lodged in her subconscious because she never gave him another thought after they'd parted at the end of that summer. She met his incredible eyes.

'Your dad taught me to swim,' she told him.

'You always had your nose in a book.'

'You never did,' she countered.

He shrugged. 'Too many fun things to do outside…'

Their conversation petered out. Right, she remembered they'd struggled to connect back then, too. She'd barely seen him that summer: he woke early, spent all of his time at the beach or on a bike his father bought him, and he'd made friends with a gang of kids he'd met somewhere. In his eyes, she'd barely existed and was way beneath his notice.

Now Golly was expecting her to share the cottage with him on the very flimsy basis that they'd once shared a room? Was her godma rowing with only one oar in the water?

Why couldn't Golly refund Gib his money and send him on his way? And, dammit, why did he make her skin prickle? He looked like Pip all grown up, and his voice made her think of long kisses under a velvet moon. A velvet moon? Jesus! She was a writer but that was way too much purple prose.

The point?

He was a *stranger*, and she didn't share beds with *strangers*. Dear God, Golly was ridiculously free thinking, but this was patent nonsense.

Gib spoke before she could. 'I'm not moving. I paid my money, and I like the cottage. I also like my privacy.'

He lifted an arrogant eyebrow, and his eyes met Bea's. Her stomach did a complicated backflip. Stupid thing.

'I'm sure there's a couch you can sleep on in the main house,' he added.

'Nobody is sleeping on any couches in my house,' Golly told him, her tone suggesting he not argue. 'I have not, and never will, let people sleep on my furniture. That's what beds are for.'

'You're shit out of luck then,' Gib told Bea.

Bea glared at him and thought fast. There were two couches in the cottage's lounge. One was a horsehair-stuffed divan of questionable origin. Sleeping on it was like lying on springs and nails, and it left bruises on butts and backs. The other couch, an Art Deco sofa, was more beautiful than it was comfortable, and sleeping on it would require four sessions at a chiropractor when she returned to London.

Bea had a thousand things to do this weekend, she'd be useless if she didn't get a solid night's sleep. With Gib taking the big bed in the room next door and her lying on one of the couches-from-hell, there was no way she was going to get enough rest. But she didn't have time to argue the point. 'I'll sleep on a couch in the lounge,' she muttered, annoyed she was conceding.

'No!' Gib responded. 'I hired the cottage, and I'd like to have it to myself.'

Bea ignored him, as did Golly. She handed Bea her toiletry bag. 'Actually, I had to burn one of the couches, it was riddled with woodworm.'

Freaking marvellous. 'Crap,' Bea muttered, thinking of the Art Deco couch and chiropractor bills. On the bright side, that horsehair POS-divan was finally gone. Fifty years too late, but yay!

'I'm sure you can find somewhere else to stay,' Gib told her.

Golly placed her pink and orange-tipped fingers on Gib's huge bicep. 'Absolutely not! This is Bea's home, and she needs to be on-site to arrange things for me. Now do stop being difficult, darling.'

'I am not the one who—' Gib threw up his hands as

Golly walked away. He looked at Bea, obviously irritated. 'I was talking to her.'

'She got bored with the conversation,' Bea replied. She suspected it had been a long time since anyone had walked away from Gib mid-conversation.

Bloody hell, who would've thought that annoying kid with a sunburned nose, chapped lips and thin arms and legs would grow up into someone seriously gorgeous?

And masculine.

And he made her, for the first time in years, want. His arms around her, her mouth under his... She wanted to jump him. But he was too good-looking, too cool, too charismatic to look at her twice. If she was a four, maybe a five on good days, he was a friggin' eleven. *Thousand.*

And no, she wasn't putting herself down, at least, no more than usual. Her mother was stunning, Golly was glamorous, and Bea had been in a long-term relationship with the walking, talking definition of hipster cool. Realistically, Bea's shoulder-length hair was thick but brown, her nose a little flat. Her eyes were a mix of grey and blue, and her teeth were good. She still carried the extra seven kilos Gerry had begged her to lose, telling her that no one wanted to nail a fat girl.

She sighed and dragged her hands over her face. Embarrassed by her thoughts, and sure that he could read her expression, she tugged at her heavy case again. It didn't budge. Gib walked over to her, slammed the handle down, and picked it up with one hand. He plucked the toiletry bag from her hand and told Bea to grab her clothes bag. She automatically, and infuriatingly, obeyed his instruction. Argh! Annoying.

Reena turned around to tell her lunch would be served in the kitchen in thirty minutes.

'G&T's right now,' Golly said, walking backwards, her good humour restored. Bea scowled at her, which Golly countered with a huge grin. Her godmother was up to something, and that something wasn't good. It never was.

She'd have to have a come-to-Jesus talk with her as soon as she could shake Mr Muscles. 'Don't let me keep you from the beach,' Bea told Gib. 'That was where you were going, right?'

'I think we first need to resolve the question of who is moving, and where to,' he said, his voice hard. 'And, newsflash, it's not gonna be me. But it's hot, so we'll continue this discussion in the cottage.'

Bea was hardwired, conditioned by her childhood to put everyone else's needs before her own – it was the primary reason she'd stayed with Gerry for much longer than she should've – and she often experienced guilt when she annoyed people, something she tried very hard not to do.

But, very strangely, she wasn't going to move heaven and earth to accommodate this man, to find another place to stay. The cottage was *her* space, the place she needed and wanted to be. She wrote a good portion of her first book while sitting at the small wooden table on the deck, banging out the scenes while occasionally lifting her head to look out to sea as she searched for a word, a sentence or inspiration.

Too bad that Gib had paid Golly, even though she could refund him in a matter of minutes. And Bea knew there was a hotel, room or stable somewhere on the island where he could stay. Or he could hop on a ferry and go to Mykonos or Eos. He could go anywhere, he just needed to leave her in peace.

She had a party to organise, a new series to plan – her rough notes needed to be typed up and she suspected her premise needed a top-to-toe overhaul – and at some point, she grudgingly supposed she needed to think about finding a new agent, one who would understand her need to stay incognito.

Bea desperately wanted to sleep in that big California King alone, to breathe the island air, to calm her nervous system.

He needed to go. And she intended to make that very clear to him.

Her godmother, *her* cottage.

Chapter Three

In the exquisitely decorated cottage, she found the five-foot long and two-foot-wide divan –AKA the horsehair seat from hell – squatting opposite two exquisitely decorated chairs. Where was the Art Deco couch? Bea winced. She'd assumed the *fugly* divan had been chucked, and not the pretty couch. Dammit. And wasn't burning it a rather drastic step? Couldn't Golly have had it fumigated instead?

She rubbed her forehead with the tips of her fingers; her head was pounding. Did she still have any aspirin? She'd emptied a box this morning, did she chuck another in her suitcase before she left? She couldn't remember.

Bea looked around, taking in the recent changes to the cottage. The walls were now a delicate sage green, and the two chairs a soft grey. The carpet under the wooden coffee table was new, a swirly pattern of greens and warm creams, a nice contrast to the dark slate floors. If she ignored the boil-like divan, vomit-yellow and blergh-brown, it was a pretty, pretty room. Why redecorate so beautifully but leave the divan? Or, at the very least, why didn't Golly replace the Art Deco couch? The mind boggled.

The kitchen had also been remodelled and the breakfast bar removed. In its place was a warm wooden table with bench seats on either side. Golly had also bought a new pale blue fridge, and the counters had been replaced with white granite.

Despite beating her to the villa by only ten or fifteen minutes, Gib had already made himself at home. His wallet and phone sat on the kitchen counter, and his laptop on the glass and wood coffee table. She suspected his clothes were packed away in the bedroom cupboard, his toiletries on the bathroom shelves.

Well, he could simply pack them all up again. She wasn't budging on this. Bea frowned, confused by the strength of her feelings. She genuinely didn't recognise herself; this wasn't like her. The teeny-tiny part of her that wasn't shocked by her uncharacteristic bolshiness was doing high kicks and waving pompoms, proud she was standing up for herself.

Bea turned to face him and looked up into his hard-as-nails, inscrutable face. 'I'll help you pack your stuff.'

He had the gall to, almost, smile. Well, she presumed it was a smile because the corners of his sexy mouth lifted a fraction. 'That won't be necessary because I'm not going anywhere,' he calmly responded. 'I like this cottage, I like the location. I had the best time that summer twenty-five years ago and I've been looking forward to being here for *weeks*. But I am very happy to call my assistant and ask her to find you a room on the island. There should be something.'

'Of course there is, and you can move, not me,' she retorted. Scrubbing her hands down her face, she plopped down on the arm of one wingback chair. 'You're being ridiculously stubborn, Mr Caddell. This is my home, my cottage. I need to be here, while you are just a visitor to the island. There are many places as nice as this.'

He shrugged, unmoved by her argument. 'As I've said a bunch of times now, I paid Golly a considerable amount of money to stay here, we made a deal. I am not going anywhere.'

'Well, neither am I.'

She lifted her chin, digging in her metaphorical heels. Why now and why with this man? He was big, intimidating and annoyed but instead of trying to please and placate him, her default mode, she was defying him.

'You'll have to kill me while I sleep because it's the only way you're going to get my body out of this cottage!'

'There's no need to be dramatic. I could always just pick you up, toss you out, and lock the door behind you.'

Ha! 'The patio doors don't have locks, and neither does the bathroom window,' she retorted. 'I'll be back inside and in that big bed before your head hits the pillow.'

'Are you that desperate to sleep with me?'

The air between them changed and started to sizzle. Bea knew he didn't mean his comment to sound sexually charged, but it hung there, tiny bolts of electricity coating every word. She wanted to mock him, tell him that he had an overactive imagination, but the hell of it was that she couldn't stop thinking about him. Naked.

He'd be glorious, and she could easily imagine his big muscles moving under tanned skin. The scratch of his stubble against her breasts, between her legs. Those big hands on her skin, sliding under her butt to lift her hips as he positioned himself between her thighs—

Shit! *Shitshitdamn.*

What the hell was she thinking? But, judging by his pained expression and his fuller-than-before package, she wasn't the only one riding this crazy train.

Gib groaned, sank to sit down on a chair and rested his forearms on his thighs, his hands and head dangling. He released another set of creative curses, something about this being a shitastrophy (she couldn't argue with him there), and ended his imaginative cursing with a deep, loud sigh.

'Despite sharing a room when we were kids, we barely connected back then. I'm a stranger to you, so why aren't you running for the hills?' he demanded, his voice rougher than before.

She met his eyes. She knew that if she even hinted at her being wary of him, he'd pack up his stuff and leave. It was tempting to use that as an excuse to get her way, to make him leave. But she didn't want to resort to subterfuge. She felt strong and vital, and was reluctant to taint her burst of bravery by being underhanded.

She wasn't scared of him, she knew – and don't ask her

how – that he was utterly … what was the word … honourable. Despite the heat in his eyes and the way they kept dropping to her mouth, she was convinced he'd never make an unwelcome advance.

He seemed honest and was very direct. So … *clean*. No artifice and no hidden meanings and innuendo.

The walls of the cottage seemed to expand and contract along with her ribs. After what seemed like a million years, he lifted his head to look at her properly, and she caught a hint of resignation in his eyes. 'You're not going to leave, are you?'

She shook her head. No, not this time. This time, this *one* time, she was going to do what felt right for her, and that meant sticking and staying.

'No. I told you, this is where I want to be.'

Another lift of those huge shoulders. 'I guess we're just gonna have to share that bed. As Golly said, it could sleep four.'

Oh, wait, hold on a second now. She jabbed her index finger at him. '*You* need to leave the cottage, *you* need to find another place to stay.'

'Not happening.' He sat up straight, and his silver-blue eyes drilled into and through her. 'I'm dammed if I am going to be chased out of accommodation I paid for.' He jerked his thumb over his shoulder. 'I'm sleeping in that bed. Whether you sleep in it too is up to you.'

Caught on the back foot, she shot up and paced the area between the chair and the fugly couch. 'That's not going to work for me.'

JOSS WOOD

'Tough.' He didn't soften his gaze. 'The way I see it, you have three choices: sleep somewhere else, sleep on that,' he nodded to the divan, 'or sleep in the bed.'

She hadn't shared a bed with a man in nearly five years. She slept like a starfish, and maybe she snored or, even worse, farted, in her sleep.

'You can—'

'Not arguing anymore,' he snapped. 'It's over. Three choices, what's it going to be?'

She rocked on her heels, biting the inside of her cheek as she ran through her options. 'I doubt we'll see that much of each other. I'm organising the weekend so there's lots to do,' she said, grasping at straws. 'I'll probably be out of here early most mornings. If I'm not, I'll be working on the deck.'

She was not, *not*, going to give up her writing spot.

He repeated his question. 'Bed, that ugly-as-shit thing or somewhere else?'

He wasn't backing down, dammit, and it was obvious that, despite his hot gaze raising baby blisters on her skin, he expected her to. As the CEO of a huge company, he was used to being obeyed and expected his minions to ask how high and far they should jump when he spoke. But she wasn't going to cave, not this time.

She eyed the California King through the open bedroom door. The bed was huge, and there were layers of cushions, so if she needed a barrier between them, she could use those. Hell, maybe a barrier would be a good idea, as there was a chance she might, accidentally on purpose, roll over and land on top of him.

She shook her head, annoyed by her casual deceit. As she knew, and knew *well*, there were no accidents when it came to sex. *'It happened by accident, Bea!'* was Gerry's favourite excuse to explain his infidelities. He always rolled his eyes when she reminded him that he couldn't *accidentally* trip and fall into someone's vagina. From the first flirtation, the first text message, the first kiss, infidelity was a series of choices, with sex being the final one.

And when she slept with a man again, it would be because she wanted to.

Pushing away her thoughts about a naked Gib – so hard to do! – she pulled her attention back to the bed.

'This whole situation would be a lot easier if you were less stubborn!' she snapped.

'Right back at you, sweetheart.'

She wasn't, generally, inflexible. All her life, she'd drifted along with the current, terrified of being criticised, hating herself for not being strong enough to stand up for herself, for making sure everyone – specifically her father and Gerry – were happy. Usually at the expense of her peace of mind and happiness. Not that either of them had ever noticed.

She lifted her head and met his eyes. 'I'm staying,' she told him, cursing her shaky voice. 'And I'm sleeping in that bed, *sweetheart*.'

His eyes clashed with hers. 'So am I.'

Well, *shit*.

But she couldn't back down now. 'Fine.'

'Fine.'

Bea gritted her teeth at the note of amusement she heard in his voice. She wanted to blast him but knew she'd lose any ground – if she'd gained any at all – if she continued to argue. She didn't have enough facts and hadn't researched how to deal with intractable, assertive men. She was ill-equipped to argue with a man who, she was sure, had mastered the art of negotiation. He hadn't given an inch…

But, it was worth noting, neither had she. And damn, she was proud of herself for not backing down.

But she would still have to share the bed and the cottage with him, and that, for the record, was anything but *fine*.

———

After unpacking her clothes and putting her toiletries in the bathroom – all done in icy silence – Bea told him she was going up to the main house to eat with Golly and Reena.

That suited Gib, so he headed to the beach with his kayak and spent the bulk of the afternoon paddling past the weird pumice cliffs of Vlychada and marvelling at the speckled grey-and-white pebbled beach. He enjoyed a beer and a snack at a laid-back beach bar, before paddling back to where he'd left his rented Jeep. He'd had an excellent workout and his shoulders and neck felt looser, his body less tense.

After a shower at the empty cottage, he'd headed into Oia and had a long, solitary, *amazing* meal of grilled octopus followed by moussaka. It was now shortly past ten and time to see whether bright-eyed Bea had had a change of heart in the day and moved out. He was surprised by his intransigence. Obviously, it made sense for him to find another place, and despite the wedding of some mega-wealthy guy's daughter, he knew he'd find something decent, somewhere. He had resources, and when money wasn't a problem, obstacles tended to melt away.

But the minute he'd stepped out of the Jeep and seen the house again, he immediately relaxed, feeling like, strangely, he'd come home. A memory of him and his dad playing football on the beach flipped over into one of them laughing ... he couldn't remember at what, but he knew his stomach had ached when they were done. Days spent in the sun, eating great food, sitting in the courtyard as a record player played some lame music in the background.

He and his dad had connected during their boys' away holiday – something he and his mom never did – and it was the best memory he had of the man he'd adored. He hadn't thought about Greece in years, and now that he was here, he wanted to remember everything he could. He'd love to recapture some of that childish freedom; although impossible, he still wanted to try.

To do that, he'd have to be on the estate and share this cottage with Bea. He supposed history repeating itself gave his visit back here some authenticity. She'd been a strange little girl, quiet and reserved, happy to fade into the background. They'd shared a room, but he barely knew she was there. Her bed was always made, and her side of the room was tidy, while his looked like he was living in a war zone. She'd read her books and left him alone, and he'd considered that a win.

Gib pushed his hand through his hair, remembering their conversation earlier. He was used to keeping his expression unreadable, he rarely gave anyone a hint of what he was feeling, but it took all his willpower to keep his surprise in check when she'd told him they'd be sharing the bed. *Huh.*

It was the last thing he'd expected. Somewhere along the line, that little mouse had grown a set of balls.

Gib walked down the path to the cottage, thinking that while he didn't want to share the bed or cottage, he was desperate to have her under him, over him, up against the nearest wall.

He rubbed his hands over his face. He'd been having sex for more than half his life, but he'd never had such a quick, visceral reaction to a woman before. And why with Bea, who was so unlike anyone he'd ever been attracted to in the past? She wasn't glossy or glamorous, neither was she sophisticated...

She was ... *what?*

Normal. Real. Down to earth. Her face was makeup free, except for some smudged mascara, and her plump, pink lips didn't need any lipstick. She wasn't fat, but neither was she rake thin, or a gym bunny. She was a girl who looked like she enjoyed a piece of chocolate cake, a beer, or a few glasses of wine. A girl who ate carbs and who didn't count calories. Healthy. Someone who wouldn't give him shit if he wanted to skip a workout to sloth on the couch and binge-watch a Formula One documentary (previous fling). Neither would she invite him over for dinner and serve him a protein-free couscous salad, followed by a yoghurt smoothie for dessert (fling before that).

As easily as he could imagine them rolling around naked together, he could also see himself watching a ballgame, and eating ribs with her, sauce rolling down her chin, her fingers sticky and her smile wide. Along with tasting every inch of her body, he wanted to see what she looked like with bed hair and with sleep in her fantastic eyes, have her fall asleep on his chest as they watched TV.

Fuck. He was in a metric shitload of trouble here. He needed a punch in the head.

Relationships, even quick flings, required some measure of conversation, a little back and forth about who you were, what you did, and what you liked. Even basic, mild, getting-to-know-you questions were sandpaper on his soul.

That's what happened when you were raised by the parental equivalent of the National Security Agency. His German mom had no concept of boundaries, and because he was an only child he'd been the complete focus of her attention. He knew she loved him, but her love was all-consuming and overwhelming. Dr Mom—she was a psychologist—needed to know where he was every second of the day, and if he deviated from his routine, she freaked. She demanded to know who his friends were, why he liked them, why they liked him.

Every aspect of his life was open for analysis, from girls to exercise to schoolwork to his friends. His life was dissected and discussed, frequently the only topic of conversation. Her constant prying and her follow-up pseudo-therapy sessions telling him why he shouldn't feel that way, or asking him why he reacted one way and not another, or whether he could've handled a situation better, left him feeling exposed and judged. His mother's personal science experiment.

His father never told her to back off, or supported Gib's right to privacy. His dad was a completely different person around his mom to the person he had been in Greece; in the States he was quieter, harsher … sadder.

Gib hauled in some air. He still felt extraordinarily guilty about his initial rush of relief when he'd heard his parents had died. For a minute, or maybe just seconds, he revelled in the idea that he'd never have to explain his thoughts and feelings again and would never be judged for feeling one way and not another. Then reality sat in and he realised he was, at sixteen, an orphan.

After his grief faded a little, he realised how much he owed his Uncle Hugh – a long-divorced, single dad – for taking him in. At sixteen, he would've been OK on his own – hell, kids in the First World War went to fight at that age – but Hugh gave him stability and security. Gib was grateful to him for giving him a home, and a few more years to be a kid. Gib's going to school and earning his MBA, working a thousand hours a week at CI, and running a huge, successful company, went a little way to thank his uncle for his unquestionable support.

And the best thing about moving in with two guys,

Hugh and Navy, had been that they never made him have heart-to-heart conversations. They ran with him, sat with him, and, when things got bad and he needed to release pent-up anger, hopped into the boxing ring with him. What they didn't do was pry and poke and scratch around his mind like a poor, panicking prospector looking for gold.

His mom's unrelenting demands to crawl inside his mind had made him wary of friendships and intimacy, and he never shared his true self with others. Navy and Hugh got more of him than most, but Gib had sky-high walls around his heart, convinced that revealing his innermost thoughts and feelings could, and would, only lead to criticism and pain. It was safer to keep feelings and emotions locked away.

Gib walked into the cottage and tossed his phone, wallet and keys into the bright turquoise bowl sitting on the table next to the front door. Bea's closed laptop stood on the breakfast counter, her phone charging next to it – and both meant he was about to share a bed with the most attractive woman he'd met in a long time.

He banged his forehead against the nearest wall. *Freaking fucking fabulous.*

Taking a deep breath, Gib walked to the closed bedroom door and knocked lightly. When he didn't get a reply, he eased the door open and looked into the room. He saw Bea leaning back against the huge headboard on *his* side of the bed – he always slept on the side closest to the door – her eyes fixed on the book resting on her knees. She wore a loose white T-shirt, and he could see the outline of a tank top or sports bra beneath it. No doubt she was wearing panties or, more likely, pyjama shorts. Her hair was pulled into a high ponytail and her face was scrubbed clean, but her lips looked a little glossy.

'Are you wearing lip gloss?' he demanded.

She didn't look up or acknowledge him. Right, he was getting the silent treatment. Excellent. If he had to share a cottage with someone, he far preferred a silent someone than a chatty, have-to-make-conversation someone.

He should feel happier than he did. Was he looking for a reaction from her? And why? Yes, and he didn't know. How old was he? Eleven again and looking to pick a fight?

Gib sighed, pushed open the door, and stepped into the room. When he'd first inspected the cottage earlier that day, the California King was stacked high with pillows – four rows at least, including one as long as the bed was wide. The pillows now precisely bisected the bed, forming a barrier between her side and his.

OK, then. They were doing this.

Her eyes didn't leave her book, though he doubted she was doing any reading. She was ignoring him, and that didn't bother him at all. Whistling, he reached back to pull his shirt over his head and tossed it toward the chair in the corner. He missed and it fell to the floor. Oh, *dear*.

Out of the corner of his eye, he saw her watching him. She frowned and started to speak, before biting her lip to keep her words from escaping.

She so wanted to tell him to pick it up, to hang it up. Smiling, he turned his back to her and undid the belt to his chinos shorts and unzipped, stepping out of his flip flops and kicking the shorts in the direction of his shirt. He heard her gasp, and her low rumble of annoyance. Oh, she had no idea what was coming next…

Still whistling, he walked into the bathroom in his briefs and flipped on the taps to the shower. Deliberately leaving the door open, not enough for her to see him, but enough for any sounds to carry, he shucked his underwear and stepped into the glass cubicle.

She didn't ask him to close the door.

The water slid over his head and down his back. He pushed his hair back and looked at the range of toiletries she'd placed on the shelf. He picked up a bottle of shower gel, lifted it to his nose – nice – and squirted some into his hand. He scrubbed his face with it, before rinsing off.

Enjoying the unisex scent, he washed the rest of his body before reaching for his bottle of generic, much less interesting shampoo. He quickly washed his hair, rinsed off and shut off the taps. He saw her towel hanging on the rail and wrinkled his nose.

'Hey, Bea, where can I find a towel? Can you toss me one?' Her silence was an unspoken 'no' and not unexpected. Shrugging, he reached for her still damp towel and rubbed his wet head. He pulled it down his chest, between his legs, and up his back before wrapping it around his hips. 'Don't worry, I'll just use yours.'

Still no reply. She was tougher than he thought.

After brushing his teeth, he pushed his hair off his forehead and hung the towel up on the rail to dry. Grinning, he walked back into the room, as naked as the day he was born.

As he expected, Bea slapped her hand over her eyes and released an anguished wail. 'For God's sake, put something on!' she shouted.

The one good thing about being brought up in a house where nudity – mental and physical – had been encouraged was that he now had no compunction about walking around in the buff. Compared to his mom's mental mind-probes, being physically naked wasn't that big of a deal. He pulled back the light cotton throw covering the bed, then the sheet, and climbed into bed. 'I sleep naked,' he informed her, turning his head to look at her.

She was an interesting colour, hot pink in places, scarlet in others. One hand still covered her eyes.

'You can look now,' he told her, amused.

She lowered her hand and fixed him with a cold, hard stare. 'You are *not* sleeping naked,' she informed him. 'Put on some shorts. And a T-shirt.'

He bent his knees and folded his arms, looking at her across the shoulder-high wall of pillows. 'Not happening,' he told her. 'But feel free to leave and sleep somewhere else if you don't like it.'

She growled, actually growled. Unfortunately for her, she sounded like a puppy and wouldn't intimidate a grasshopper. He grinned.

'You also left your clothes on the floor and the bathroom and bedroom door open,' she said, her voice colder than a Siberian witch's tit in the dead of winter.

'And, you bastard, you used my very expensive Creed shower gel! Golly bought it for me last Christmas! Judging by how amazing the room smells, you used half the bottle.'

Maybe a third. And she was right, the smells wafting in from the bathroom were incredible. If he remembered, and he probably wouldn't, he should take a photo of the stuff and order the same brand when he got home.

'Do *not* mess with my stuff,' she told him, her posh English accent becoming more pronounced as her irritation levels rose. 'And. Pick. Up. Your. Clothes. I won't be able to go to sleep knowing they're just lying there.'

Normally he would, he wasn't a slob, but annoying her was fun, and a means to an end. If he did it well, and he did everything well, she'd leave and give him the solitude he craved.

'If it bothers you, please feel free to do something about it.' He slid down the bed, bunched his pillow beneath his head, and she disappeared from view. He yawned, surprised by his exhaustion given it wasn't even eleven yet. Normally he'd still be at his desk, blowing through reports or spreadsheets.

He wasn't used to sharing his space, and he thought he'd be more keyed up, more annoyed than he was. All he felt was tired. Mentally and physically drained.

'Get up and pick up your stuff! And close the damn doors!'

Not a chance. This bed was incredibly comfortable, and he was struggling to keep his eyes open. Hell, even if she got naked and asked him to do her, he might choose sleep over sex. Might being the operative word.

'Not happening. Besides, if I do, I'll still be naked and you'll get another eyeful,' he replied, around a long yawn.

He heard the sound of covers rustling and lifted his head just high enough to see her sliding out of bed. She stomped her way around the bed, it was ridiculously big, and he eyed her long legs peeking out from short tartan sleeping shorts. He took in her round ass as she bent over to pick up his shirt and shorts, stomping into the bathroom to dump them in the laundry basket.

Neat freak. That hadn't changed. She slammed the bathroom door closed, then the bedroom door, her body stiff with annoyance. He felt the bed move as she climbed back under the covers, heard her adorable huff of irritation and with one last yawn, slid into sleep.

———

For the second night in a row, Bea didn't sleep well. At all.

At around one a.m., or it might've been two, she sat up and looked at Gib on the other side of her Great Wall of Pillows. He lay on his stomach, his hands under his pillow, the sheet and light cotton throw barely covering his world-class ass. The moon was half full and bright, and beaming light into the room from the open window – she'd forgotten to lower the shade – and she could see him clearly. She took in his big arms, and his muscled back tapered into narrow hips. Because he went to bed with his hair wet, it resembled a bird's nest, and the thick scruff on his jaw looked soft.

He slept silently, deeply, utterly relaxed.

At one point, almost in tears because she was so tired, she considered putting a pillow over his face and sitting on it. A judge familiar with the psychotic effects of insomnia would understand her struggle and would probably only sentence her to a year at a sleep clinic.

Now sitting at the small desk on the deck, her laptop in front of her and a blank Word document mocking her, she placed her elbows on the table, and wondered if a third cup of coffee was indulgent or necessary. It might make her feel reasonably human. But she couldn't muster the energy to walk to the kitchen. Just like she couldn't find the energy to write or check her emails. She'd spent the two hours since dressing zoning out by staring at the amazing view of the sea between the olive trees, doodling in her notebook and scrolling social media.

She'd had, maybe, two hours of sleep last night, three the night before and Bea felt like a walking zombie. She couldn't spend another night in *that* bed, not sleeping. She'd been super aware of Gib both nights. The room was five degrees hotter than normal from the heat rolling off him and images of his naked body – better than she'd imagined and she had, according to the professionals, a damn fine imagination! – kept flashing up on the big screen of her mind. Huge shoulders, ridged stomach, a *very* fine bum.

The jerk knew he had a good body and wasn't afraid to show it off.

Unlike her. She'd never undressed in front of Gerry, and sex, back when they were both interested enough to bother, happened under the cover of darkness. Bea suspected Gib was a 'do it in bright sunlight' and 'on the nearest flat surface' type of guy.

Gib was the first guy, in a long, long time, to make her ovaries sit up and start chittering. Like over-excited meerkats, they were on their hindquarters, their heads swivelling, telling each other that their girls were desperate to meet his boys. Or, at the very least, that they wanted to see some action, of the naked, horizontal kind. Of *any* kind.

She didn't like feeling out of control, at the mercy of her sexual urges. Feeling like this made her wonder whether she was more like her mother than she wanted to be. In her weekly column, sex was one of Lou's favourite topics, and she wasn't shy about telling the world how much she loved it and how difficult it was to limit herself to one sexual partner at a time. *We're not supposed to be monogamous, people! We need variety!* Was that something Lou learnt from Golly? Maybe.

Lou's oft-stated position was that women who had hangups about the act (and their bodies) were weak, old-fashioned, and foolish. Bea was the exact opposite of her sultry, earthy, pleasure-seeking mother. And Gib was dangerous because he made her want to explore that hedonistic (albeit tiny) part of her personality, the side that she normally ruthlessly pushed down and away...

She, the thirty-year-old who hadn't had sex for the last five years was desperate to roll around naked. With Gib.

That was why he was dangerous, why having him around – sharing that blasted bed!– was problematic. She liked her life the way it was, she liked the normality of it, the ease of it, the worlds she controlled, both IRL and in fiction. She did not need a six-foot-something, sexy man to upend her carefully constructed apple cart!

But she was in deep danger of flipping tits over arse...

Would you please get a grip, Bea? The Urban Explorers, who'd unexpectedly returned to occasionally dance on the edges of her mind, stuck their fingers down their throats and gagged. Their hormones hadn't kicked in yet and, thank God, never would.

Right, she'd been contemplating her lack of sleep, and she'd veered off into thinking about Mr Muscles again. Pride and stubbornness be damned, she couldn't spend another night *not* sleeping next to him. So what were her options? She could drive to Fira and buy a camping mattress, or she could pad the fugly divan with blankets and sleep on that bed of nails.

Or she could rent another room...

What she wouldn't be able to do was get Gib to move. Displacing him would require an SAS team and, possibly, a horse tranquilliser. Sleep was necessary for her to human and to adult, and she wasn't going to keep sharing a bed with him. So – dammit, shit, and fuck – she was going to have to back down.

Not move out, she wasn't going to give him the satisfaction of doing *that*. She still needed to be able to work at this desk, to escape here when Golly became too demanding, when she felt overwhelmed. Despite Gib's presence, this cottage was still her safe space. But tonight, she'd spend the night on the floor on a mattress, or on the divan getting poked and prodded by God knows what.

Also, she couldn't spend the next week trading barbs with Gib, fighting him every step of the way. Fighting wasn't what she did, who she was, and arguing with him drained her mental batteries.

It took two to fight, and she could've been nicer, and less … abrasive. A lot less confrontational. More like her normal self.

She didn't want him leaving Santorini thinking she was a bitch on wheels. Neither did she want Navy Caddell to hear that Golly's niece had the personality of a rabid porcupine. That was something Gib's agent cousin would remember and repeat.

That reminded her, she wanted to know more about Navy Caddell. Opening her computer, she banged his name into a search engine, added 'literary agent' and within seconds her screen flashed with results. She clicked on the link and landed on his agency's website, her eyes raising at his profile picture. The Caddell men were attractive; it was obvious they'd hit the good-looks jackpot.

She skimmed through his bio, read his wish list, and whistled when she took in his clients. He'd managed to net some big names in a short time, and she was impressed. He was clearly a man who was making waves in the literary world.

'Why are you stalking my cousin?'

Bea jumped a foot in the air and her elbow knocked over her mug, spilling her cold coffee over her open notebook, the one holding her notes on her new series and book ten.

She rushed inside to grab a dish towel to mop up the coffee and came back out to see Gib holding her notebook upright, coffee dripping from the pages onto the wooden deck and splashing his bare feet. He'd pulled on a pair of plain black, board shorts that hung low on his hips, just a fraction off indecent, and yet again he was shirtless.

Holy hotness. Hand her a fan!

'God, your handwriting is terrible,' Gib commented, peering at her scribbled notes.

Jerked back to her senses, she snatched the notebook out of his hand and grimaced when she read what she'd written. *GMC*, circled three times. *Series arc. Riding the rapids. Hettie falls, Pip reacts!* She'd also made a note to send out a newsletter. Thank God her writing was awful.

Seeing that her laptop was still open, Bea slammed it shut before wiping the coffee off her notebook, cursing when she saw several pages had stuck together. Normally, she'd be in tears, but her notes were drivel and most of the ideas on those pages were unusable.

Bea mopped up the coffee, and remembered her resolve to be nicer to Gib and looked for something to say. 'Sleep well?' she asked.

He scratched his chest, his finger sliding into the thin layer of hair covering his pecs. 'Much better than I expected to,' he said, squinting as he looked out to sea. 'What's the time?'

'A little after nine.'

'That's the latest I've slept in years.' Gib walked to the edge of the deck and gripped the railing, lifting his face to the morning sun, and closing his eyes. Muscled, good-looking, masculine ... the Greek gods would approve. Anybody with a pulse and a fondness for hot, half-naked men, would.

Really, Bea? Enough now.

'Can I get you some coffee?'

He slowly turned and arched one thick eyebrow. 'Why aren't you shouting at me for startling you and causing you to spill your coffee over your notebook? And why are you offering to make me coffee? Who are you and what did you do with shrew you?'

Shrew? That was a bit harsh. 'You haven't been all goodness and light, either,' she pointed out.

'I rented the cottage, you're the usurper.'

Bea tightened her grip on the dish towel, refusing to take the bait. He was looking for a fight, but she wasn't going to give him one. 'Do you want coffee or not?'

'Yeah, black and strong. Thanks.'

Of course, he took his coffee without anything that made it taste good. He probably ripped the heads off bats and drank the blood of virgins...

Bea stomped back into the cottage and walked over to the coffee machine, another of Golly's recent purchases to bring the cottage into the twenty-first century. Since coffee was as important as oxygen, Bea very much approved.

While the machine made its coffee-making sounds – was

there anything better than the sound and smell of grinding beans? – she scowled at the divan. Why was it still in the cottage? Why was Golly holding on to it? She made a mental note to ask her godma.

Talking about notes ... was there anything in her notebook that directly linked her to Parker Kane? Unless Gib picked up one of her books – and why should he, he didn't fall into her ten-to-fourteen demographic – he wouldn't recognise the characters or link them to her series.

She was pretty sure he wouldn't make the connection. Parker Kane-wise, she was in the clear. Sleeping wise, sharing this cottage wise?

She was still in the weeds.

Chapter Four

T he thing about having bad handwriting himself was that Gib could easily read the chicken scrawl of others...

He was also a speed reader, so he'd managed to read a couple of lines of Bea's notes before she snatched the book away. What did she do that required her to send out a newsletter? And what did the initials GMC mean?

Gib picked up his phone and plugged the acronym into his search engine, not surprised when it came up with about a billion responses, most of them referencing the car brand. Someone who couldn't change a tyre wouldn't make notes about a car brand. He sent a quick message to Navy. Hopefully he'd still be awake.

> If you saw GMC and a newsletter in someone's notebook, what would you think? Don't think cars.

Navy's reply was instantaneous.

Goal, motivation, conflict. Writer or
wannabe writer. Why?

Gib didn't reply because Bea was back and shoving a
cup of coffee into his hand. It was hot and smelled
delicious. He took a sip and felt his brain cells perk up.
'Thanks. Good coffee.'

'Life is too short for bad coffee,' Bea told him. She
joined him and leaned against the railing. 'I'm going to
either buy a blow-up mattress or sleep on the divan
tonight.'

Disappointment ran through him, as sharp as a knife
blade. What the hell was that about? It was what he wanted,
right?

'Why?' he asked her. 'I slept really well last night.'

'Well, I didn't, and I need to,' Bea snapped. There were
dark smudges under her amazing eyes, and she looked a
little pale. Funny that he'd had the best sleep in a long time,
yet she hadn't.

Had she been scared of him? Worried that he'd make an
unwelcome move, cop a feel?

Bea met his eyes and after a few Ice Ages had passed,
she spoke again. 'I haven't shared a bed, or my space, with
anyone for a long time. It feels … strange.'

Funny that, to him, sharing a bed with her felt
completely … well, he didn't want to say right, or natural
… but it hadn't been a big deal.

Bea waved her words away. 'I'm not leaving the cottage,

but you can have the bed. If I don't manage to get into Fira today, I'll sleep on the divan.'

Gib looked into the cottage and saw the butt-ugly couch-with-no-back. It looked like a medieval torture rack. He walked over to it and sat. It creaked ominously as the wood shifted. Seriously? He lifted his eyebrows and lay down on it, his feet dangling off the end and his shoulders nearly as wide as it was.

Don't do it, Caddell, don't…

'It's damn uncomfortable.' Using his core muscles, and hoping Bea wouldn't notice, he lifted his body an inch and slammed it back down under the pretence of shifting his weight as he tried to get comfortable. As he expected, and just as Bea walked back into the cottage, a sharp crack ricocheted through the cottage and his butt fell into a deep dip in the divan.

'Crap,' he said, looking up at her. Had he really gone out of his way to sabotage a piece of furniture so that she would have no option but to share the bed with him? Had the little time he spent in the Greek sun fried his brain? This wasn't who he was, what he did. What was next? Was he going to sabotage her rental so she couldn't drive anywhere?

It would be easy enough to remove a spark plug… Jesus, he was losing his shit.

When he'd seen her standing next to her car talking to Golly and Reena two days ago, her wavy hair blowing in the wind, his heart had bounced off his ribcage. Looking at her, something unfurled within him, a recognition he never expected to experience. He could bullshit and tell himself he remembered her from his childhood, but that wasn't the source of what he was feeling. It went deeper than that, and wasn't wanted or welcomed. Something he'd never experienced before.

He'd only ever indulged in surface-skimming relationships. They suited him, and he didn't have to worry about how many hours he worked a week or checking in with someone when he abruptly left for a business trip. He loved his slam-the-door-closed-and-leave life, and how it didn't matter if he spent six weeks in New York when he'd only intended to stay a week. The only people he checked in with were Hugh and Navy.

He was a free agent, and he *liked* his life.

But Bea... Jesus, there was something about her. She intrigued him. Her fabulous blue-grey eyes, the colour of mist reflecting off the sea, held a thousand secrets and he wanted to know each and every one. How did she come to be Golly's goddaughter? Where did she go to school? Was she a morning person or a night owl? Did she sob or scream when she came?

He loathed personal questions, but he wanted to know everything about her.

Gib frowned. He wasn't thinking straight. She wasn't *that* fascinating, she couldn't be. He'd dated female CEOs and catwalk models, ballerinas and professional athletes. Bea wasn't his type...

He was overreacting, possibly because he hadn't had sex for far too long. And this place, God, you couldn't help noticing how fucking romantic it was. It was timeless. The buildings, the flowers, and the breath-stealing views of the aqua-blue-green water and the wild beaches, the rocks and the endless sky made one think of the romance of sunny days and long, balmy nights.

It was also the one place where he'd experienced true, soul-deep happiness. Uncomfortable with the direction of his thoughts, Gib pushed himself out of the broken divan and rolled to his feet. He eyed the couch. It really was a piece of shit. He lifted it with ease and peered at the fabric underneath. A piece of wood poked through the ratty fabric.

Gib lowered the couch to the floor. 'Guess I'll be buying your godmother another...' He shrugged, then winced. 'I don't know what to call this?'

'A hot mess?' she suggested, shaking her head. 'And there is no way I'll let you replace it, it should've been tossed away fifty years ago. I can't think why it hasn't been, other than the fact that up until now, the cottage has always been a repository for furniture Golly didn't know what else to do with. Besides, I think I can still sleep on it, I'm not as big as you.'

There was no way he was going to let her spend the night on it, but he'd argue about that later. He knew what battles to pick and crucially, when to pick them. So he changed the subject. 'What are your plans for the day?'

She sent a longing look towards her computer before wrinkling her nose. 'I need to sort out the lights for the cocktail party. And help Cassie with the set-up.' She sipped her coffee and looked at him over the rim of the pottery mug. 'Oh, there's something I need to ask you. Last night at dinner Golly told me to invite you to lunch today. And be warned, she's going to invite you to her cocktail party tonight, so have a good excuse ready.'

'You're assuming I wouldn't want to go?' He didn't, but he was interested to find out why she thought he'd baulk.

'You said you wanted privacy and quiet. I presumed that attending a cocktail party was the opposite of that.'

She'd presumed right.

'Why are you craving solitude, Gib? Are you running away from an ex, did you have a breakdown, are you in trouble with the law?'

Personal questions, even when asked in a jokey tone, made him itchy – they were nails across his mental chalkboard – so he looked past her to the view of the bright sea behind her.

'I didn't ask you what your bank balance is or what your worst memory is,' Bea prodded when he didn't answer.

He opened his mouth to tell her he was overworked and peopled-out but snapped it shut, keeping the explanation behind his teeth. He wanted her, was attracted to her, he wanted to breach her wall of pillows. But he'd been attracted to a lot of other women, slept with many of them and he never felt the urge to open up. Why Bea?

Bea shifted on her feet and rubbed the back of her neck. 'Right. None of my business.'

She looked around, saw her flip flops by the front door and moved towards them. She slid her feet into them, and he eyed her legs, long and lovely below the band of the hem of her fitted, sky-blue cotton shorts. She'd loosely knotted a button-up shirt and her face was makeup free, showing off the light freckles on her nose and cheeks.

He scrubbed his hand over his face. Maybe he should go back to bed to reboot his brain, because it sure as hell was glitching.

'Lunch is at one, in the kitchen at the villa. If you don't pitch up, I'll see you when I see you.'

He wouldn't be going to lunch, or to the cocktail party. Until his brain was bug-free, he would avoid Bea as much as possible.

Later that morning, Bea, back from Fira, sans a blow-up mattress, left her car and smiled at Golly's Folly, built in the mid 1930s by a wealthy Englishman as his summer home. With its incredible views, Bea understood why the original owner chose to build where he did. The house itself was two floors of perfection, immaculately decorated by Jack Farrow, with the art provided by his sister Jacqui.

Golly did, occasionally, rent the place out as a wedding venue, but only when she thought the couple highbrow, interesting, or influential enough for her to bother.

Bea sighed at the warm brown, stone building with its rectangular windows and terracotta roof. It looked rich, but not ostentatious, old but not ancient. Built in an H layout, with an amazing courtyard in the centre of the two wings, it was a perfect event location; in Golly's case, her birthday and retirement party. From the courtyard, guests could walk through her garden – peppered with ceramic pots overflowing with flowers – and onto a lookout point, with its amazing view of the caldera. The esplanade was the perfect spot to watch the brilliant Santorini sunsets.

Golly's Greek home was lovely and gracious … and bloody romantic.

Something she didn't normally think about. And it was all Gib's fault.

Dammit.

'Bea!'

Bea spun around and saw Gib jogging towards her. She placed her hands above her eyes to block out the still-hot Greek sun. It was obvious he'd just come back from the beach, as his hair and board shorts were still damp.

She waited for him to reach her, and when he did, he lifted his eyebrows at the erotic stature of a maiden standing between them and the imposing front door, a hand between her legs and a blissful smile on her face. 'I thought I'd join you for lunch.'

And wasn't that a surprise?

Crap. She remembered Reena telling Nadia last night that she'd take care of lunch, and that meant a blow-your-head-off chilli dish. Spicy food was all Reena could make.

'Maybe you should eat in Oia, there are some fantastic restaurants still open.' Eating in Oia was a *much* safer option.

'Why are you so desperate to get rid of me?' he drawled. The breeze picked up the tails of his loose shirt and once again she caught a glimpse of his rock-hard, tanned stomach, and those sexy hip muscles that took hard gym workouts to attain. She could easily imagine her fingers dancing across his stomach, sliding lower.

'*Bea-darling*!'

Bea spun around, her heart sinking to see Golly walking from the direction of the swimming pool. She and Reena tended to spend most of the morning by the pool sunbathing, turning their already wrinkly and brown-as-leather skin darker in the process. She'd warned them about skin cancer, but her entreaties to wear a hat and sunblock fell on deaf-by-design ears.

'I just went for a quick dip,' Golly told them as she tucked her sarong over her chest. It reached her knobbly knees and was transparent enough to show she was wearing a bikini. Thank God, because Golly was fond of swimming naked.

Golly's bright eyes fell on Gib. 'I'm so happy you're here, Gib. You look so much like your dad.' Gib smiled at her, the first proper smile she'd see from him, and it almost stopped her heart. Golly let out a fluttery, 'Oh, my', and Bea understood her reaction and her dazed expression. It was a helluva smile, designed to stop air traffic and drop panties.

When he smiled like that, he could power the sun, create balls of light made from sunbeams and moondust, move mountains and drain seas. It made Bea want to know how his lips felt on hers, his tongue on her breasts, his fingers between her legs, whether the colour of his eyes changed when he slid into her...

She'd never had such an intense reaction to a man before and she didn't like it. She wasn't a fan of her world being rocked, her libido being prodded. She liked her uncomplicated life, and getting tangled up with Gib Caddell was the equivalent of prodding a semi-poisonous snake with her foot. She might not die from the bite, but life would, temporarily at least, change. And it would hurt.

No, she had enough on her plate without adding another element of confusion and complication. She had to make sure that, in the tumult of change, her identity as Parker Kane remained a secret, and find a way to get her writing mojo back. She needed to protect her creativity and her imaginary gang of five. Both were infinitely precious and had been, in many ways, a lifesaver after her relationship, and her world, collapsed.

Her life might, to some, seem boring, but she spent a great part of the day in another world, following Pip and the gang as they found hidden worlds in the gritty area of Edmonton Green. She went on adventures, fought ghosts and dragons, and laughed and cried with the gang. Because she had this rich inner world, she didn't feel she was missing out on anything. OK, sometimes she thought sex would be nice, but her vibrator took care of those urges when she was desperate. In the real world, she had Golly and Reena, a few casual friends. Did she need anyone else? Up until today, she didn't think so.

She'd met Gib the day before yesterday and he was already making her question her carefully planned life. *Madness!*

Golly's snapping fingers brought her back to the present. In her bright eyes, Bea saw her curiosity and a healthy dose of amusement. She liked men, and she loved flirting with them. Maybe Golly could keep Gib entertained while she ran down to the pool to take a quick dip. She desperately needed a reset, and a swim would do the trick.

'You seem far away, Bea-darling,' Golly complained. 'What on earth are you thinking about?'

Your party, Gib's abs, the one-bed situation, your retirement, my new proposal, this weekend, the future, an unexpected cocktail party, lights in the courtyard, Gib's abs, Gib's hands on my non-existent abs ...

Should she explain the length of her to-do list? No, she wasn't going to whine, she'd agreed to help Golly make this weekend amazing and she wasn't going to bitch. Or if she did, she'd keep it to herself.

'Just thinking about everything I have to do,' Bea replied.

Golly tucked her hand into Gib's elbow and Gib shortened his long stride to match hers. 'What would you like to drink, Gib? A beer? A G&T? A Martini?' she asked, as they approached the front door.

Gib patted her tanned and wrinkled hand. 'It's a bit early for me, Golly. But I wouldn't say no to a bottle of water.'

'You young people and your water. If I put any water into my system, my liver would think it was under attack.'

Bea caught his subtle smile. 'We're not nearly as strong as your generation, Golly,' he said.

83

Golly led them into the imposing front hall, with its double-volume ceiling and handcrafted wooden staircase. The floors were black-and-white marble tiles, and the hall table was circa 1750 and held a bronze bust by the mid-twentieth century artist, Elizabeth Frink. The expensive, masculine bronze wore a garland of wilting daisies. The massive vase on a marble plinth at the bottom of the stairs contained brown and withered flowers. Bea added finding fresh flowers to her to-do list.

Bea watched Gib out of the corner of her eye; waiting for his reaction when he clocked the ten-foot nude on the wall above the hall table. It was sexy and sinuous and a little erotic.

Instead of commenting on the subject, he stepped forward and peered at the signature in the corner of the painting. 'It's a Heppel, probably painted in the late sixties or early seventies. Something about it makes me want to link it to his famous Nudes of New York series, but it's too abstract to fit in there. And his next six paintings were more realistic, and the subjects were easily identifiable.'

Bea stared at him, surprised by his knowledge. While well known to connoisseurs, Heppel wasn't a name that sprang to everyone's lips when they saw the painting. Gib looked from the painting to Golly and back to the painting. 'How did you come to model for Heppel?' he asked.

Golly laughed and clapped her hands, delighted. 'How did you know it was me?'

'The tilt of the subject's head. It's the way you look at people a lot taller than you, you did it to me outside.'

Golly patted his big bicep. 'You clever man.'

Damn. It was bad enough that he was sexy, she didn't need him to be intelligent, and *interesting*, too. If he turned out to be nice, she might have to ram a dagger into her heart and be done with it.

You're not going to do this, Bea, you're not.

'I met Heppel in New York, when I first started work in a publishing house on Broadway, as an intern. Interns weren't paid back then, and I was short of money. A friend of a friend told me he was looking for models, so I went along, and he hired me.' Golly waved her hand at the painting. 'Of course, he only painted that after we started sleeping together.' She pulled a face. 'He was a good artist, but a lousy lay. I forgave him when he realised he preferred men.'

Before any of them could respond to that, Golly spoke again. 'Then the dick went to Vietnam and got injured over there. Stupid man.'

'I don't think he wanted to get hurt, Godma,' Bea pointed out.

'War is stupid,' Golly said, placing her small fists on her jutting hips. 'Women should run the world; we'd make a far better job of it than men.'

'I've always said women are the smarter species,' Gib smoothly replied.

Bea would bet her next quarter royalties he'd never said anything of the sort. She narrowed her eyes at him, and he smiled. She gripped the back of an elegant chair, next to which was a wooden wine barrel holding a collection of never-used walking sticks.

Gib gestured to Golly's portrait. 'I presume he gave you the painting as a gift?'

'Jacqui Farrow bought it at auction a few years ago and harangued me to buy it from her. I didn't want to, because I was still mad at him for going to Vietnam.' Golly shrugged. 'I don't remember him painting it. Or me. There were lots of artists, lots of nude modelling, lots of dope, booze, and sex before, during and after those sessions... I was,' she proudly admitted, 'a bit of a slut!'

Bea rolled her eyes. 'We don't use that word anymore, Golly,' she reminded her. Trying to get Golly to be more politically correct was an uphill struggle.

'Well, I do! I was a loose woman, a bit of a nympho,' she told Gib, with not a hint of embarrassment. 'I love sex. Haven't had much of it lately, though.'

Right, too much information. To his credit, Gib's expression didn't change, except that his silver-blue eyes brightened with mirth. Golly had no shame, and no filter, but she was never normally *this* forthcoming with strangers.

Before anyone could say anything more, Reena walked into the hall, wiping her wet hands on a tea towel. 'Since Nadia and Cassie are trying to get things sorted for the cocktail party tonight, I made Chicken 65.'

Bea's eyes widened in horror. Chicken 65 was one of the spiciest dishes in India, an intensely spiced fried chicken that routinely made grown men cry. She'd been introduced to

Reena's spicy cooking when she was ten and had had twenty years for her taste buds to shrivel up and die. If Gib ate the Chicken 65, he wouldn't be able to walk and talk for days.

'I love fried chicken,' Gib responded. 'And hot food. I spent the morning on the water and I'm starving.'

Dear God. Bea closed her eyes in dismay. She could see a lawsuit in Reena's immediate future.

Reena clapped her hands, delighted. 'Good, give me ten minutes.' Reena took two steps, turned and returned to grab Golly's hand. 'You need to help me.'

'With what?' Golly demanded. 'You know I'm not domesticated, Reen!'

'Yes, I know you were made to drink wine while you watch people cook for you. But come.' Reena didn't release her grip on her hand and Golly had no option but to start walking. Bea was reminded of a carthorse leading a Shetland pony.

When they were gone, she shook her head and looked at Gib. 'How are you doing? Are you OK or do you want to run back to the cottage, desperate to get out of the madhouse? You can, it's a perfectly reasonable response.'

'Your godmother is…' Gib stopped, looking for the word. He finally settled on 'entertaining'.

'She's batshit eccentric,' Bea retorted. 'She has no filter, at all. I'm sorry about the sex talk. She doesn't respect other people's boundaries.'

Gib didn't reply, thank God. 'Can I take a look around?' he asked. 'Reacquaint myself?'

She appreciated him changing the subject. 'Sure, I'll give you a quick tour.'

Bea led him down the passage that ran at ninety degrees to the one Reena and Golly had disappeared down, except that this one had rooms to one side – the huge reception and dining rooms, and a study – and glass walls on the other. Beyond the glass wall was an extensive courtyard, large enough to seat all the guests for the party. Lemon trees in expensive pots lined the edge of the courtyard and Bea heard Gib whistle. He looked impressed.

As he should be, it was an extraordinary space.

Bea pushed open one of the many glass doors and walked outside, Gib on her heels. He stopped and slid his hands into the pockets of his shorts.

'It was smaller, and darker when we were kids,' he commented.

'Golly did a huge renovation about fifteen years ago. She put in the glass doors and revamped the courtyard to make this enormous entertainment space.'

'It's amazing.'

Bea'd written the bulk of book number four here, the book she loved the most. 'Isn't it? Golly's Folly is my happy place. I feel so inspired here.'

'And what do you need inspiration for?' Gib asked.

He was sharper than a spear and she had to watch her words around him. She couldn't run her mouth and risk outing herself as Parker Kane. She shrugged. 'Doesn't everyone need inspiration occasionally?'

His piercing look cut through the layers of bullshit and

pulled her apart, leaving her feeling exposed. Wanting to move on, she gestured to the arches and the shadowed veranda beyond them. She'd spent many afternoons lying on the couches and loungers, keeping her fair skin out of the strong Greek sun.

'On Saturday night the bar will be on the left side, the food on the other,' she said. 'The starters will be finger food, the pudding as well. The main meal will be served, with guests sitting at long tables.'

She was gabbling because she was nervous, not because she thought Gib had any interest in Saturday night's set-up.

'Sometimes Golly hires this place out to friends and friends of friends for an event, sometimes for a ridiculous amount of money, sometimes for free.'

'I can't figure her out,' he said. 'She acts like she's ditsy, but then she does or says something, and I think she's as sharp as a scalpel blade. I think she's deliberately outrageous because she gets a reaction that way. Or she does it to test boundaries.'

It had taken Bea years and therapy to work out that much, yet Gib already had Golly sussed. But she didn't want him to think Golly was only self-absorbed and attention-seeking. Well, she was, but she could also be sweet, kind and funny.

'Golly is complicated, a curious mix of wild and contemplative, funny and ferocious. She…' Bea bit her lip, wondering if he'd get what she was about to say next, or whether he'd dismiss her words without thought.

'Go on,' he said, curious.

Oh, well. If he dismissed her, it would be so much easier to dismiss *him*. If he didn't, then she'd sink deeper into…

Into whatever madness this was.

'Golly is glamorous, self-involved, and selfish, but she's also generous and interested and concerned. She frequently does things and gives things – advice, time and money, her interest – with no expectation of repayment. She runs into a situation, sprinkles her magic, and retreats again.' Bea looked at him, suddenly serious. 'That Heppel painting? What Golly didn't tell you is that she spent a month at Heppel's bedside when he was dying of AIDS in the eighties. He left her that painting in his will, but Golly sold it and donated the money to AIDS research. She then bought it again when it came back on the market. And when Reena was in danger of losing her house and, more importantly, her stables, Golly stepped in and paid off her mortgage.'

'My Uncle Hugh and cousin Navy are the same. They're both quietly involved in foundations and philanthropic work,' he replied softly, and Bea was surprised he'd said that much.

'And you?'

He looked at her. 'What about me?'

'Are you open and accepting, or suspicious and cynical?' He didn't need to answer her question, it was written all over his face. 'Don't bother to answer that. You have a layer of charm, but you don't give anything away. Also, there's lots happening under the surface.'

'I could say the same for you.'

One Bed

Shock at his words glued her feet to the courtyard's large cobblestones. 'What do you mean?' she demanded.

'You're hiding something,' he said, in a voice so bland he could've been ordering coffee. 'You watch your words, as if you're scared to let something slip.'

How…? *How* did he know that? Did he suspect she was Parker Kane? But how could he? They'd only recently met! Was he just super perceptive or did every emotion skitter across her face? She suspected it was a combination of the two, a little of the first, and a lot of the second.

'I'm not interesting enough to have secrets,' she told him.

'Oh, I disagree,' he drawled. His gaze drifted over her face, making her feel hot and cold and her heart rate accelerated. Why did he have such an effect on her and how was she going to get herself under control?

Bea blushed. Suddenly she was standing on the edge of a bubbling volcano, both mesmerised and terrified. She stepped back and whipped her eyes away. She desperately needed to put some distance, mental and physical, between her and Gib.

'You're a lot spikier than you were when you were six.'

'There's this new concept, I don't know if you've heard about it, it's called growing up.'

He almost smiled. 'More sarcastic, too. And you're still a neat freak. I remember you making your bed every day and stacking your books in perfect piles.'

'And you barely remembered to brush your teeth,' she shot back. 'Did you shower once during those six weeks?'

He smiled. 'I was swimming so much, I didn't see the point. Dad and I had a few arguments about that. And about me coming home way after curfew.'

'I know, dinner was delayed night after night,' she grumbled.

He didn't seem to hear her. 'God, that summer … it was amazing.'

'Life is easier when you're young. Ten or eleven is the perfect age. Not old enough for hormones to have kicked in, young enough not to care what people think about you. Insanely curious, deeply loyal. Energetic and interested in the world around you.'

'You must've had a hell of a year when you were ten,' he said.

Actually, no. Ten was when she'd segued into becoming a mini adult, when she realised that other kids didn't know how to make scrambled eggs and macaroni cheese, or how to order food and household necessities online using their father's credit card. It was the year she'd realised she lived in a different world from her peers, an adult world, and started to pull back from her friends, to create her own world on paper. Shortly after her tenth birthday, Bea started writing letters to Pip, her imaginary penpal. Describing the adventures they could have was her steam valve, a means of escape. It was from those lonely letters that the Urban Explorers were born

She now clearly remembered Gib back then, his hair lightened by the sun, his light eyes a perfect contrast to his nut-brown body. He must have been lurking in her subconscious for years, manifesting as her beloved Pip down the line.

And, yes, that freaked her out. She'd think about that later, (possibly never), it was too much to take in, to work through, now. She crossed her arms over her chest and rocked on her heels. 'We should go in, Golly is a stickler for punctuality.'

And because life kept throwing shade at her, she still had to eat Reena's fiery Chicken 65.

Joy.

Chapter Five

The kitchen in the villa was, by far, Bea's favourite room. A battered, well-scrubbed twelve-seater pine table with mismatched chairs tucked under it stood in the middle of the room, its sturdy legs resting on greeny-ochre limestone tiles. Herbs grew in pots on the windowsill. The granite counters mimicked the floor and bright colours in the splashback – Mediterranean reds, oranges and yellows added pops of colour. There were two copper sinks and a huge sea-blue fridge. Like so much in the house, the contrasting colours shouldn't work, but they did.

Bea drained the glass of freshly squeezed lemonade Reena handed her, and after kicking off her sandals, she lifted the lid to the serving dish sitting on the table, wincing when the smell incinerated the inside of her nose. She could tell, from the colour and the aroma, that the fried chicken was way hotter than normal.

'What happened?' she asked.

Reena grimaced. 'A slight measurement problem.'

Bea took the clean fork Reena held out to her and peeled back a sliver of chicken. It was barely warm and would be a perfect filling, if edible, for the thick slabs of freshly baked sourdough Nadia made earlier. Bea lifted the fork to her lips and took a cautious bite.

The heat rolled over her tongue and caught at the back of her throat. *Hoo-boy!* She waved her hand in front of her mouth, thinking that she might end up with blisters on her tongue.

Reena sent her an anxious look. 'Too hot?'

'Holy crap, Reen,' Bea replied, still waving her mouth.

'Can we serve it to Gib?'

Bea winced. 'It's a *lot* hotter than you usually make it.' The guy annoyed, irritated, and attracted her in equal measure, but she wanted him to be able to walk and talk.

Golly breezed into the kitchen. 'Hello, my babies,' she sing-songed, heading straight for a cupboard and taking out four wine glasses. She sat them on the table and opened the fridge. She pulled out a bottle of white wine and squinted at the label. 'Yes, a Chardonnay. *Perfect*. Where's Gib?'

'Washing his hands.' Bea looked at the chicken and frowned. 'I think he should stick to bread and salad.'

'Pfft! It's not that hot,' Reena told her. 'Do stop fussing, Bea!'

'I just don't want you to be sued for inflicting gross bodily harm,' Bea shot back, sliding into her normal seat at the table.

'You are so dramatic,' Reena whipped back, as Golly

poured a healthy amount of wine into her glass. Well, the chilli might affect Gib's ability to walk and talk, but the wine, thanks to an already long day and not much sleep over the past few weeks, and barely any last night, would do the same to her.

At this rate, she might not even notice the six-foot-something man sharing her bed.

Talking about people sharing beds … there was something she needed to ask her godma.

'Before Gib comes back, Golly … I need to know if you're in any could-cause-you-trouble relationships at the moment?'

'That's hurtful,' Golly replied, not looking, or sounding, the least bit wounded.

'C'mon, Golly, you know what I'm asking…' More than one event had ended with the other half realising that their partner was colouring outside of their relationship lines with Golly. 'If I know, I can try and keep you separated. Though, you know, it might be a good policy if you don't sleep with people who are in committed relationships.'

'I'm not cheating, they are,' Golly replied, as she always did. 'It's their karma, not mine.'

Bea was pretty sure karma didn't work that way.

'I am still, and always will be, gloriously single, Bea-darling,' Golly replied, not in the least embarrassed.

'And why did you mention your sex life to Gib? Dammit, Golly, you seriously need to stop with that shit!'

Golly drained some of her wine, and mischief jumped into her eyes. 'With those looks, I bet he gets laid quite often. I wonder how many people he's slept with. I think I'll ask him.'

Bea barely knew the man, but understood she had more chance of falling pregnant by an alien than she had of Gib opening up and sharing something so personal. Or, frankly, anything at all. If she was a closed book, he was the human equivalent of the Swiss Fort Knox.

'I will stab you with a fork,' Bea warned her. She was ninety per cent sure Golly was winding her up, but she couldn't take the chance.

Thankfully, they were all helping themselves to salad, fried chicken and bread when Gib walked into the kitchen. Bea immediately noticed his hair was damp; he'd probably run wet hands through it. She, on the other hand, looked like she'd been dragged through a bush backwards. Her hair refused to stay in its ponytail and kept falling and sticking to her face. She was also red from a mixture of exasperation, excitement and stress.

And she was deeply, deeply worried about Gib's reaction to Reena's chilli.

Please, please, let him not be too emotionally attached to his tastebuds.

'Something smells amazing,' Gib said, taking the seat opposite her at the kitchen table. He took the glass of wine Golly pushed on him and thanked her. He lifted it. 'Here's hoping you have a marvellous weekend, Golly.'

God, he was smooth. No, that wasn't fair, it was a nice toast. It was pitch perfect, he certainly knew what to say at the right time. But it was impossible to see below that urbane, corporate CEO surface. Golly grinned at him as they all clinked glasses.

Bea leaned forward and waited for Gib to look at her. When he did, she suggested, as serious as a torpedo strike, that he avoid Reena's chicken. 'I *strongly* advise you stick to bread and salad,' she insisted.

Gib smiled at her and slid a piece of bread onto his plate. 'I'm not missing out on the fried chicken. It smells amazing.'

'Maybe, but it has the kick of a bionic superhero.'

Gib sipped his wine. 'Bea, whenever I go to a new city, whether it's Mumbai or Beijing, I always ask the locals where I should eat. Their food is always spicier than what they serve the tourists and I've never had a problem.'

Maybe, but he'd yet to taste Reena's Chicken 65. While tasty, she was sure it measured about a trillion on the Scoville measurement scale. She was used to Reena's spicy cooking, but she'd only managed a tiny sliver of chicken before throwing in the towel.

OK, well, if he was going to be stubborn about this. She sat back, folded her arms, and lifted her chin. 'Don't say I didn't warn you.'

Bea watched as Gib picked up a chicken leg and bit into it. Three sets of eyes were on him as he chewed, then swallowed.

'No big deal,' he said. He took another bite, his teeth sinking into the red, crispy skin. Bea watched as he turned white, then red, then white again. And there it was…

'Feeling the burn, Gib?' she asked, her tone super sweet.

He looked down at his plate and droplets of sweat appeared on his forehead. 'Holy hell,' he croaked.

'It gets better the more you eat,' Reena told him, her mouth full. No. It didn't. Eating more of it was like shoving the red-hot end of a poker into your eye after accidentally burning your leg with it.

Gib, because he was a man and had more pride than sense, went in for another bite. He chewed, swallowed, reached for his glass of wine, and downed it in one. 'Shit,' he rasped, staring at his plate, wild-eyed.

'Good, right?' Reena said, pleased. Bea considered telling her that it wasn't a compliment, but stayed silent and spread butter on her bread.

Golly reached for a wing and took a small, delicate bite. 'Jesus, Reena, you could sell that to a warlord as a chemical weapon!'

'It's not *that* bad,' Reena protested.

'I think I'm dying,' Gib croaked. Bea filled up his wine glass and pushed it into his hand. He downed it and placed his head in his hands.

'Are you OK, Gib?' Bea asked, now a little anxious.

He was changing colours again, like an over-anxious chameleon. Red, then white, then a pastel-vomit colour, and back to white. She was fascinated and more than a little worried. That wasn't normal, right?

Bea stood and walked over to the counter and pulled a teaspoon out of the cutlery drawer. Reaching for the honey, courtesy of a hive on a neighbour's property, she opened the jar as she walked back to the table. She twisted honey around the spoon and handed it to Gib. His eyes now looked like the badly congested roads on a satnav map.

Oh, dear. Gib ate the honey and eventually nodded. Few people knew honey was one of the best remedies for chilli, one she'd discovered a few years ago when Reena put too many ghost peppers in a gumbo dish.

'Do you know that the Caroline Reaper is no longer the hottest chilli?' Reena asked, ignoring Gib's reaction. 'The new kid on the block is called Pepper X and it's nearly five hundred thousand Scoville units hotter than the Carolina Reaper.'

'And I have every one of those units blistering my tongue right now,' Gib croaked, laying his cheek on the cool table.

'My chilli doesn't even register on the Scoville scale,' Reena cheerfully told him.

Oh, it most definitely did.

'It tastes like *pain*, Reena,' Gib told her. Bea was happy to see that his colour was stabilising. Now he was simply pale. And perspiration still dotted his forehead. 'I'm pretty sure it's given me brain damage.'

Reena rolled her eyes. 'Stop being dramatic, it wasn't that bad.'

It was that bad. Gib reached for the honey and took another spoonful. 'I once heard a guy describing his experience with hot food as feeling like someone had put a grenade in his mouth and pulled the pin. That's where I am right now.'

Reena patted him on the head. 'You'll soon get used to it.'

'I really won't,' Gib assured her. 'Mostly because I'm pretty sure you destroyed every one of my tastebuds.'

Reena frowned at him. 'But you said you could handle chilli, Gib.'

Gib frowned at her. 'Normal chilli, not something that can burn holes through titanium!' he protested.

Reena dished up another helping of chicken and tucked into her food. Now that she knew Gib wasn't dying, Bea felt like she could finish her salad sandwich. She gestured to the fruit bowl, piled high with oranges, grenadillas, and ripe, round peaches. 'There's fruit if you're still hungry,' she told him as he pushed his plate away. 'Or salad. Cold meats in the fridge.'

Gib helped himself to another teaspoon of honey. 'Jesus, that was intense,' he told them, while massaging his throat.

He reached for a peach from the bowl in the centre of the table, and looked at it, debating whether he was up to eating or not.

'So, are you coming to my cocktail party tonight?' Golly asked him.

He cut the peach with a sharp knife Reena handed him. After popping a piece into his mouth, he cocked his head, his face still pale. 'What's the occasion?' he asked.

'Do we need a reason to drink champagne?' Golly demanded, before shrugging. 'Some friends are in town already and it seemed silly for us to be doing our own thing when they could be here with me, telling me how wonderful they think I am.'

Yep, she was going to milk this weekend for all it was worth. Gib leaned back and placed his ankle on his knee. 'You really should work on your confidence and self-esteem, Golly,' he said, lifting another sliver of peach into his mouth.

She cackled, enjoying him. 'I know I'm a bit much, but if I don't blow my own horn, then no one is going to do it for me.' They laughed and Reena stood up to gather their now empty plates. 'So, are you going to join us?'

Gib shook his head. 'Don't feel offended, Golly, but I'm going to sit this one out.'

Golly pouted. 'Why?' she demanded, as truculent as an overtired toddler.

'I came to Santorini to get away from people.'

Golly leaned forward. 'Again, why?'

Bea's interest sharpened. Maybe he'd let something personal slip with Golly.

'I'll just stay in the cottage and read,' he calmly replied.

Damn, no dice.

Golly cocked her head to the side. 'You intrigue me, Gib Caddell. Still waters run deep.'

Gib placed his peach on his plate and reached for a slice of bread. 'Did you say there are cold cuts in the fridge?' he asked, adroitly changing the subject. He stood and walked over to the fridge. Before Golly could ask a follow-up question, or continue her interrogation, he spoke again. 'So,

Reena, have you ever killed someone with your chilli chicken? Or put them in hospital?'

Reena protested with a loud squawk and Bea met Golly's inquisitive, slightly annoyed eyes. Her godmother was used to getting her own way, having her questions answered, her curiosity assuaged. Golly lifted her eyebrows and Bea knew what she was asking – what is he hiding? Bea shrugged. She had no idea, but she figured that in Gib, Golly'd met her match.

He wasn't going to be charmed, hassled or manipulated into giving answers or information.

Pity.

Bea walked out of the bedroom of the cottage, her fingers at her right ear, trying to attach the butterfly to the back of the pin of the diamond earrings Golly had given her for her twenty-first birthday. She'd heard cars arriving, and the chatter of voices from the guests on the path as they walked up the esplanade.

Golly said she'd told people to arrive at six, but her concept of time was fluid, and Bea couldn't guarantee Golly would be on hand to greet her guests. She was fond of making an entrance. Bea couldn't rely on Reena to act as a host either, as she'd been known to answer the door in torn-at-the-seat jodhpurs, with straw in her hair and horse shit on her boots.

'*Shit, shit, shit,*' Bea muttered, holding onto the

bedroom's door frame to slide one black heel onto her foot. 'Why am I always late?'

'It's only a quarter to, Bea, and you look…'

She lifted her head, looking around the room to find Gib. He stood at the half-open doors leading onto the small deck. His feet were bare, he smelt familiar – the bloody man had used her Creed shower gel again – and he held a glass of red wine in his hand. Her heart sighed, and her womb rolled over.

Seriously?

Bea swapped feet and teetered as she tried to hook her shoe over her toes. She waited for him to complete his sentence, and wished he'd hurry up. How did she look? Harried? Stressed? Annoyed with her godmother? Like she wished she was in her pyjamas and curled up on the couch with a romance novel?

'Stunning,' Gib stated, walking into the cottage. He stopped and gave her a long up-and-down look. 'That's a lovely dress, Bea.'

Oh, he had a good line in bullshit because this dress was off the rack and was on sale when she bought it. It had sheer, cap sleeves and a scalloped neckline, and its hemline was made more interesting by a black gauze insert, but it wasn't anything special. It certainly wasn't designer.

'You don't believe me,' he stated, cocking his head to the side.

She met his eyes and shrugged. 'I think you know the right thing to say at the appropriate time.'

His eyes darkened to pewter. 'I don't say things I don't

mean.' His tone held a note of don't-test-me-on-this and she blushed at her churlish response.

'Then, thank you, I guess.' She started to pull her lip between her teeth and remembered that she didn't want to smudge her lipstick. She rarely wore the stuff and hated how it felt on her lips. She resisted the urge to ask him to kiss it off. *Bad girl, Bea.*

He reached for a light hoodie lying on the back of a wingback chair and pulled it over his head. 'Don't you need a wrap? There's a cool breeze coming off the sea.'

'If I start to get cold, I'll run up to Golly's room and steal one of her pashminas.'

'If I was going, I would've loaned you my jacket.'

If he was going, his jacket would cover her dress, would smell of his light, citrus-and sea cologne, and would be warm from his body heat. Much nicer than a pashmina. *Not helping, Bea.*

Lifting his wrist, she pushed back the sleeve of his hoodie to look at his watch, which seemed like it had been worn a time or two. Its face said Rolex Oyster. Wasn't that the same one she saw on *Antiques Roadshow* that was worth a few fortunes?

'Nice watch,' she told him. 'It looks old.'

'It was my father's.'

There was a story there, one she was desperate to know. But he wouldn't ever tell her. Gib wasn't the talking type.

Bea finally took in the time and grimaced. 'I need to get going.'

He nodded at her shoes. 'You're walking on rough paths in those?'

'My godmother would have several kittens if I attended her cocktail party in anything but heels, Gib.'

He walked over to the door and picked up the flip flops she'd stepped out of earlier. 'Wear these on the path and slip into your heels at the end of it.' When she hesitated, he shook his head. 'I think you have enough to do without having to deal with a sprained ankle.'

She looked at the flip flops in his big hand, unexpectedly touched. Gerry had never thought about her or considered her comfort. She'd always been the one ten steps ahead who remembered to put petrol in the car and slide an umbrella into her bag on overcast days. The one who'd locked up their flat and done the grocery shopping. Gerry was an 'artist', a 'creative' and couldn't, *shouldn't*, be expected to remember the mundane. Ironic that her stories sold, and his songs never did.

It felt weird, and lovely, to be the object of a man's thoughtfulness. Using his arm to balance, she swapped shoes, surprised when Gib tugged her heels out of her hands and let them dangle from his fingers. 'Thank you,' she whispered. It was such a little thing, but it meant so much.

'I'll walk you up.' Gib went over to the front door, pulling it open and using her shoes to gesture to her to go before him. Manners, too. He flipped off the light switch and pulled the door closed behind him and they walked out into the kind of magical light that could only be found at the end of a still-hot Greek day.

Gib placed his hand on her back and guided her onto the path that led to the pergola and the outdoor entertainment area overlooking the caldera. It was a spectacular place to hold a cocktail party and the perfect place to watch God paint the sky with blues and purples, oranges, reds and pinks. Bea shook her head at her romantic thoughts—*this is not a romcom, Beatrice!*

'Who will be at that party tonight?' Gib asked her, dropping his hand. She immediately missed it.

She had to think. 'God knows. A few of Golly's friends, the ones who are in Santorini already. Some of Golly's local friends, too, I imagine. She's been coming here for a long time, and she's well-known on the island.'

He was quiet and Bea inhaled deeply, the air tinged with lavender and oregano and the sea, mixed with Gib's delicious scent. The breeze was cool – she kept forgetting it was autumn! – but it would die down when the sun sank below the horizon. She saw hints of purples and pinks in the sky and knew Golly's guests would be treated to a spectacular sunset. Of course they would, Golly wouldn't stand for anything less.

'Are you looking forward to the party this weekend?' Gib asked, his deep voice rumbling over her skin. 'Will you know a lot of the people coming?'

'Yes, I've met many of them through Golly.'

'I keep meaning to ask you what you do for a living.'

Shit. *Shit.* She thought she'd dodged that question. So

she trotted out her bog-standard answer, hating, for some reason, the need to lie to him. 'I inherited some money from my father when he died, and I work part-time as Golly's assistant,' she told him. Inheriting money wasn't a lie, but Golly had an assistant back in London who was brutally efficient and practically ran her agency.

There was something about Gib that made her want to confide in him, to tell him who she was. And that was so strange, because she was very used to keeping everything tightly controlled, locked away in its separate compartments. But here he was strolling through her mind and picking open those locked chambers, trying to peep inside.

And she wanted him to.

God, she was in a world of trouble here. And she'd only met this guy *forty-eight hours ago!*

'It looks like the path smooths out here,' he said. 'Do you want to swap shoes?'

Just around the corner was the esplanade, pergola and outdoor bar. The happy sounds of people talking and laughing rose and fell, and a violinist played modern classics on her hauntingly beautiful instrument. Finding someone to provide music, as Golly demanded, had been difficult, but the young girl Cass had hired was talented.

'Did I ask Cass to pay her?' Bea mused out aloud.

Gib didn't miss a beat. 'Remind her when you see her. You need to put on your heels, Bea.'

She nodded, held onto his arm again, and swapped out her shoes. She left her flip flops on the side of the path for the return trip later and stepped onto the smooth concrete path that wound up the slight incline to the top of the hill. She looked at Gib, his face in the shadows.

'I wish you'd said yes to coming,' she impulsively told him. When was the last time she'd attended a party with a gorgeous guy on her arm? Gerry and Golly had hated each other, so she'd kept them apart, which meant going to Golly's parties alone.

And Gerry's idea of a good time was a pot smoke-filled pub with music either sad enough to make you weep, or screechy enough to make your ears bleed.

Gib gave her that half smile she was coming to love. 'I'll see you later, Bea.'

She was on her own again. Situation normal. Gib melted into the shadows and Bea walked up to Golly's esplanade. Below them, the fairy lights created a pretty wave over the villa's courtyard, and the lamps in the garden threw light up the walls of the villa and it glowed. Lovely, classy ... sophisticated. Tonight was a dry run for the party on Saturday night.

So far, so good.

'Line 'em up, bub, because I plan on starting this weekend off right by getting shitfaced!'

Bea braked and tipped her head back to look at the streaked pink and purple sky. Trust her godmother, and woman of the hour, to bring her back to earth with a thump.

Chapter Six

Fifteen minutes later, Bea leaned her shoulder into one of the pergola's uprights, a glass of chardonnay in her hand, thinking that if this cocktail party was a precursor to the main event on Saturday, she was toast.

She heard a masculine snort of laughter behind her and turned to see Gib shaking his head. Her eyes widened as she took in his stone-coloured suit. Instead of a shirt and tie, he wore the same black T-shirt he'd had on earlier, with cap-toed, suede and leather trainers on his feet. He was *GQ* perfect. He looked imperturbable as always, but his eyes, full of laughter, gave him away.

'It's not funny,' she insisted.

'No, she's *not* funny. She's hysterical.'

He gestured to the pergola, where Golly sat *on* the bar, her bare legs and feet swinging. All the guests had made an effort to look nice – except Bea's godmother and Reena. Golly'd slapped a tiara – real sapphires or not? Who knew?

– onto her head and swiped on some bold fuchsia-pink lipstick. But she still wore the same sarong from earlier, tightly knotted above her bikini-top covered boobs. Heavy silver bangles adorned her slim wrists, and the silver chain around her neck was baby-finger thick.

Reena didn't look much better. She was in the same jodhpurs she'd been wearing all day: frayed at the knee and tucked into low-heeled riding boots. She'd pulled on a man's button-down and rolled up the sleeves, one of which had a long tear at the elbow.

'Pour those tequilas, sweetheart!' Golly told the bartender.

He did as ordered and filled a row of shot glasses lined up in military precision on the bar. Four? No. *Five*. Jesus.

'Cheers to Golly, she's true blue, she's a pis-shead through and through!' Reena chanted, handing Golly a tequila. No lemon and salt for her, she was a hardcore drinker.

'She's a bastard so they say, she tried to go to heaven, but she went the other way. Down! Down!'

The group by the bar joined in the chant as Golly threw back one tequila after the other, slapping the third glass on the bar with a triumphant yell. Reena, bless her, pushed the other two behind Golly's back where she couldn't see them.

'It's like a septuagenarian frat party,' Gib said, laughing.

It was an accurate description. Bea shook her head. 'Welcome to my life with Golly,' she told him. She squared her shoulders and straightened her spine. 'Time to do damage control. If she carries on tossing shots back, she won't make eight o'clock.'

As she approached the bar, she wondered how to get Golly down, and how to con her into drinking some water. She smiled at people she knew, kissed cheeks, all while keeping an eye on her godmother, who was leaning sideways to listen to a man with a handlebar moustache. If she leaned too far, she'd lose her centre of balance and tip over – and the concrete floor would turn her head into a smashed melon.

Bea knew she couldn't storm in there and demand Golly get down, she didn't want to embarrass her. No, she had to be subtle and sneaky, and make Golly think that getting down was her idea. And God, she needed to get her away from the bar. Being in close proximity to that amount of alcohol was dangerous.

Bea caught Reena's eye and scowled at her. Reena just lifted her shoulder in a 'what can I do?' gesture. True, Golly didn't listen to anyone, ever.

As Bea stepped between Golly and her admirers, Gib moved closer to the bar, his arms opened wide. 'Golly, my gorgeous. I heard that there was a beautiful woman holding court at the bar, and I'm not surprised to see it's you.'

Before she could reply, he placed his hands on her narrow hips, and easily lifted her off the bar. Golly giggled and held onto his arm as he placed her on her feet. She was, Bea noticed, with grudging admiration, a lot steadier on her feet after three tequilas than Bea had been when she'd swapped her flip flops for her heels earlier.

Golly reached up and patted his face. 'If only I were twenty years younger, you wouldn't be able to keep up with me, young man.'

He lifted her hand and gallantly kissed her knuckles. 'I can't keep up with you now.' He threaded her hand through his elbow. 'Now, come with me, and let's go watch the sun set. I think it's going to be a beauty.'

Golly nodded. 'They always are. Yes, let's all go watch nature paint the sky.' As Gib passed her, Bea grabbed his free hand and squeezed.

When his eyes met hers, she mouthed a 'thank you'. He'd handled the situation perfectly, without embarrassing her godmother. He came across as being debonair and assured, supremely confident, but, nobody would suspect how closed off he was, how much he hated answering personal questions.

Why was he at the party? He'd told her he was desperate to be alone, that he needed solitude, and she thought he would've jumped at the chance to have a couple of Bea-free hours alone in the cottage.

But here he was, charming her grandmother, shaking hands and smiling as Golly introduced him to her guests. It was like he'd pulled on a cloak, and Bea suspected he'd flipped into corporate CEO mode. He hadn't wanted to attend this party, and Gib Caddell wasn't someone who did things he didn't want to do.

So … *why*?

With his hand on Golly's lower back, Gib guided her to the stone wall. A waiter distributed flutes of champagne, and Gib pulled up a chair. Golly sank into it and placed her bare feet on the wall. Bea stood behind her, her shoulder connecting with Gib's bicep, her eyes on the quickly changing sky in front of them.

There were streaks of reds and pinks, which deepened to purple. The dying sun tossed yellow sparkles onto the sea, which faded to silver and then disappeared beneath the flat surface. Stars popped out, cubes of light on a swathe of rich, blue-velvet sky.

As the day faded into darkness, Cass's crew lit fat candles and pretty lanterns, and soft light spilt from the pergola. The violinist segued into soft rock and a few couples swayed in time to the beat.

Bea pushed her way into the space between Golly and the wall and dropped to her haunches. She couldn't balance well in her heels, so she gripped the arm of Golly's chair.

Golly pouted. 'I know, I know, I should've showered, changed. And I shouldn't be slamming back tequilas. That's what you want to say, isn't it?'

Bea frowned, shaking her head. Did she really nag so much? 'Actually, no. I want to know if you're OK.' She gestured to her clothes. 'It's unlike you not to spend hours on your clothes and makeup.'

Golly shook her head and looked out to sea. 'I thought I'd lie down for a quick nap, and I fell asleep. I didn't have enough time to shower and change so I thought, fuck it. I slapped on my tiara, some lippy, and came out here.'

Bea frowned. Her godma had never been a need-a-nap person. 'Are you feeling OK?' she asked, resisting the urge to check if Golly had a temperature. If she did that, she'd have a layer of skin stripped off her and her hand slapped.

But the reality was that Golly was growing old, and one day, sooner than Bea'd like, she'd have to live in a world without her. The thought made her feel a little light-headed. Why was she even considering Golly's mortality? Everyone knew God and the devil needed more time to argue about where Golly would spend eternity – God didn't want her corrupting Heaven, and Satan was worried she'd upend Hell. Their inability to concede would give her another few decades together and a birthday card for Golly from the King.

Bea wanted to tell her she loved her, but Golly wasn't sentimental and wouldn't appreciate her getting soppy. Before she could speak again, Golly slapped her hands against her thighs and stood up, bumping her knee against Bea's, who wobbled on her heels. Needing every bit of her core strength, of which she had none, Bea held onto the chair and pushed her way to her feet, wincing at her complaining knees. She was thirty, surely she wasn't old enough to have dodgy knees?

Bea sighed as Golly strode over to the bar, a woman on a mission to get this party started. Rubbing her hands over her face, Bea pushed back her shoulders and swallowed a yawn, thinking she'd like nothing more than to go to bed.

A shower, a pair of men's boxer shorts and a loose vest, a good romcom on her eReader … she couldn't think of anything better. Actually, that was a big fat lie. She tipped her head to look at Gib, who was talking to Reena and a tall, thin man with a goatee. Gib, naked and touching her, would be a very decent alternative.

But, thanks to her five-year bed-based-fun drought, she wasn't sure she'd know what to do with him if they dropped their clothes. Was sex like riding a bike? Did you automatically remember how to do it? Or was a refresher course required? If yes, where did you go to get one? Or was that foreplay? Did Gib like to kiss, to taste and savour, to take his sweet, sweet time, or was he an in-and-get-it-done lover? Despite their years together, Gerry had never managed to give Bea an orgasm without her input.

As Golly always said, you can't do epic shit with basic people. With Gerry, even mediocre sex had been out of the question.

The clinking of a spoon against a crystal glass caught her attention. Bea wasn't surprised to see it was Golly demanding attention. Who else would it be?

Bea's eyes danced over the crowds and stopped on Gib, standing just outside the pergola, his expression one of mild amusement. Feeling her gaze on him, he turned his head, his eyes slamming into hers. In his, she caught the heady combination of want and need and lust. And as they traded eye-fucks – because there was no other word for what they were doing – a klaxon blared in her head flashing 'BEWARE!' in huge letters.

Despite their ultra-brief acquaintance, she knew, deep inside, that Gib was a threat to her independence, her lifestyle, to her need to keep herself apart. Something in him called to her and she fought the urge to walk over to him and step into his arms. She wanted to lie to herself, to say that she was simply attracted to him, that it was pheromones or a need for sex, that it was being in Greece, where the innate sensuality of the island heightened emotions...

But from the moment she first saw him walking towards her, she knew an adventure was about to begin.

And tonight, she also, simply, liked him. Liked that he'd sized up a situation, and then did what was needed. Gerry had been blissfully, selfishly unconcerned about anything and anyone that didn't involve him, and he would never think of her swapping her shoes to minimise her discomfort, or rescuing Golly from her perch on a bar. Instead of talking about himself, as Gerry often did – he was his own favourite subject – Gib gave nothing away about who he was, what he did and how he felt.

Yes, his reticence was frustrating, but he was a refreshing change from her self-involved ex.

'Calm the hell down, peasants!' Golly shouted. The crowd laughed but did as she said. Golly's tiara sat crookedly in her messy pink hair and her eyes blazed with vigour. Her godma was the embodiment of the saying 'pocket rocket'.

'A toast!' Golly raised her wineglass in the air. 'It matters not if the wine glass is half empty or half full, clearly there's room for more! Here's to me!'

Glasses were lifted in the air and a series of 'to Golly' floated down the hill, to the purple-black sea.

And they were off.

As the last of Golly's guests walked down the path to their cars and waiting taxis, Bea sat on the stone wall and slipped her feet out of her shoes. She wiggled her toes and winced as blood made its way into her scrunched digits, the arches of her feet, and her heels.

Cass, their event manager, sat next to her and crossed one long leg over the other. She wore a plain black shift dress and black hightops, eminently sensible since she'd been scurrying around for hours. She placed two massive margaritas on the wall between them.

'It's a beautiful night,' she said, tipping her head back to look at the stars.

'It is,' Bea agreed. The waiters and bar staff buzzed around them, collecting glasses and plates of half-eaten food. Most of the platters were empty, and she was grateful. Her imaginary gang of five lived on the poverty line and throwing away food, in real life and in fiction, annoyed her.

'Good job on estimating how much food we needed, Cass.'

'Thanks. But, to be honest, I told Nadia to under-cater because, unlike other places where we work, I wasn't able to find an organisation to take the leftover food.'

And there was another reason why she liked this woman so much. Bea sent her a sideways glance and nibbled the inside of her cheek. She wasn't good at putting herself out there, but would Cass think it weird if she asked whether she and Nadia would be keen to grab a coffee, maybe even dinner, when they returned to London? She wrinkled her nose. No, she was being silly. Why would they?

They probably had an active social life, and as they often travelled, they probably liked to spend their London time catching up with friends and chilling. It was easier to not ask than to risk being rejected.

Rejection, in any form, sucked.

Bea picked up her margarita and sipped, enjoying the tart liquid sliding over her tongue and down her throat. 'Where's Nadia?' she asked.

'She went to bed ages ago,' Cass replied. 'She's an introvert and would far prefer to have her nose in a book than talk to strangers.'

'Me, too!' Bea fervently agreed.

The waitstaff called out cheerful goodnights and Cassie laughingly refused their offer to join them at a club in Fira. 'I used to work late, then only go out clubbing around midnight or one. Now all I want to do is drink my drink, and amble down the hill and snuggle up to my wife,' she said.

Even when she and Gerry were younger, Bea had never spent much time partying into the early hours of the morning. Before she was published, she worked at a sports goods shop during the day and wrote at night. Gerry spent a good part of the money she earned on music and acting lessons and class A drugs, assuring her his big break was just around the corner.

Bea took another huge gulp of her drink. She'd told

herself she wasn't going to think about the past and yet here she was, allowing the memories to slide on in. Now wasn't the time to look back. For the next ten days or so, she was going to live in the present, and not worry about the future. She was going to celebrate Golly's birthday, not think about her retirement, while also trying to keep this weekend from descending into chaos.

Cassie nudged her and nodded at Golly who was walking over to them in a not-so-straight line, puffing on her cigarillo. Her sarong had been retied and she looked sex-satisfied. Oh, God. Who had she been snogging or worse? And where? Actually, *no*. No details required.

Reena, who was lying on the wall, a precarious habit and one nobody could break her of, sat up and narrowed her eyes at her old friend. 'You are such a tart,' she stated, rolling her eyes.

Golly blew on her nails and grinned. 'I've still got moves, Reen.'

Bea really didn't need to know about Golly's moves, not *ever*. Then Golly picked up her margarita, took a healthy sip and perched on Bea's thighs. *Oomph.*

Reena made her way over to them and placed her riding boot on the wall next to Cassie. She rested her forearm on her thigh and looked out to sea. 'We're going to miss this when we're dead, Gols.'

'We might not, depending on what the next place is like. It might be amazing,' Golly blithely responded.

'Or hot.'

Golly ignored Reena's pithy response. 'If I go first, I'll let you lot know I'm still around if I can. I'll flick some lights, throw some pans, bang on walls.'

Golly was promising to haunt her after she died, par for the course. Reena and Golly started talking about someone's divorce settlement, and Bea tuned them out.

She was bone-deep tired, emotionally depleted, and she still had to decide where she was sleeping. The idea of sleeping on the half-broken divan made her body ache. She wanted a decent night's sleep in a decent bed. Preferably after some amazing, ground-shaking, earth-tilting sex.

She hadn't seen Gib for a while. Where was he, anyway? Had he had enough of being sociable and gone back to the cottage? And if he was still awake when she returned, how awkward would the rest of the evening be? Would he try and talk her out of sleeping on the Bed of Horrors? There was a good chance he'd tell her she was stupid because she'd created the Berlin Wall of pillows between them. She didn't want another argument with him, but that's what they would have if she insisted on sleeping on the divan.

On the other hand, she didn't want to go back to the cottage to find Gib in bed, fast asleep and not remotely concerned about where she was and what she was doing.

'Divorce Settlement broke a leg,' Golly replied, helping herself to the rest of Bea's margarita.

'Had to be shot. Never realised his potential,' Reena added, sounding bleak. 'Such a damned waste.'

Ah. Divorce Settlement was a *horse.*

'Oh, look, Gib's back...' Golly said, wiggling again. Dammit, she had a bony arse.

Right, so Gib had stuck around. What did that mean? If anything.

Gib looked at the group sitting on the wall, their faces lit by the lights of the burned-down candles on the low tables around them. The dim light smoothed Golly and Reena's aged skin, and softened Cass's angular face.

Bea looked...

Shit. She looked enchanting in her figure-hugging dress ending two inches from her knees. Her hair was half out of its loose knot and lay on her smooth shoulders. Her eyes held laughter-tinged frustration. Or frustration-tinged laughter.

Her arms were around her godmother's waist, and Gib noticed the small kiss she dropped on Golly's shoulder, the quick brush of her cheek against her wrinkled arm.

They had a bond that ran deep and true and had been built, he was sure, by tears and talking, fights and frustration. Bea's impossible high heels lay on the flagstones, and she flexed her bright aqua-tipped toes. He tightened his grip on her flip flops, glad he'd picked them up on his way back from walking the mayor, and his wife, to their car. They'd looked a little lost and he felt somebody should.

Gib kept his eyes on Bea, who'd yet to notice his approach. On coming closer, he saw she looked tired, a drooping woodland sprite who'd spent a long day in a forest doing whatever sprites did. Golly spotted him and Bea looked past her and smiled.

It went straight to his gut and his world tilted, just a little.

Fuck, he'd just met her, they hadn't even kissed, had yet to make love. But he couldn't, not for one minute, help thinking this woman would change his life. How, he'd just have to wait and see.

He scrubbed his hand over his face. He had to be reacting like this because, like Golly – and wasn't that information he didn't need to know! – he hadn't had sex in a while, and he was missing it.

Logic dictated that his reaction to Bea could be connected to his lack of sex, his stay on this romantic, tranquil Greek island and being forced to step away from work, to slow down, just a little.

OK, he'd only spent two full days on Santorini, but they'd been totally different to his high-pressure, high-octane lifestyle. Since leaving college and joining Caddell International, he'd put in long hours at work, determined to prove he had something to offer the company. And that he was anything but a Nepo-baby.

Hugh encouraged all Caddell employees to embrace a work/life balance, but since Gib wasn't interested in settling down, having a wife and 2.6 kids, his work was his life. It was his number one priority.

If he felt like this after just a couple of days – loose and relaxed – Hugh might have to use a taser to shock him back into work mode after his vacation.

'Ladies.' Gib lifted an eyebrow at the bowl-sized glasses of margaritas on the wall, hoping they weren't as strong as they looked. Bea had told him she had a full day ahead of her tomorrow and he knew from experience that working with a hangover was shit on wheels. Why was he worried? He wasn't her brother or her boyfriend, and she was an adult who could make her own choices. She didn't need his protection.

When he joined them, he looked at Bea's bare feet and handed her her flip flops. 'I thought you might need these.'

He saw surprise and confusion skitter across Bea's face. She took them tentatively, caught off guard by his gesture.

'Thank you,' she said, slipping them onto her feet with obvious relief. 'God, why do women wear stupid shoes?'

'Beats me,' Reena replied.

'Because they make our legs look fabulous,' Cass replied.

Golly stood up, stretched and leaned down to hug Cass, thanking her for making her night special. 'I know that I am a demanding old bat, but you and Nadia are the best.' Golly kissed her on both cheeks before placing her hands on Bea's shoulders.

'Same goes for you, Bea-darling. I appreciate all your hard work.'

Gib caught the flash of tears in Bea's eyes, her slightly wobbling lip. 'In ten years, you're going to tell me you need another weekend bash, and another celebration. And I'm telling you now, we'll celebrate by having afternoon tea at The Savoy.'

Something as sedate as tea? He didn't believe that for a second.

Golly hauled in a deep breath and spread her arms out wide. 'No bloody chance, Bea-darling! *Old age should bloody burn and rave at close of day; Rage, rage against the dying of the fucking light.*'

You had to admire a woman who could quote Keats while swearing like a prison inmate.

'Now, I'm going to bed with a bottle of champagne and a good book,' Golly said.

'What are you reading at the moment?' Cass asked.

It was a question he'd never dare ask, mostly because he wasn't sure he wanted to know the answer. That Fifty Shades book? *The Bible, the Quran* or *the Kama Sutra*? A serial-killer suspense? How to take over the world in your seventies?

'The Rubaiyat of Omar Khayyam,' Golly told her. 'I think the Persian scholar and I would've been friends.'

'You would've been part of his harem,' Reena said, in her raspy, blunt way. Gib wasn't sure if her comment was historically correct but wasn't about to challenge her on it. Reena scared him a little.

Golly threaded her arm through Reena's. 'Honey, he would've been part of *mine*. Along with Caravaggio, pre-syphilis of course, and that sexy Spanish actress, the one who was in the film about that drug lord.'

Reena rolled her eyes, said goodnight and the two older women walked away, arm in arm. Cass picked up her glass and took a large sip of her margarita. She turned to hug Bea.

Women were such tactile creatures, so openly affectionate. He and Navy showed they didn't despise each other by ragging each other, and giving each other back slaps and shoulder punches. Only on extreme occasions – marriages, births, when they scored a goal at indoor soccer – did they resort to quick, one-armed hugs.

'I'll see you in the morning, Bea.' Cass held Bea's face in her hands, her smile soft. 'Get some sleep, sweetheart, you look like you need it.'

'I'm so glad you're here, and I promise that bonus is going to be super big,' Bea told her, holding her wrists.

Cass kissed her forehead and when she stood up, she handed Gib a smile. 'Good night, Gib. If you get bored, I can always use a pair of free hands.'

Tomorrow, Gib intended to hit the beach, paddle for a couple of hours, and have a mid-morning nap. He wanted to use every minute of his time on Santorini relaxing in peace and solitude. 'I'll keep that in mind,' he told her.

Cass sauntered away and Gib sat down on the wall next to Bea and stretched out his legs. He picked up Cass's glass, took a sip and swallowed. There was enough tequila in there to sedate a horse.

He handed it to Bea and she shuddered. 'If I have any more, I will be less than useless tomorrow,' she told him, crossing one leg over the other, her bright yellow flip flop dangling from her pretty foot. She had a high instep and long toes...

What the hell? He'd never noticed a woman's feet before.

127

The fairy lights decorating the pergola still twinkled, and a couple of candles still had a little way to go before they burned out. The sky was in an inky, purple blue, the heavy texture of expensive velvet. The slight sea breeze danced across the ocean, up the cliffs and rolled over them. The lights of Oia twinkled in the distance. It was tranquil, lovely, and God, so tempting. As was Bea…

It didn't mean anything, it couldn't. But it did. It could.

Gib leaned forward and rubbed his hand over his face. His skin prickled at her proximity. Too close…

But not close enough.

He turned his head, and her face was right there. What else could he do but mimic Cass's gesture and hold her face in his hands? His thumbs stroked her cheekbones, and he watched her amazing eyes widen, and her lips parted. She gripped his wrists, her fingernails digging into his skin. The pulse point in her neck jumped and his heart echoed the erratic thumping of hers.

He wanted her.

'Gib…' she whispered. 'What are we doing?'

That question had layers of meaning and he had no fucking idea. 'Right now, I'm about to kiss you.' His voice sounded deeper, rougher, like he'd smoked an entire pack of cigarettes.

'OK, good. Just checking.'

He was taking that as a yes. Gib slanted his lips over hers and his heart settled, and his stomach stopped its roller-coaster ride around his body. He knew how to do this, how to make her feel good. Not because he was experienced, not because he'd loved a lot of women and knew his way around a female body, but because he felt like he knew her, that somewhere and somehow, they'd crossed paths before.

And not just as kids, but in another world, another lifetime...

Fuck!

This night, and Bea, were playing havoc with him. He wasn't a guy who waxed lyrical, he didn't look for deeper meanings. He didn't fucking *talk*.

Find your balls and get with the program, asshole. This was about attraction and sex, about their mutual need to chase pleasure.

He pulled back to look at her, taking in her gorgeous mouth and lust-swamped eyes. She hooked her arm around his neck and edged closer, her mouth landing on his again. Her tongue traced the seam of his mouth and slipped inside...

Pure fucking magic.

This time he didn't hesitate, he took what he wanted, plunging his tongue inside her mouth to discover her. She tasted of lemons and tequila, and he swiped a speck of salt off her bottom lip. Underneath the margarita, he tasted sin and temptation. Deeper and darker than he'd expected.

Needing her closer, Gib wound his arm around her waist and hauled her onto his lap, positioning her so that she was facing him, the inside of her thighs resting against his hips, the skirt of her dress lying over the crotch of his pants. He needed to feel her, so he yanked her to him and her warm mound hit his so-hard cock. Instead of pulling back, she ground against him, pushing her breasts into his chest at the same time.

This woman, so full of secrets and layers, confounded and confused him. He was used to walking the linear track to bed, no frills and no fuss. Dinner, sex, leave. But Bea was a tangled knot, a complicated puzzle … a place where he started in the middle and had no idea where he would end.

Pulling his mouth off hers, he scraped his teeth over the line of her jaw, his fingers pulling down her dress's zip. When he had enough play on her dress, he pulled it down to reveal her lacy black bra over her small but lovely breasts; he placed his hand over one and swiped her sweet nipple with his tongue. Through the lace, he felt her tighten. His hand replaced his mouth and pulled the lace down. His thumb swiped her pebbled nipple.

Bea moaned and her eyes opened, locking with his. She looked a little confused, a lot turned on, rosy and lovely and feminine. He'd never wanted anyone more than he did her, right then.

It was *just* sex, his dick talking, it didn't mean anything. He wouldn't let it.

'What are we doing, Gib?'

Her question, the same as before, and the turmoil in her voice, made him drop his hand and place it on her hip. Instead of answering her, he rested his forehead on hers and closed his eyes, trying to get air into his lungs. Bea scuttled back and pulled her dress back onto her shoulders, her eyes lowered and her long lashes casting shadows onto her cheek.

'It's so soon,' she whispered, playing with the leather and steel bracelet on his right wrist. 'I don't... This is madness.'

He agreed. And he made it a point of never stepping into a situation he didn't fully understand. He never made business deals unless he knew every facet of the agreement, and had sussed out every possible outcome. He only slept with a woman after he'd made it crystal clear he wasn't in it for the long term, that a few dates, a few weeks – no going deep and getting personal – was all he could give.

It wasn't the right time to discuss the parameters of their non-relationship, something that could only ever be a fling. She'd had a tough day and the huge yawn she'd just tried to hide, told him she needed sleep, and lots of it. They needed to drop the temperature and slow down...

People got burned when they rushed into fires.

Wrapping an arm around her, he stood up, and her legs fell from his hips. He slowly lowered her to the ground – she weighed next to nothing – and gently turned her around to zip up her dress.

'Should I apologise?' he asked, when she looked up at him.

He would if she demanded it, but she'd been as into their kiss as he was. When she shook her head, his respect rose. He liked women – people – who took responsibility for their actions.

Bea tucked her hair behind her ears and shoved her feet

into her flip flops. 'It's been a very long day, and I need sleep. I didn't get much last night.'

It wasn't that late, just a little past eleven, and he rarely went to bed before one. He wasn't a great sleeper – the last two nights had been the exception to the rule – and after years of practice, he could function just fine with three or four hours. But there were shadows under Bea's eyes, and she looked pale.

She wasn't drunk, a little tipsy maybe, but tiredness was a contributing factor. Her defences were down, and he should back away. He should give her some space, some time to think, and decide whether she wanted to sleep with him or not. If she was still awake when he got back, if she gave him the slightest encouragement, he'd have her naked so fast her head would spin. So would his.

But God, if she was in that bed asleep or pretending to sleep when he got back, the rest of his night would be hell. The last thing he wanted to do was to lie awake with a hard-as-fuck erection and watch her sleep.

But a hard dick wouldn't kill him. He didn't think. 'I'm going to go for a walk, maybe even head into Oia and see if there's a pub open.'

Gib didn't think it possible to look relieved and disappointed at the same time, but Bea made it work. 'Um, OK.'

He had no idea why her words held a hint of ice. 'I'll see you later?' *Please be awake.*

'Sure.'

Something was wrong, but he had no idea what it could

be. Did she *want* him to come back with her? And if so, for what? She said she was exhausted. Wasn't that girl code for sex being off the table?

At sea, in a place he wasn't familiar with – it pissed him off to feel as unsure as a fifteen-year-old trying to cop a feel – he watched Bea force a smile onto her face. 'Have a good time. There's a little pub near the big church, down the alley next to the bakery on the northeast corner of the square. Go there, they have a fabulous selection of beers on tap and a great wine list.'

Now she was playing Ms Tourist Guide? What the hell?

Bea surprised him by standing on her tiptoes to kiss his cheek. 'I'll try not to wake you up in the morning.'

With that sally, she strode away in the direction of the cottage.

And he was left with the suspicion that something had shifted, but he had no idea what.

Chapter Seven

M *en are pigs. All of them.*

Bea stomped her way into the cottage and slammed the door behind her. She kicked off her shoes, sending one flip flop flying across the room. It landed on the table against the far wall, nearly knocking a blue-green bohemian vase to the floor.

She touched her lips, still able to taste Gib, still able to feel his hand on her breast. Everything stopped after he touched her boob…

And that wasn't a surprise. How many arguments did she and Gerry have about her breasts? Or lack thereof. The tool often complained she had 'boy boobs' and demanded she get plastic surgery. Even if she'd wanted one, a breast enhancement was never an option when they could barely afford to pay rent and keep themselves fed.

Gib hadn't expressed his disappointment, he was too

much of a gentleman to be that crass, but how could he *not* be dissatisfied?

Flopping into the chair, she couldn't get Gerry's words out of her head – *fucking you is like doing it with an ironing board*. Bea wrapped her arms around her chest and wished that men weren't so stupid. If they didn't like her boobs, they could skirt them and head south. The rest of her was perfectly, as far as she knew, normal.

But what really killed her was her suspicion that Gib was heading into Oia to look for some action. He'd been steel-pipe hard when she sat on his lap and when she left him, his enormous erection still tented his pants.

A guy like him – good looking and successful – could walk into the nearest pub, snap his fingers and have a queue of women begging to go home with him. Or jump onto Tinder and find a hook-up almost instantaneously. Why, just because she'd backed away, should he do without?

They weren't lovers, they weren't even friends – she'd only met him, as adults, on Sunday! – but the idea of him having sex with someone else and then coming back to share a bed with her, even if it was platonic and temporary, made bile creep up her throat. Bea closed her eyes and was transported back to when Gerry used to roll in drunk or stoned, smelling of pot, beer and cheap perfume, with another woman's lipstick on the side of his mouth, or on his neck.

Oblivious to her shouting or screaming, he'd crawl into their bed and pass out, leaving her mentally and psychologically battered. To her shame, it happened way too many times before she finally kicked his entitled, scrawny arse out of her flat.

Gerry had cheated on her, taken her for granted, and treated her like his own personal cash back machine, but she still hadn't been prepared for the level of hurt he, and her mum, inflicted on her in the weeks and months after their breakup.

But this wasn't about Gerry. She was over him, and he wasn't worth any more of her energy. She and Gib weren't lovers, they were barely friends, and they'd only shared a kiss. A mind-blowing kiss, but still just a kiss.

But sharing a bed with him was *not* happening. She'd rather sleep on the floor. Or that ugly, broken divan.

After washing off her makeup and brushing her teeth, she changed into sleeping shorts and a T-shirt and ignored the siren call of the super comfortable bed. She cursed quietly and stomped back into the lounge of the cottage, carrying a blanket and a pillow she'd swiped off the bed.

She eyed the dip in the divan, and when she sat down on the edge, it only creaked a little. She lay down, trying not to roll into the hole. She wiggled her butt and folded her arms across her chest. If she lay on her back and stayed still, she *might* be able to fall asleep.

She'd make do tonight and make another plan in the morning. Actually, Gib could make another plan. He could move out. And she could have the cottage to herself.

From tomorrow on, she'd have as little to do with him as possible. Hopefully, he'd soon be bored with the slow pace of the out-of-season island, and he'd leave to go back to wherever he lived.

And she would never think about him again.

The next morning, Gib walked into the cottage's small kitchen, slightly damp and a lot annoyed. And looking so damn sexy her heart hurt.

His sleeveless vest revealed impressive biceps, and the damp circles under his arms and around his neck told her he'd run hard and for a long time. The scruff on his jaw was darker this morning, his lips thinner.

And his eyes were the silver of a light sabre dialled to destroy.

Bea wished she hadn't stumbled from the couch to the coffee machine. She was still dressed in her old T-shirt, her sleeping shorts had a torn hem and she knew her bedhead was at its best. A glance in the reflective surface of the kettle told her she also had dark rings around her eyes and a crease from her pillow embedded in her cheek.

To say that she hadn't slept well was an understatement of epic proportions. Sleeping on the divan was the Santorini equivalent of sleeping on the pebbles at Kamari Beach. She'd tumbled, more than once, into the hole and found herself in an uncomfortable V shape.

She'd still been awake when Gib walked back into the cottage, after midnight, but she'd kept her eyes shut and her breathing light. She felt his heat as he loomed over her, and heard his low, frustrated 'for fuck's sake, seriously?' remark. Then he'd walked into the bedroom and slammed the door closed, suggesting he knew she was awake.

It took her at least an hour to fall asleep after that. Only to be woken by the bed-from-hell at least three times after that. Her back hurt, her bum hurt, and her neck was a breath away from going into a spasm. She was so tired she couldn't even be arsed to feel embarrassed about looking like death warmed up.

Besides, he'd probs got lucky the night before, and burned off all his excess testosterone. He wouldn't find her sexy now.

'Morning.'

Bea lifted her coffee cup in his direction and sat down at the kitchen table, resisting the urge to lay her head on her arms and go back to sleep. Through the open doors leading onto the deck, she watched a fishing boat heading out to sea. She wished she could spend the day snoozing on the beach, but she had things to do.

Bea cradled her coffee cup in her hand, ignoring Gib as he stomped to the bedroom, chugging water from the bottle he'd snagged out of the fridge. She presumed he'd gone to shower, but he returned a few minutes later in a fresh T-shirt, barefoot and rubbing his wet head with a hand towel.

Sliding his leg over the bench on the opposite side of the table, he spun his water bottle on its rim. 'Right. What's up with you?'

A straightforward question, and one she didn't expect. 'I'm fine,' she spluttered.

Gib frowned at her standard, cop out response. 'Bull*shit*.' He drank more water, replaced the cap and pointed the bottle at her. 'Last night we kissed. You seemed hesitant to take it further, so we stepped back. I said I was going for a walk, maybe to have a drink in a bar, and that pissed you off.'

Bea wanted to look away but couldn't. It was a pretty accurate summation of the events.

'I thought I'd give you some space to shower, to get into bed, to avoid feeling awkward after we shared the hottest kiss this side of the sun. But when I came back you were perched on the side of that fucking stupid couch, pretending to be asleep.'

Crap. She had to work on her acting skills. Bea nibbled on the inside of her cheek and thought about a way to get out of this uncomfortable and frankly miserable conversation. 'I'll go into Fira today and buy a mattress, or I'll sleep on a couch in the house.'

Gib reached across the table and held her wrist in a firm grip. 'Stop it, Bea! Just tell me what happened to change your mind about trusting me.'

'I never said I trusted you!'

'You would never have suggested us sharing a bed if you didn't,' Gib shot back. OK, damn him, that was true. 'Tell me the truth, Bea.'

She looked down at his fingers gripping her wrist, long and broad, with neatly clipped nails. His grip was light, as if he was conscious of his strength, and of his size. What should she do? Tell him the truth – that she'd freaked out at the idea of sharing the bed with someone who'd just got lucky? – or brush off his concerns and allow him to walk away?

'Talk to me, Bea. Help me understand.'

Beas lifted a shoulder to her ear. She was too tired to argue. 'We kissed, and, as you said, I backed away. I felt a bit overwhelmed and shocked at my response.' Her embarrassment level was already high, so what would a little extra truth matter? 'I haven't dated for a long time, many years rather than many months, and I'm very out of practice.'

He nodded. 'OK. For the record, you wanting to go slow wasn't an issue for me.'

She winced and twisted her lips. 'But you still went into Oia.'

He lifted his hands, obviously confused. 'Yeah. I went to the bar you recommended for a beer. Walked around the town for a while. Came back.'

Was it possible that he hadn't got any action? 'You didn't meet anyone?' she asked, her voice higher than normal.

'I spoke to two older gents from Dublin, and I bought them a beer.'

He was going to make her say it, to spell out her fears. 'You left here frustrated... *Shit!*' She placed her hands on her face, peering at him through her fingers.

Understanding jumped into his eyes. 'Are you asking me if I met another woman, if I picked someone up for sex?'

She stared at his water bottle like it was the most fascinating thing in the world. 'Like I said, you were ...

frustrated when you left. I thought you'd want to finish what we started. Even if we hadn't kissed, I still wouldn't want to sleep next to you after you'd had sex with someone else.'

He was quiet for so long that Bea had to look at him, and when she did, she saw the anger in his eyes, his thin lips and the muscle ticking in his jaw. Oh, God, he was properly pissed. But what else was she supposed to think? She'd lived with a man who routinely moved from her bed to someone else's, who treated sex the same way people treated takeaway coffee. She'd been out of the dating game for a while and, for all she knew, that was acceptable hook-up behaviour these days. The dating world moved fast.

'I'm going to say this just once… I did *not* sleep with anyone else last night.'

OK, good. *Phew.*

'I would never disrespect someone like that, sharing a bed with one woman – even if it's only because of a stupid arrangement cooked up by your godmother – and sleeping with another. I am *not* a disrespectful prick.'

She believed him and the layer of ice surrounding her heart melted. Maybe Gerry was the exception to the rule. That made her feel a little better about the male species. Or maybe Gib was one of a kind.

'Thanks for that.' Wanting to move on – conversations like this made her feel she was rolling in poison ivy – she asked him why he thought Golly was up to something.

'No, you're not going to squirm out of an explanation.'

Fuckshitdamn.

He lifted his finger and pointed it at her nose. 'Why

would you think that of me? Apart from refusing to leave the cottage I hired, I have been nothing but respectful of you and this situation. So what's going on in that pretty, but frustrating, head of yours?'

Gerry made her feel inadequate, frequently told her she was a terrible lover, and that she'd never been able to satisfy him in bed. (Or in life.) Last night, tired and overwhelmed, her insecurities had welled up, and she'd assumed Gib was like her ex and that he'd left her to go trawling for some action. But she couldn't tell him any of that. Not now, or at any time in the future.

She'd endured enough humiliation on that front, thank you very much.

She'd worked through their relationship, and had some therapy to deal with the pain of him and her mother hooking up – a double betrayal. She also now understood that she'd been less than enthusiastic about sex because her life had been demanding. It was hard to work a full day, write at night, juggle the bills and pick up after her man-child partner. It was hard to feel sexy when you were overwhelmed and lacked support, when you were the one who held up the sky so it didn't collapse on their heads. She'd done that as a child, and had continued to do it with Gerrie.

And also, sex for her, and many women, started in her head; a conversation, a little laughter, and maybe, if she was lucky, some flirting. Gerry hadn't been fluent in any language but grunt.

Gib's huge sigh reminded her he was waiting for an

answer. An answer she couldn't give him. He pushed his hand through his wet hair and pushed up from the table. '*Jesus*. OK, then, I'll get my stuff together. I should be out of your hair in fifteen minutes, maybe even less.'

He was leaving? What the hell? Standing up so quickly that she pushed the bench over, she grabbed his arm. He stopped, looked down at her and lifted one eyebrow.

Letting him go would be easy, he could walk out of her life, and she could carry on as normal. But normal was very boring, and very safe. Yes, she liked her routine, and her independence, feeling safe. If she didn't engage with people, she couldn't disappoint them and she couldn't be criticised or, worse, hurt.

But Gib had brought colour and a lot of excitement into her life. Something about him made her feel strong and, weirdly, secure. In the short time she'd spent with him, she'd felt more like her authentic self, like the woman she would've been if she'd had a normal childhood. She felt that through him, she was meeting herself…

Bottom line, she didn't want him to go. Not now. Not yet.

'I'm sorry,' she said, dropping her hand. 'I'm sorry I thought that.'

'Why did you?'

So he wasn't going to let her off easily. Bea bit the inside of her cheek, thinking. OK, she'd cracked open the door to her heart, but there was no chance of her flinging it wide open and allowing him to see the mess inside. 'Can I just say that I'm used to being disappointed, and am very used to people acting badly, and leave it at that?'

He crossed his big arms, his frown not as deep as it was before. 'If that's the case, then you need to start hanging out with better people.'

She couldn't argue with that. She stared down at her toes, wishing she could sink into the floor. 'And I'd like you to stay,' she quietly stated.

Admitting that much was hard and if he said no, it would sting.

'Where are we on sex?'

She lifted one shoulder and looked at him. 'Not sure yet.'

'Fair enough. Sharing the bed?'

She couldn't spend another minute on that divan. 'That I can do.'

A few beats later, the corners of his mouth lifted, just a little, and his eyes lightened. He pushed his hands through his hair and sighed. 'You're going to be trouble, aren't you?'

'Probably. I am, after all, Golly's goddaughter,' she reminded him, and the rumble of his laughter melted the remaining ice between them.

He thought she was trouble? Man, he was confusion, complication and chaos – and craving – in one six-foot-plus package.

An hour later, Bea and Gib walked into the kitchen of the villa and found Golly and Reena sitting at the vast wooden table, looking like they'd been dragged through the bougainvillaea backwards. Golly was wrapped in an oversized men's bathrobe that skimmed the floor and Reena was dressed in leggings and a long white, slightly grubby T-shirt.

Both had massive cups of black coffee in front of them and Golly was tucking into the contents of the pot she cradled in her elbow, eating like she'd just ended a month-long hunger strike. Reena's eyes looked a little glassy, and she swayed to music only she could hear.

Having lived with Gerry, Bea instantly recognised two people as high as kites. Her eyes swung round to Cass, who looked on the verge of tears.

'What's going on?' she asked, though she was pretty sure she knew.

Cass wrung her hands together. 'We messed up.'

At her nod, Bea turned to see Nadia standing in the door to the pantry. She tipped a rectangular cake tin and Bea saw what looked to be a thin, mangled, half-eaten layer of chocolate cake. Wait, were those chocolate brownies? *Yum.* Cass walked over and wrapped her arm around her wife, who looked like she wanted to walk into a wall and disappear. Nadia was a brilliant cook but tended to keep her distance from her employer and her guests. There seemed to be a lot of that going around.

And what did they mean they'd messed up? And how badly? Did they forget to order the lobster for the seafood platters? Had they double-booked and were going off back to the UK? Had they inadvertently poisoned the wrinklies?

'What's the problem?' Bea demanded, her voice and panic rising.

Bea felt Gib's hand on her back, his touch grounding her. Her heart rate dropped from 1,000 to 990, and she asked Cass to explain.

'Is there any more of this?' Golly interrupted, holding out her pot to Cass. Her dressing gown was only loosely tied, and Bea caught a flash of a naked, wrinkly boob. Too much, too early.

Walking over to stand in front of her, Bea pulled the dressing gown together and tightened the belt. She looked into the pot and frowned. The contents were yellow and gooey; it wasn't porridge.

Golly slapped her hand away and tapped the pot's rim with the back of her spoon. 'More?'

'I can make you some, Golly,' Nadia softly replied. 'But cheese sauce takes a little time. What about some oatmeal?'

Golly's bottom lip pushed out. 'I want cheese sauce, not oatmeal.'

Reena waved a hand in front of her face. 'I can feel the colours, Gols. And the back of my head is prickling.'

'I want to feel the colours, too! I want another brownie, Nadia. Why did you take them away from me?'

Bea looked at Gib, who was standing by the big free-range stove, his hand over his mouth and his shoulders shaking. Yeah, yeah, the old people were Burj Khalifa high. This wasn't their first drug rodeo, but she didn't expect them to be stoned at – she squinted at the dial on Gib's fancy watch, he'd swapped his Rolex for something high tech – 8.17 a.m.

She looked at Cass. 'Want to explain?' she asked, heading towards the coffee machine and pushing a cup under its spout. Staying with the drug theme, she knew she'd be mainlining espressos today.

Cass took Nadia's hand. 'Nadia suffers from lupus, and she takes micro-doses of cannabis to keep the inflammation down.'

'I came down early this morning and made a batch of dope cookies.' Nadia's voice was so low Bea had to strain to hear her. 'I left the slab cooling in the cake tin and went back upstairs to get dressed.'

Cass bit her lip. 'I asked Nadia if she wanted to come for a walk with me, so we headed into town.' She lifted her chin, looking a little defiant. 'Knowing how crazy the rest of the weekend would be, we decided to take some time out.'

And why shouldn't they? They'd worked their butts off to pull off a last-minute event last night.

'I came back, intending to cut up the brownies into bite-sized portions,' Nadia said, lifting the cake tin. 'And I found this.'

Bea winced at the ripped apart cake. Golly and Reena hadn't used a knife, choosing to pull the brownie mixture apart with their fingers. Damn, it did look yum, and Bea could do with a hit of sugar and chocolate.

'Don't even think about it, *Bea-darling*,' Gib murmured, laughter in his voice.

Bea-darling? Was him using her nickname supposed to mean something? No, they'd only recently met up again –it felt like they'd known each other for weeks, not days! – so it couldn't. Mean anything, that is. Reena and Golly called her Bea-darling, and he'd just picked it up from them.

She stepped away from the plate and clasped her hands behind her back because, damn, the brownies looked *fabulous*.

'I take it that they ate far more than they should've?' she asked Nadia, resigned to the idea of Golly and Reena going back to bed for the morning. Possibly for most of the day.

'A *lot* more,' Cass stated. 'Nadia only takes a half-inch square, and she's used to the stuff. If I ate what she does, I would float off the ceiling.'

And the Terrible Twosome ate half the tray. *Shit.*

'I'm really sorry, Bea. I didn't think they'd be down so early, they never are usually,' Cass gabbled.

'They chose to eat the cake, Cassie,' Gib quietly reminded her.

Cass tossed him a grateful glance. 'Do you think we should take them to a doctor or something?'

Bea shook her head. 'They're just high, Cass, they aren't dying. And, honestly, I'm pretty sure they've tried worse.'

'I once ate magic mushrooms at Burning Man, and I loved Molly when I was younger,' Golly grandly declared. 'I've always been able to handle drugs.'

Since she was dipping her fingers into her coffee mug and trying to suck the liquid off her fingers, Bea wasn't convinced. And Reena, head on the table, was out like a light. Bea pushed her fingertips into her forehead. 'Jesus, Golly,' she muttered. 'You don't need to brag about it!'

'If I don't blow my own trumpet, who will?' Golly demanded. Her eyes, sort of, focused on Bea's face. 'Oh, you look so very pretty this morning, Bea-darling.'

Since she was dressed in another pair of shorts, and a sleeveless cotton shirt, this was definitely the drugs talking. OK, it was time to get her godma horizontal. 'Let's get you up to bed, Gols.'

Cassie bit her bottom lip. 'Um, Bea…'

'Yes?'

'Does that mean that we're not fired?' Cass tentatively asked, her eyes reflecting her worry.

Horror made Bea's throat constrict. 'God, *no*! If anything, I'm terrified you're going to resign,' she admitted. 'Please don't resign,' she begged them.

They both laughed and Bea knew that one crisis was over. With Golly, it wouldn't be long before another arrived. 'Can someone wake Reena up and get her onto her feet?' Bea asked Cass and Nadia.

Cass nodded and Nadia turned away to put the plate in the pantry, on the highest shelf and behind a big bag of flour. Good plan. She wouldn't put it past the two of them to go looking for more when they sobered up.

Bea walked over to Golly, put her hand under her arm and told her to stand up. Golly swayed and Bea locked her knees and wrapped her arm around her waist. She met Gib's eyes. 'Are you sure you want to stay here? This is a madhouse, and I can't guarantee it will get any better.'

His eyes softened and his mouth quirked up into that smile potent enough to melt hearts and pantie elastic. 'Are you kidding? This is the most fun I've had for years.'

He strode over to them, bent his knees and scooped Golly into his arms. Golly, being Golly, ran her hand over his biceps, and murmured a low hum of approval.

'Behave yourself, Godma,' Bea told her. 'Up the stairs, turn left and her room is at the end of the corridor on your right, Gib. Just dump her on the bed. Slap her hand if she gets fresh.'

He nodded and looked over at Reena. Cass was shaking her shoulder, but the older woman was dead to the world. 'Leave her, Cass,' he said. 'I'll dump Golly and I'll come back for her,'

'She's heavy, Gib,' Bea told him, wincing. Reena was tall and more muscly than Golly.

'Then I'll toss her over my shoulder,' Gib replied, unfazed. 'It's not like she's going to know, is she?'

That was a solid-gold truth. And if Reena didn't want to be lugged around in a fireman's hold, then she should've *just said no!*

Bea smiled at Gib. 'Thanks. I knew your muscles would come in handy at some point.'

His eyes heated, she blushed, and knew he was thinking about that kiss they'd shared, the way she'd run her hands up and down his thick arms, over his chest, down his back. She'd made the most of the little time she'd had to explore his body, and running her hands over his was the sexual equivalent of riding a lightning bolt. Why had they stopped? She couldn't remember…

Gib turned away and dammit, his back view, in another pair of board shorts and a simple sky-blue T-shirt, looked as good as his front. She sighed, and when she finally, years later, remembered where she was and what they were doing, she turned to see Nadia and Cass looking a little mesmerised, too.

'He's such a hottie,' Nadia said with a sigh, surprising the hell out of Bea.

'He really is,' Cass agreed. 'If I was into men, I'd fight you for him, Bea.'

Bea shook her head so hard she heard her spine creak. 'No, I – we … um—'

'No … I … we … um?' Cass mimicked her. 'Have you lost your power to speak?'

'I haven't seen him since I was six years old, he's little more than a stranger, Cass!' Bea said, holding onto the back of a chair, her knuckles white.

'Me and Cass slept together the night we met, got engaged two weeks later and were married two weeks after that,' Nadia told her. 'Time is irrelevant when the heart wants what it wants.'

Her heart wasn't allowed to want anything, its only job was to pump blood around her body. And when did Nadia turn into Miss Chatty? She'd barely said anything since they first met, now she was commenting on Bea's love life. Bea didn't mind, though, and was glad Nadia felt more at ease. Anyway, she didn't have a love life. She and Gib had merely shared a bed and a kiss. That was it. They were all being ridiculous, her life was ridiculous...

And as an exclamation to that thought, Reena released a loud and noxious fart.

'Good God!' Bea waved her hand in front of her face, grabbed her shirt and pulled it up and over her nose.

Cass pushed the kitchen door and windows open as wide as they could go, and Bea welcomed the gust of fresh air. Cass looked at Reena. 'We're sorry about this, Bea.'

It wasn't their fault. How were they to know that Golly and Reena together were, at heart, precocious teenagers with access to far too much money? That they both lacked sense and even the smallest measure of self-preservation? 'I don't blame you, at *all*. They are wild at the best of times, and this weekend is an excuse for them to misbehave. I am dreading Saturday.'

'You've nixed all her bad ideas, Bea.' Cass reminded her. 'It's going to be a perfectly normal party.'

Oh, to be so optimistic and so naïve! 'You haven't spent enough time with my godmother,' she muttered. 'Wait until she persuades everyone to a skinny dip at midnight, to a tequila-drinking contest or to do a Coyote Ugly routine on the bar and someone falls off and breaks a hip.'

'And you think that might happen?' Nadia asked, pulling ingredients out of the fridge and piling them onto the table. Eggs, ham, cheese, chives ... was she about to make an omelette? Bea thought she could eat a couple. Or five.

'I know *something* will happen,' she said, pulling out a

chair and sitting down. 'Golly will do something, start something or nail someone, and will make it memorable.' She looked at their confused faces and sighed. 'Golly often seduces the married or committed. Because she's wildly indiscreet and doesn't give a flying fig about what people think, the news of the affair invariably gets back to the cheated party and...' Bea mimicked an explosion. 'I love her dearly, but she can be impossible.'

Cass leaned back against the counter and her feet. She nodded at Reena. 'Are they ... you know?'

'Together?' Bea asked. She looked at her godmother's best friend, her mouth open and grey hair sticking up. 'To be honest, I don't know. Golly's had affairs with women before, but I've never asked, and they've never told me. I just know they've been friends for years.'

'Fifty,' Reena muttered, 'and she's asked me many times. I said no.' She wiped her hand across her mouth, swiping drool over her chin. *Lovely.*

Bea's wide eyes met Cass's, then Nadia's. Oh, this was just getting better and better. Reena had turned down Golly? 'Why?' she asked, intrigued.

'Don't fancy women, and your godmother is damn hard work. Best friend but *very* dramatic. Got a fella back home, and he's very good in the sack. We like a bit of slap and tickle, do Charlie and I.'

OK, who was Charlie and why had she never met him?

Bea spread her hands out wide, shocked. Cass slapped her hand over Nadia's mouth to muffle her giggle.

'Thanks for that, Reena,' Bea said, hearing Gib jogging down the stairs.

He strode into the kitchen and flashed Bea a smile. 'Golly's out like a light.'

'Thanks.' She leaned over the table and poked Reena's shoulder. 'Hey, Reena, it's time to wake up.' She looked at Gib. 'She was talking to us a minute ago. Reena, *wake up!*'

Reena turned her head away from Bea and buried her face in her armpit. Then she released a low snore, and when Bea shook her shoulder again, she didn't respond. She placed her hands on her hips and stared down at Reena. 'I suppose we could leave her there and eat at the other end of the table.'

Nadia waved an expensive-looking kitchen blade in her direction. It was one of her fancy ones that lived in rolled-up material. 'No, I have too much to do today, and I need her out of my kitchen.'

Gib made a production of stretching his arms and his back, and they laughed.

'I've got this,' he told her before grimacing. 'But if I hurt my back, I expect to be waited on hand and foot.'

'Dream on,' Cass scoffed, amused. 'We might toss a piece of bread your way if you're lucky.'

'Such a hard woman,' Gib said, as he pulled Reena's chair away from the table. As she flopped forward, he boosted her up and over his shoulder, where she lay, like a loose rag doll. 'Where am I taking her, Bea?'

She followed him to the stairs. 'Turn right on the landing, she's in the east wing.'

Bea followed him down the long hallway, the walls covered with art and photographs and even framed finger paintings Bea had done in kindergarten. There was no rhyme or reason to the way Golly assembled her pictures, but somehow it simply worked.

'Should they both be this out of it?' Gib asked, shifting Reena higher onto his shoulder.

'They were both drinking heavily last night, and I know they carried on after the cocktail party ended. Golly posted a picture on Instagram of them laughing at around two-thirty, and they looked like they were still going strong. And they did eat way more dope brownies than they should've. I think the combination of drugs and booze knocked them out.'

'Do you not think that Golly, at some point, should consider her age and start slowing down?'

Bea opened the door to Reena's bedroom. 'Oh, I very much do, but Golly doesn't listen to anything I say. Feel free to suggest that to her, but there's a chance she'll rip off your head.'

'Noted.' Gib laid Reena down on her large bed and tucked a pillow under her head. He was surprisingly gentle. 'Are either of them taking any medication that might interact with the drugs and the booze?'

'No, nothing,' Bea shook her head. 'They're both incredibly healthy. Reena takes nothing, but Golly takes vitamins and cod liver oil.'

Gib grimaced. 'Ugh.'

Bea agreed, it was vile stuff. 'Even if she did have a

health issue, Golly wouldn't take the meds. She's never been a fan of Big Pharma, and if there's a homoeopathic way to treat an illness, she'll try that first. I remember having to eat copious amounts of garlic and parsley when I had a summer cold.'

Gib opened the door for her, and they stepped into the hallway. He pulled the door shut behind them. 'Did it work?'

'Eventually, but I'm pretty sure conventional medicine would've had me sorted in two days rather than six.' Bea walked over to the window at the far end of the hallway and leaned her shoulder into the wall. This was a good view of groves of olive and almond trees and Profitis Ilias, the highest hill on the island.

Gib stood next to her, relaxed and at ease in his body and skin. He looked nothing like the CEO of one of the biggest and best talent, production and entertainment agencies in the world.

'Thanks for lugging them up here. I owe you.'

He put his hands on his lower back and faked a wince. 'I think I pulled a muscle in my back. I might need you to give me a massage.'

Bea nudged him in the ribs with her elbow and rolled her eyes at his over-egged 'Oof.' He was absolutely fine. In every way possible.

'Stop being a drama queen, Caddell. I have enough of those in the house, thank you very much.'

Chapter Eight

Dinner on Wednesday night was a lovely paella, made by Nadia, thank God. Reena offered some of her red-hot, homemade chilli sauce as a condiment and Nadia threatened to kick her out of the kitchen for spoiling her food. Nadia had found her voice, and it was *loud*.

Golly, now fully recovered from sleeping yesterday away, sat at the head of the kitchen table, a glass of red wine at her elbow.

She looked happy, and a happy Golly was fun. Dangerous but fun. Bea's godma loved Santorini's climate, the secret coves and the clear, bright sea. She had friends here, expats like her, and the locals were also incredibly friendly. But there was only so much of the laid back island island life Golly could tolerate and soon she'd be itching to get back to her cosmopolitan London (and New York) life of eating at restaurants, attending gallery openings and auctions, charity events and house parties in the Hamptons and Hampshire. Causing havoc on two continents, unhampered by the demands of her author clients.

Bea was well aware that if Golly never had to check an email, read a contract, or be the bridge between the publishing world and her authors again, she'd be ecstatic. She recalled Golly first raising the subject of retiring a couple of years ago, but Bea accidentally-on-purpose ignored their agreement that Golly would only act as her agent until she found someone else. She hadn't made much of an effort to find another agent – correction, *any* effort.

Bea leaned back in her chair, the pad of her index finger skimming the rim of her wine glass. Things were changing, and far too fast. And she needed to change with them. But it was hard, so hard, to step out of the shadows and into the sunlight, hard to have eyes on you, to allow others to judge you. If she stepped out from behind her pseudonym, she'd open herself up – herself, *not* Parker Kane – to criticism and comments, with people judging her and her decisions. The thought of being publicly judged, of being so vulnerable, turned her blood to ice.

But, at the very least, and at some point, she would have to reveal her Parker Kane identity to a new agent. How would she find her? Or him?

Should she find an agent first, or should she bite the bullet and reveal she was Parker Kane first? Bea's skin turned clammy, and her throat constricted, but she needed to consider her options.

Nobody knew how her literary 'coming out' would affect her book sales. Golly seemed to think they might take a minuscule dip initially, but Bea's connection to her mother, Lou – someone who was a professional shit-stirrer – would soon fade from everyone's minds. Golly believed that as long as Bea kept producing fun adventures for her crew, her readers (and their parents) wouldn't care who she was related to and what happened in the past. And hey, parents wanted to get their kids to read, and kids wanted to read about Pip and the gang, so they'd buy the books.

Golly said it wouldn't be nearly as big a deal as Bea thought it would be. Bea wasn't so sure.

She looked across the table to Gib, who'd pushed his chair away from the table, as if distancing himself from the lively conversation. She'd been surprised, shocked even, when he'd accepted Golly's invitation to join them for dinner tonight. But she supposed he felt that since he'd stayed in her house as a kid, and had been a recipient of her hospitality so long ago, he couldn't say no. After helping her with Golly and Reena earlier, he'd eaten the omelette Nadia'd made him, told Bea he'd see her later and disappeared for the rest of the day.

Exhausted, she'd enjoyed an afternoon nap, and then tidied the cottage. She'd made both sides of the bed and washed their coffee cups and the dishes. Seeing the overly full laundry basket, a mixture of Gib's clothes and hers, she'd carried it up to the laundry room at the villa and threw their clothes into Golly's big and quick washer and tumble dryer. Before coming up to the villa for a sundowner, she'd folded their laundry and left his on the chair next to the bed.

She wished she could leave the bedroom in a mess, his clothes on the floor and his dishes in the sink, but she was wired through the circumstances of her childhood to make a situation as good as it could be, to be the caregiver and problem solver. It was what she did.

She bit her lip, wondering what Gib thought of her cleaning up after him. Did he even notice? He probably didn't, assuming Golly employed a maid to clean up after him.

Bea desperately hoped it wouldn't be awkward or weird tonight when she and Gib returned to the cottage. She couldn't help wondering if he'd kiss her again. Would she let him? Would he sweep her off her sexual feet and would they make love? She didn't know: a part of her was desperate to know him that way, but her brain was telling her to calm the hell down, to take a breath, to *think*.

Whatever happened, she hoped she'd be able to sleep with him breathing just a short distance from her, that she'd feel warm and safe rather than agitated and off balance.

She caught his eye, and his half smile drilled through her, melting away layers of skin, muscle and bone until it reached her core and started to melt that, too. She'd never had this reaction to Gerry, or any other man. Gib made her feel...

Just that. He made her *feel*. Like a woman. Like she was noticed, like she mattered.

And that was bloody dangerous. Because those sorts of feelings opened cracks in her walls, and he could shatter her defences more easily from the inside. *He's dropping in and out of your life, Bea. He's not staying.*

'Where are Jack and Jacqui?' Golly demanded, looking at the big clock on the wall behind Gib's head. 'They are ridiculously late!'

Jack and Jacqui – fifty-plus, twins and inseparable – friends of Golly's from way back, had said they'd be at the villa by seven. It was now eight and Golly was starting to get anxious.

'I'm sure they made a detour into Oia,' Golly complained, the wine in her glass sloshing. 'That's so like them, easily distracted.'

And wasn't that the pot calling the kettle pitch-black?

'Do you want dessert now, or shall we wait for them to arrive?' Nadia asked.

'We'll wait for them,' Golly replied. 'Bea-darling, call them and tell them to get their asses out of whatever bar they are in!'

She slid her phone down the long table. It skittered off the bottle of hand-pressed olive oil and bumped into a plate. Gib picked it up and leaned over the table to hand it to Bea.

In so many ways Golly was a child who had no patience for delayed gratification. She wanted what she wanted *now*. Immediately. It had always been that way. Having never married, nor lived with anyone on a permanent basis, she had no concept of compromise, of waiting or of patience. The world revolved around her all the time.

Would she have been more accommodating if she'd had

children, if she'd had a long-term relationship? Partners, longtime lovers and children had a way of shaving off those hard edges, of making people a little more thoughtful, able to bend a little. Marriages and partnerships made people realise the world did not spin for them alone, and not everything was about them. Sometimes, most times, compromise and patience were required. Those weren't lessons Golly ever learnt.

But Bea? She'd learnt that lesson and taken it to the extreme.

Because she'd been happy to have someone sharing her home, her own man, thrilled to return to the comfort and security of what she knew how to do – and that was to look after someone – she'd never allowed Gerry to learn that lesson, either. She'd bent and buckled, all the time. Her life with Gerry, like her life with her dad, had revolved around keeping him happy and comfortable.

Gerry'd been a sloth, a serial cheater, and a man-child, but because she'd been so desperate to feel useful again, believing she could only be loved because of what she did, not who she was, she'd given him everything, including a licence to walk all over her.

Was she, by picking up after Gib, sliding back into those old bad habits?

God, what a terrifying thought!

She looked at Gib and found he was watching her. He lifted an eyebrow, silently asking if she was OK. Why did he want to know? Why did he care? And why did her heart lift every time he showed a little consideration when he noticed her? He was simply dressed, in tailored shorts and an open-collared shirt, sleeves rolled back to show off his delicious, muscled forearms. He'd shaved this morning, but a hint of stubble now dusted his jaw and chin, and his nose was a little sunburnt from spending too much time outside.

Hot, handsome, confident, charismatic … he made her stomach tumble and her core warm. She could cope better if it was simple attraction and lust … but he was also intelligent, reticent, impatient, solid. Snarky. And she *liked* him. Far more than she should.

Golly lit up a cigarillo and looked from Bea to Gib. 'So, how did you two sort out your sleeping arrangements?'

Bea glared at her, annoyed by the intrusive question. She didn't look at Gib, but knew he'd loathe Golly's probing, too. 'That's got nothing to do with you, Golly,' she snapped.

She wasn't surprised when Gib stood up and pushed his chair under the table. His face was as hard as granite, and his eyes conveyed his annoyance. Yep, the man hated being questioned. On this occasion she didn't blame him, Golly had stepped way over the line.

'You're not going to stay for dessert?' Nadia asked him.

His reply was curt, his words clipped. 'Thanks, but no.'

It was obvious, to Bea at least, that he'd had enough and desperately needed some peace and quiet, to not talk to anyone. She was surprised he'd lasted this long. She looked at him, caught his eye and mouthed a quick 'Sorry.'

His shrug was tiny, but there. She saw him glance at the kitchen door and knew he wanted to bolt.

'Goodnight, Gib,' she said, understanding his need to leave.

His eyes flashed his gratitude. He took a minute to thank Golly, a little curtly, said a brief goodnight and left the room. Bea watched him and as soon as he opened the door, his shoulders dropped an inch.

When she knew he was out of earshot, she looked at Golly and shook her head. 'Seriously?'

'What did I do?' Golly asked, confused.

'Gib doesn't like personal questions, and he hates people prying. Just give him some space, OK? I know that's a foreign concept to you, but please *try*.'

Golly looked at her through a haze of smoke. 'What's his story?'

Bea didn't know and even if she did, whatever Gib told her (and she didn't expect him to say anything at all) would stay between him and her. She pointed a finger at Golly. 'He's not a puzzle you need to solve.'

It was a good reminder for her, too.

'Good God, there's no reason to bite my head off,' Golly snapped.

Bea thought she was being remarkably restrained. She was stressed, determined to make sure this weekend went off well, and she was sharing a bed with a man who could be another Hemsworth brother, someone she was stupidly, massively attracted to. She had hard career decisions to make, and she hadn't made any progress on plotting book ten, or her new series. She wanted to run down the road screaming, possibly naked, but she was holding it all together with gossamer-fine threads.

Bea remembered that she was going to call the twins, and swiped Golly's screen. She looked at her godmother. 'Why am *I* doing this, by the way?'

'You came to live with me when you were sixteen and you can't make a call for me?'

Bea rolled her eyes. After her dad's death, she'd wanted to stay on her own, something her mother supported, but Golly wouldn't hear of it, so she'd moved her into her Belgravia house. Unlike her mother, Golly wanted Bea with her, so she didn't take her passive-aggressive comment seriously. With Golly, you had to look at what she did, not what she said.

Golly cocked her head, her expression brightening. 'I'm sure I heard a car. The twins are here! Oh, by the way, Bea, your mother wants to join the party on Saturday night,' she added, far too casually.

She had to be joking. And if she was, it was a shitty one. 'Not funny, Golly.'

'Not joking, Beatrice.'

Golly couldn't seriously be thinking of allowing Lou to visit, could she? This weekend – and her life – was currently complicated enough without adding her horrible and toxic mother to the proceedings. 'Golly, please don't let her come. I have so much to do, and I can't deal with her, too. Please tell her she's not welcome—'

'Hey, anyone here? Golly, where are you?'

JOSS WOOD

Everyone whipped around at the masculine voice drifting down the passage, followed by footsteps. As the twins walked into the kitchen, bearing bags from Harrods and Fortnum & Mason, Bea realised she hadn't got the reassurance she so desperately needed from Golly. That Lou wasn't going to rock up and ruin the weekend, and Bea's holiday.

Dammit. And now Golly would use the arrival of the Two Jacks, as she called them, to delay having that conversation.

While Golly introduced the twins to Cass and Nadia, and Nadia started hauling edible goodies out of the bags, including olives from Lesbos and cheese from an artisanal dealer in Yorkshire, Bea picked up Golly's phone and swiped the screen.

If Golly wouldn't give her mother the heave-ho, she would. She was typing the message when Reena gently tugged the phone out of her hands.

'It's not your phone, and it's not up to you to reply to your mother. This is Golly's house, this weekend is for her, and you have no say in who she invites,' Reena added.

'Reena, *come on*! You know Lou poisons everything she touches!' Bea hissed.

'Don't do it, Bea. It's wrong, and you know it's wrong. And you'll regret it.'

The thing about Reena was that she so rarely interfered, when she did, her words carried a lot of weight. And, *shit*, she was right. Bea had no right to respond on Golly's behalf. It was her life and her party, and she could invite whom she wanted, even if that person was Bea's narcissistic, selfish, uncaring, had-the-maternal-instincts-of-a-black-widow-spider mother.

Before she could argue any further, she found herself in Jack's arms, being lifted off her feet and whirled around. Her feet touched the floor again, and she heard the noise levels in the kitchen rise. Golly told Cass to open another bottle of wine – what the hell, two – and just like that Bea knew that, like Gib, she needed some quiet.

When the attention was off her, she followed in Gib's footsteps, slipping out of the kitchen and into the night.

―――――――

Gib found himself waiting for Bea, annoyed by his inability to settle down, read his book, and enjoy the quiet. When she didn't return to the cottage after an hour, he decided to walk off some of his irrational frustration.

Pulling on a thin hoodie, he ambled through the olive grove, his hands in his pockets. Emerging between the house and the cottage, he walked through the courtyard that would, on Saturday night, be covered in tables, and no doubt exquisitely decorated by Cass. For now, unlit lights were draped from one wing to the other, the moonlight glinting off the occasional bulb. Veering into the garden, Gib cursed when a stray bougainvillaea branch snagged his shirt and his skin, its sharp thorn pulling blood to the surface.

The moon peeked out between UFO-looking clouds, and

the sea made a soft whoosh-whoosh sound in the distance. It was a cool, but lovely night.

How long had it been since he'd noticed the nuances of his environment? The way the moonlight bounced off the sea, the deep blue of the night, the pop of starlight? He couldn't remember the last time he'd walked through the countryside in the dark.

He was so far from his real life, a million miles from the hustle of Nashville, London and New York City. He'd deliberately on purpose forgotten to charge his phone, so he was unaware of what emails had landed, whether there were fires he needed to put out, clients he needed to reassure, or employees he needed to promote or fire.

He'd have to check in tomorrow, but tonight he'd give himself the gift of being free of work-related worries.

He'd stepped out of his own life and instead of having a relaxing holiday and getting to know the island as an adult, he'd stumbled into Bea's world. He'd enjoyed dinner earlier – Nadia was a fantastic cook! – and had been content to listen to the lively conversation. But when Golly had turned her spotlight onto him, he'd immediately removed himself.

Unlike his Uncle Hugh and Navy, Gib wasn't good with people. He knew he could only cope with Golly in small, very small, doses. He was an excellent manager, he knew that to be true, he gave clear instructions, and didn't ask for the impossible or the inane. He didn't play games, but he expected people to give their best, and then some. He was the boss, and he didn't socialise with his employees after hours. But, despite striving to keep his distance, he still had to network, to meet with clients, investors and partners, with suppliers. He was constantly pressing hands, making small talk, negotiating deals.

The CEO position required him to become an extroverted introvert and after nearly burning out this year, he knew he needed time away from people and drama, solitude and quiet, to recharge his batteries.

Yet, here he was, standing on the outside, watching Bea's family drama. Why? Why wasn't he taking the opportunity for some solitude? Why was he still in the cottage? Why the hell hadn't he demanded a refund from Golly and found another place to stay?

Because … *Bea*.

She *fascinated* him. She was a study in contrasts … prickly and sweet, tangy and hot. Her eyes held secrets and pain. What caused the light frown marks between her eyebrows, the tiny creases at the corner of her eyes? Why was her smile sometimes hesitant, why did it seldom reach her eyes?

And why did it seem she was always waiting for the other shoe to drop?

He approached the wooden deck built over the edge of the swimming pool, designed to resemble a wild pond. In the darkness, he could see the shadows of the water plants poking through the nooks and crannies between the boulders surrounding the pool. And sitting on the edge of the deck, her bare feet dangling in the water sat Bea, holding the weight of the world on her slim shoulders.

He should back away, leave her in peace, but … *fuck*. Not gonna happen.

At the edge of the deck, he kicked off his flip flops and stepped onto the smooth planks, still warm from the sun. Instead of sitting beside her, he slid in behind Bea, his thighs on either side of her hips. His toes skimmed the surface of the water. It was warmer than expected, and he realised the pool was heated.

Bea tensed, and he told her to relax. He kept his left hand on her hip while he picked up the wine bottle beside her. He recognised it as the nearly full one from dinner earlier and removed the cork with his teeth. He handed her the bottle of chilled Chenin Blanc and rested his chin on her shoulder while she took a deep sip from the bottle, then another.

He knew the value of silence, so he simply wrapped his arms around her waist and waited. She'd either talk or she wouldn't, he couldn't force her. He hated people prying into his mind, loathed being peppered with intrusive questions, so he'd let her be.

'I don't want to talk, Gib,' she told him, her husky voice telling him that she'd shed a tear or two.

He got that in ways she didn't understand. And never would. 'That's OK,' he murmured, pulling her hair off her neck to place his lips on her skin. There were different ways to comfort someone, and this was another. And, in his opinion, just as effective.

Bea tipped her head to the side to give him better access to her neck, and he nibbled his way up, and across to her jaw. On her so-smooth skin, he smelled flowers – he was a guy and couldn't identify what kind if you held a gun to his head – and when she turned her head so his lips could reach hers, he tasted wine on her luscious lips, on her tongue. Not wanting to push, he kept their kiss soft, undemanding…

He suspected she felt like things were out of her control, so he wanted to give her a measure of it here, to let her set the pace. He was a take-charge guy, someone who liked having the upper hand in bed, but he knew when to stand back and just wait. Bea returned his lazy kiss, but he clocked an uptick of need in her, and when she placed her hand on his leg and squeezed his thigh, he knew she wanted more.

Maybe she wanted to forget, maybe she wanted to step out of her life, maybe she simply needed to lose herself in the moment. Whatever her reason, he didn't care; he was just happy to sit here, and take anything she offered.

He lifted her onto his lap and allowed his eyes the pleasure of roaming over her face. Not classical pretty, definitely not perfect … but, man, *gorgeous*. Interesting. A face you could study a thousand times, and still find something captivating. And while looking at her was a pleasure, kissing her was better. He skimmed her mouth with his, wanting to prolong the anticipation, and build up a little more tension, before finally locking his mouth on hers. When his tongue slid against hers, Bea released a part-mewl, part-groan and he was lost.

And found.

Needing more, wanting everything, he took their kiss deeper and darker, and in a movement that was as old as time, and twice as natural, he covered her breast with his hand. His thumb found her already taut nipple and teased it with a slow stroke. He pulled her T-shirt up, and the palm of his hand settled on her breast, small but lovely, perfectly formed.

They said that time stopped on Santorini, but on this island tonight, with Bea in his arms, her lovely, sweet 'n spicy mouth under his, nothing else mattered. Just Bea, and the way she made him feel. He was the plug and she the source of power.

He craved more of her, needed everything, needed to taste her, to feel her in his mouth, her nipple against her tongue. Pulling her shirt up her body and over her head, he dropped it to the deck and reached behind her to twist open her bra's clasp. While still kissing him – God, her mouth was a revelation, sexy as sin and twice as hot – she tossed her bra over his shoulder and sat up. She straddled him, moonlight on her lovely torso. She swiped his mouth with hers, her breath warm.

'This is just a bit of fun, right?' she whispered.

He pulled back and stroked the hair off her face. That was his line, and it felt strange to hear the words he so frequently uttered falling from her lips. And yes, of course, it was. Fast and fun, he was a master of the concept.

'Gib?'

She was still waiting for an answer. And why was he hesitating? He nodded. 'It would be a lot more fun if we were naked,' he stated. 'And if we were back in the cottage, rolling around that huge bed.'

'We'll get there.' Bea placed her hand on his cheek. 'When was the last time you made out on a deck at night, Gib?' she whispered.

He was conscious of her hot core pressing against his steel-hard dick, so thinking was hard. 'I must've been seventeen, she was nineteen, an older woman. It was summer, and we went skinny dipping.'

Bea's mouth curved. 'Wanna do that?'

Without waiting for his answer, and using his shoulder for leverage, she stood and shed her shorts and what looked to be a white, lacy thong. Before he could see more, take in her beautiful body, she whipped around and dived into the pond.

It took her a while to surface and when she did, she slicked her wet hair off her face, grinning. 'It's lovely,' she told him. 'Come on in.'

If the pay-off was getting up close and personal with a naked Bea, he'd swim the fucking English Channel. Gib rolled to his feet, gripped the back of his shirt and pulled it off in a one-handed move. He undid the button of his shorts, unzipped and pulled down his briefs and shorts in one economical movement. He was hard, painfully so.

Not knowing how deep the pool was, he sat down on the edge of the deck, risking splinters in his ass by sliding off into the water but Bea's soft voice drifting over to him immediately distracted him. 'You've got such a gorgeous body, Gib.'

He met her eyes, and he swallowed down the lump in his throat. Hers would be lovelier. He cocked his eyebrow and grinned. 'Are you done ogling, or can I come in?' he asked.

'If you must,' Bea told him, laughter in her voice.

He pushed off, ducked under the water, and his feet brushed the floor. When he stood, the water hit his shoulders. He planted his feet and watched Bea swim toward him, her lips curved. He pulled her into him, and her legs wrapped around his waist, and her arms around his neck.

Instead of kissing him, she tipped her head back and looked up at the stars. 'You are a very pleasant distraction, Gib,' she murmured. 'If you weren't here, I think I would be a lot more miserable than I am.'

'I know my holiday would be a *lot* quieter.'

She tugged his wet hair.

He smiled against her lips. 'OK, I'll admit it might be more boring.'

'Boredom is the last thing you have to worry about when you're around Golly.'

Oh, he wasn't referring to her godmother's antics or the fact that she was a trouble magnet. He was only staying close to the action because he couldn't stay away from *Bea*. Because something in her called to him...

It was just attraction, just lust, just this weirdly sensual island playing tricks on his mind. If he were in New York or Nashville, or any of the other cities he knew, this wouldn't be an issue. But Santorini was magical, and when you added an attractive, trying-to-be-brave woman and out-of-control attraction things were bound to get tangled and misinterpreted.

He just had to keep his head. His big one needed to keep thinking and strategising, his little one … well, it was uncontrollable.

And right now, it needed him to stop thinking and start doing. 'I need your mouth, sweetheart,' he told her, his voice low and a little growly. He craved much more but he'd start there and work his way down.

Bea's eyes met his, and she placed her hand on his cheek and brought her mouth closer, closer…

Unable to wait, and not in the mood to be teased, he pulled her in, chest to chest, the vee of her legs pushing into his cock. Forgetting gentle, he took possession of her mouth, making it his, just as he wanted to claim her body as his, too. He needed, just for this moment, this night, to bind her to him in the most elemental way possible. He wasn't possessive, but a primal part of him, his caveman DNA, wanted to brand her as his.

Bea responded to his rough hands racing over her skin by wrapping her tongue around his and gently sucking. His cock instantly hardened – how was that even possible? – and he placed his hand on her lower back, to pull her deeper into him. Her legs widened and he felt her feminine heat. Needing to taste her, he boosted her up so that he could clamp his lips over her breast. She whimpered, and her nails dug into his shoulder blades, and the slight hit of pain only heightened his pleasure.

This was hot, real, amazing…

But he needed more. Lowering her, he told her to hold on and her legs wrapped around his hips again. He walked her out of the shallow edge of the pool and onto the deck.

'Let's take this back to the cottage,' he murmured. He put her on her feet, taking a moment to look at her, his wet woodland nymph in the moonlight.

Bea bit her bottom lip and shifted from foot to foot. He now knew her well enough to know that she was thinking … and doubting. He pushed her wet hair off her forehead and brushed his mouth across hers. 'It's chilly out here, Bea-darling, and the other night I saw Golly wandering around late at night.'

With Bea as skittish as she was, the last thing they needed was to be interrupted by Golly, or anyone else out for a late-night stroll. He wouldn't put it past Golly to give him tips on his technique. No, they needed to go back to the privacy of the cottage, to that huge bed that could accommodate his big frame.

He dressed Bea in his shirt and pulled up his shorts. Grabbing the rest of their clothes, he took her hand and fast walked her back to the cottage, stopping to kiss her at regular intervals. On her mouth, on both of her breasts… By the time they reached the cottage she was panting, and her eyes were a little glazed.

Gib shut the cottage door with his foot, dropped their clothes, scooped her up, and carried her through to the bedroom, gently lowering her onto the bed. Peeling his shirt off her was ten times better than opening a present on Christmas day…

Bea closed her eyes and tried to cover the strip of hair between her legs with her hand, to place her arm around her breasts, but Gib gently clasped her wrists and lifted them up and over her head, holding her easily with one hand. 'No, I want to look at you.'

His gaze raked her from tip to toe, and each breath he took was hotter than the one before. Keeping his control was going to be a challenge, he wanted in, *now*, but he needed to savour her more. He was making a memory and intended to take his time.

After shedding his shorts, leaving them in a pile next to the bed, he stroked her, using the back of his fingers from one breast to the other, down her sternum and across her belly button, over her mound. Her mouth dropped open and her eyes darkened, and she touched her top lip with her tongue.

Good, her embarrassment was gone… Not that she had flaws she needed to hide.

'Fuck, the things I want to do to you, Bea. Can I?'

She whispered her 'yes' and he slid his hand through her pubic hair, so soft, and danced over her folds. He found her clit and she arched her back. 'I want to kiss you, suck you, taste you coming on my tongue.'

He watched her eyes and, judging by the surprise in them, instantly realised oral sex wasn't something she'd experienced before. How the hell had she not had someone going down on her? What was wrong with the men in her life? Men in general?

Well, that was a wrong he could make right.

'Do you trust me to make you feel good, Bea-baby?'

'Uh … *yes*?'

He played with her again, loving the shock and need in her eyes. 'Can I make you come with my teeth and my tongue?'

'Um … *sure*?'

He heard hesitancy in her voice and knew he couldn't continue until he was sure she wanted this as much as he did. 'You don't sound convinced, sweetheart.'

She bit down on her lip, so hard that she left teeth marks. And embarrassment was back in her eyes. 'I just don't know what to do,' she admitted, unable to look at him.

He lifted her chin by grasping it between his finger and thumb and waited for her eyes to meet his. 'You don't have to do anything. That's kinda the whole point.'

Chapter Nine

L ying here, naked, with Gib looking at her, was miles out of Bea's zone of comfort.

He looked entranced, determined, excited, and she couldn't believe a man like him – big, bold and, crucially, experienced – could look at her with heat and want and need blazing from his eyes. Just to make sure, she glanced down and saw his huge shaft, upright and proud, weeping a little from the crown. She knew enough to know that he was ready, possibly desperate, to be inside her, but he was willing to put off his orgasm to pleasure her.

He caught her looking and smiled. 'Yeah, I want you, but I want to do this more,' he told her, his voice deeper and darker, a growl in the night.

She wished she could be bold and breezy, and tell him to go for it, but only a small, timid 'OK' left her lips. What would he do, would he start slow, or just dive on in? Was she supposed to lift her legs, widen her knees … *what?* God, why hadn't she read more books on sex? Or picked up *Cosmo* more often?

'Stop thinking, Bea-darling,' he told her, coming to lie down beside her on the bed. Despite being in the cottage, the temperature had dropped, and she was grateful for the heat rolling off Gib's truly excellent body.

Then he kissed her again, hard and hot and demanding, and when he yanked her into him, she wasn't sure where she started, and he stopped. It was a hot, drugging, kiss, one that lowered the last of her inhibitions and turned her into an aching void needing to be filled. God, she'd had more pleasure in fifteen minutes from him than she'd had from all her previous lovers combined. No, she was not going to spoil this with thoughts of the past or worries about the future. About whether she was doing it right and whether he approved. For once in her life, she was going to live in the moment … *this* moment.

Gib kissed her neck, nibbled her collarbone, stroked his hands down her sides and then his mouth latched onto her breast, sucking her nipple to the top of his mouth. A highway of sensation ran from her breast to her belly to that spot between her legs, until she was no longer built of muscle and bone, but of light, colours and sensations.

She opened her eyes when he moved, and she lifted her head to see him edging her knees wide so he could kneel between her calves. His clever mouth ran over her stomach, his tongue dipped into her belly button, and his teeth latched onto her hip. He blew into the hair on her mound, and even that soft movement inched her up a level.

Gib looked down and his fingers gently separated her folds, and she held her breath at the expression on his face … a little reverential, a lot appreciative. And in that moment, she was all the art muses in history, all the great courtesans, the models and the celebs, she was every hot woman who ever existed. Every woman who'd been loved by a man.

He *wanted* her.

Gib ducked his head, and she felt his words on her clit, rolling up her body. 'My beautiful nymph.'

Nymph or nympho? What did he mean – oh, *gawd*. Her brain emptied of thought when his tongue lathed her, hitting her spot and causing her to arch her back. His hand clamped around her thighs, keeping her from scooting up the bed as he teased her, using his teeth and his tongue to decimate her control.

'I'm going to put my fingers inside you, Bea, and you're going to love it.'

Was she? Really? One broad finger slid into her channel, then another, and she stretched to accommodate him, her muscles welcoming him in by tightening around him. The pad of his finger tapped against a spot deep inside, and she left her body. She became sensation, flipped over into light, and morphed into sound. She was everything and nothing as she climbed higher, pleasure dancing through her veins.

She'd had orgasms before, weak beats easily forgotten, but this was uncharted territory, the pulsation deep within her was something she never knew she wanted, something she'd never imagined.

Bea threaded her fingers through Gib's thick hair and held his head to her, scared he was going to leave her hanging, leave her out on a ledge with nowhere to go. 'I've got you Bea-baby,' he murmured.

He did something with his teeth and tongue, his fingers and his thumb, and then she fell, tumbling, spinning and gushing and keening in the dark, dark night.

It was heaven, it was hell, she wanted more. Her head thrashed from side to side and from a place far, far away, she felt Gib move up her body, his cock, heavy and hard and hot, between her thighs. Bea gripped his hip and she lifted hers, needing nothing but to feel him slide inside her. She waited, then waited some more.

'We don't have a condom,' Gib told her, with a tortured groan.

'Fuck,' she muttered. 'Fuck, fuck, *fuck*.'

He rested his head on her forehead. 'Or, to be accurate, no fuck,' he muttered.

'Aren't men supposed to carry condoms in their wallets or something?'

'I came to the island to be alone, sex wasn't on my mind,' he told her. 'Are you on birth control because I'm clean?'

She shook her head and heard his low groan. 'But you can, you know, pull out,' she told him, desperate for him to complete her.

'If I get inside you, there's no fucking way I'm pulling out,' he told her. He cursed, fluently and loudly and rolled onto his side. He found her hand and wrapped it around his

184

shaft, his eyes slamming shut as she squeezed. 'This is just going to have to do. For now.'

He showed her how he liked her to touch him, and she rolled her fist up his shaft, closing in on the crown, and it wept over her hand. An impulse had her lifting her hand to her mouth, needing to taste him. His eyes widened as she licked her skin, then glinted.

'Fuck, that's hot,' he muttered.

She wanted another rollicking orgasm, but she'd already had one, so she looked down at his cock. 'I could, you know…'

'Give me a blow job?' he said, finishing her sentence. 'As much as I would love that, we'll save that until later. This will do for now.'

He slid his hand between her legs, placed his thumb on her clit and worked his fingers back inside her. His mouth hovered over hers. 'Tug me harder, and faster.'

She obeyed his order, and his mouth slammed into hers, his tongue repeating the stabbing movement of his fingers down below. She rocked against him, and slid her hand up and down his cock, moving to two hands to give him the maximum amount of contact and pleasure.

She knew he was close, and so was she, and when he pulled his mouth off hers and looked deep into her eyes, she felt powerful and feminine and so damn sexy.

'You, this … feels so good … *fuck*!' Gib's eyes slammed closed, and he jerked, then jerked again, spilling over her hands. Seeing his pleasure, she tipped over herself, her orgasm rolling over her in delicious waves.

When she was done, she slumped against his chest, conscious of his rapid heartbeat and his shallow pants. She felt him kiss her hair as he pulled his fingers out of her and when he squeezed the hand still holding him, she looked up at him. 'As much as I like your hands on me, I think you can let go now, sweetheart.'

She jerked her hand away, heat flooding her cheeks. She turned her head into his neck so he wouldn't see her mortification. Gib stroked her hair, kissed her temple and, with no embarrassment, stood up and walked into the bathroom. Through the open doorway, she watched him wet a flannel and wipe himself clean, before rinsing it and walking back over to her. Embarrassed, she tried to take the flannel from him, but he held it out of reach, shaking his head.

'No, let me,' he murmured. He gently stroked the fabric over her hands and then tossed the flannel through the open door to the bathroom where it landed in the freestanding tub.

Instead of picking up his phone, or rolling over and falling asleep, Gib slid in beside her and pulled the covers over them.

His fingers tunnelled into her hair above her ear, and he softly cursed. 'Your hair is still wet.'

He rolled away again, and went back to the bathroom for a towel. He sat on the edge of the bed and gently rubbed her head with it, before scrubbing it over his.

'Better?' he asked.

'Much,' Bea replied, caught off guard by his actions.

Since she'd always been the one to look after someone, not the other way around, it made her feel...

Weird. Admittedly, it was nice, but it was definitely weird.

The towel landed on the floor, and Bea resisted the urge to hang it up. He resettled them, her head on his shoulder, his leg between hers, his big arm holding her close.

When had she last been so loved, so well looked after, so cherished?

Uh ... that would be never.

In his arms, nothing seemed to matter, and she could just be Bea. It was both liberating and lovely. She yawned and her eyes fluttered closed. She loved his body and this bed, it was the best of both worlds.

So much better than the fugly divan. She yawned again and snuggled closer to Gib. So much better than her vibrator. So much bet...

———

Gib was not a morning person. Generally, his blood didn't start to circulate until he'd been for a run or to the gym, and he was unable to form words until he'd swallowed two cups of coffee. In his normal life, all that usually happened before seven a.m., and nobody knew he needed exercise and coffee to jumpstart him in the morning.

Waking up to someone singing along to a hiphop song, the sun in his eyes and morning wood the size of a Sequoia tree – and unable to do anything about it because he had no

JOSS WOOD

goddamn condoms – made him grumpier than usual. And that was saying something.

Gib rolled onto his back and lifted his head to look down at his aching cock. Jesus. Even he was impressed by the tent it made of the sheet. But there was fuck-all he could do about it, unless he jacked off in the shower.

He might just have to, because having Bea give him a handy wouldn't work for him. He wanted to be balls deep inside her... OK, that wasn't helping.

Irritated with himself, annoyed that she'd left the bed without him noticing, frustrated in general, he sat up and looked around the spotless bedroom. Bea's side of the bed had been made, as well as it could be with him still in it. The shorts and towel he'd left on the floor last night were gone. On the whitewashed credenza sat his now closed laptop and a small vase holding what looked to be wildflowers. He didn't remember them being there last night...

Worst of all, on the chair in the corner was a neatly folded pile of his laundry. What the hell? He knew room service wasn't included in Golly's rate, neither were meals, so who'd tossed his clothes in the washer?

The same person who was, he guessed by the delicious smells wafting into the bedroom from the kitchen, frying bacon and making coffee. Annoyed – he loathed being fussed over – Gib left the bed and stalked into the bathroom. He did what he needed to, grabbed a pair of shorts from the clean laundry pile, upending Bea's carefully folded pile of clothes. Toppling the stack, he whipped out a

T-shirt, pulled it over his head, and headed into the kitchen…

He stopped abruptly and lifted his eyebrows. Bea stood in the small kitchen, humming as she pushed bacon around a pan. She wore a bright aqua bikini under a loose, long sleeved orange cotton sweater. A black sarong was knotted on her left hip. Her hair was wet again, and finger-brushed off her forehead, and her sarong showed patches of wetness on her butt. It was obvious she'd taken an early morning swim.

She turned, saw him standing there and jumped half a foot in the air. 'Jeez, you gave me a fright,' she laughed, hand on her heart. She gestured to the pan. 'I'm making breakfast. Do you want some coffee?'

Only as much as he wanted to keep breathing. And why did she have to be Sunshine Suzy so early in the morning? He walked over to the cupboard, planning on grabbing a mug to make his own coffee, but Bea beat him to it. She shoved a mug under the spout and hit the button. He noticed it was preset to dole out an espresso.

What if he wanted a latte for a change? He didn't, but that wasn't the point. Bea looked up at him, smiled and raised her chin, and Gib knew she was expecting a kiss. He'd yet to brush his teeth and was sure his breath could drop a lion at twenty yards. But that wasn't the only reason he ignored her silent request.

This was all too domesticated for him. He never slept over, and if a woman spent a night at his place, he made sure she left at the same time he went for a run. And, funny, nobody appreciated being booted out of a warm bed at five in the morning. Not his problem because he always warned them what would happen, but none of his dates believed him. Every one of the women he took home suggested he ditch his routine and stay in bed for another round, then breakfast. He never said yes.

Sex was always good, he made sure of it – if a woman was gracious enough to share her body with him, it was his job to make it good for her – but it was still just sex. A brief physical connection.

The sound of the coffee gurgling and dripping into the cup and the bacon sizzling was the only sound in the room. Not wanting to see the confusion in Bea's lovely eyes, he walked onto the deck and shook his head at what he saw.

Bea normally worked at the little table that stood directly in front of the view. Usually it was a mess of Post-it Notes, highlighters, at least three coffee cups and two notebooks full of her chicken-scratch scribbling. But this morning her stuff had been cleared away and she'd covered the table with a bright pink-and-yellow cloth, side plates and cutlery, and condiments. Another vase of flowers sat dead centre in the middle of the table.

What the *fuck* was this? Was she trying to make her own Hallmark moment? It screamed romance and he wasn't into romance. Wouldn't know what it was even if it bit him on the ass.

He sensed her behind him and whirled around to look at her. He took the mug she held out and gestured to the table. 'And this?'

Shock skittered across her face. 'Uh…' She looked back at the kitchen as if she were looking for answers there. 'I thought it would be nice for us to have breakfast out here.'

He lifted his coffee mug and took a big sip, his eyes widening as the hot liquid scorched his tongue. Maybe it was life's payback for him being a bastard. But her making him breakfast, tidying up and doing his goddamn laundry was weird as shit.

What the hell did she think she was doing? She wasn't his maid or cook.

He shook his head and banged the mug so hard on the table that the coffee splashed over the rim and stained the pretty pink tablecloth. 'I don't want breakfast.' He really did but there was no way he was going to stay here for one more minute. 'I'm going for a run.'

Bea frowned, her hand resting at the bottom of her neck, her index finger tapping her collarbone. She looked thoroughly confused and he didn't blame her. He was acting like a prize dick but didn't seem to be able to stop.

'You don't want breakfast?'

'No.'

What he wanted was for her to act like she didn't want to be here, like she had on the day they'd arrived. He needed her to have her claws out, throwing barbs at him, to look at him with scorn in her eyes. Not to look hurt, confused, sexy and so very fuckable.

And, crucially, not acting like they were in a relationship. They only met a few days ago … who *did* that? And it was 2024, why the hell was she picking up after his slobby self? That mindset belonged to the fifties and sixties! Hadn't she heard about women's lib?

'I'll grab something to eat in Oia if I get hungry.'

To her credit, she didn't try and talk him out of going. She simply lifted her shoulder and quietly told him that she was going to have a bacon butty. Because he was a contradictory bastard, he immediately wanted that English favourite – white bread, fatty bacon and ketchup, or, as the English called it tow-*mah*-tow sauce.

Bea, her back ramrod straight, stacked the side plates, picked up the cutlery from the table, walked back into the kitchen and put the items back where they belonged. She returned, picked up the condiments, pushed his cup into his hand and whipped the cloth off the table, shoving it against his chest. 'Put that into the laundry basket when you go back to the bedroom,' she told him, ice coating her words.

Gib rubbed the back of his neck and silently cursed. Yes, he was being a dick and, yes, he was astute enough to realise he'd hurt her, but who went to all this effort the morning after a night when they did little more than heavy petting? Didn't she know how flings worked? Even if this was the start of a relationship – and it most certainly was not! – everyone knew you handed out little pieces at a time, gave the minimum amount of information and effort and built your way up, over time, to something.

And her tidying up, making breakfast, and doing his laundry freaked him the fuck out. Next, she'd be asking his thoughts on religion and politics, or to tell her about his childhood. She'd want him to talk about the accident that took his parents, and how he coped after they were gone. How guilty he still felt for that initial, so selfish, spurt of relief.

He had to say something but he didn't have the first clue what. He twisted the tablecloth into a tight ball. 'Bea, I—'

Bea half turned and her look nailed his feet to the floor. 'You said you were going for a run, Gib. I suggest you do that. Before we both say, or do, something we can't come back from.'

With that, Bea headed back inside, picked up a slice of bacon from the pan on the stove and walked out the front door.

Bea felt like she'd been punched in the gut.

Pride kept her shoulders back and her back straight as she quickly walked away from the cottage, but as soon as she was out of sight, hot tears rolled down her face. She looked at the piece of bacon between her fingers and lobbed it away. In an instant, she was ten again, listening to her father express his disappointment that his scrambled eggs were burned. Twelve, and his horror at her not receiving an A for a descriptive writing essay. Fourteen, and his resignation when she told him, as she did every summer, that she was leaving to spend the summer holidays with Golly.

'If your mother doesn't want you, then you can stay here with me.'

Back then she thought she didn't know what was worse, missing out on six weeks of being a kid, or disappointing her father. As an adult, she understood that six weeks being a child, with no responsibilities, saved her sanity.

Bea swiped the tears off her cheeks, and reminded herself that she was a grown woman, and Gib's criticism was unwarranted. She shouldn't be reacting like this. But the sobs in her throat, her knotted stomach and her inability to regain her composure – all because some Neanderthal man took potshots at her – made her wonder if she'd made any progress in twenty years.

Maybe she'd always and forever be that lost and lonely, terrified to make a mistake, child.

She felt panic scour her throat and knew she needed to do some deep-breathing exercises before she lost it completely. She stomped past the pergola to sit on the wall, and placed her hand on her stomach, sucking in air, trying to get it to her toes. As her panic receded, she decided Gib's shitty attitude was his problem, not hers.

Was he pissed off because she'd tidied up, made him breakfast and set the table? Could he be that petty? It wasn't like she'd asked to move in with him or demanded a wedding ring. Maybe he was frustrated at them not being able to make love last night, but that wasn't her fault. He'd had no right, the *bastard*, to act like a dick.

But, damn, she wished she'd learnt how to defend herself better, how to be an advocate for herself. Instead of fleeing, she should've given him a blasting, told him to take his bad mood and sullen face and fuck right off.

Anger swept over her, incinerating her self-doubt and her self-pity. She was *not* a child anymore, and she refused to let him treat her like dirt under his feet. Fury dried up her tears and sent adrenaline pumping through her veins.

She didn't care who he was, or how big he was, she was going to verbally incinerate him. He'd awoken her inner dragon, and she was going to go scorched earth on his ass! And then she'd boot him off her godmother's property.

She half sprinted back to the cottage, banging the front door open so hard the table rattled, and the blue dish moved a little closer to the edge of the table. She pushed it back into place, and looked around the cottage, not seeing the object of her rage.

She stomped into the bedroom and immediately noticed his big trainers, the ones that sat next to the door, were gone. Dammit, she'd missed him. Her anger faded as she sat down on the edge of the bed, her elbows on her knees.

Calmer now, Bea scooted back on the big bed and wrapped her arms around her bended knees. She looked at his messy side of the bed and remembered how wonderful it felt to lie in his arms, listening to the steady beat of his heart.

She wasn't the type of woman who had casual sex, and she never thought she'd indulge in heavy petting in a pool her godma often used at night. She banged the heel of her palm against her forehead as she remembered Gib's face between her thighs, the way he took her clit between his teeth...

She throbbed and she squirmed at the strange feeling.

She was furious with him, so why was she thinking about how he made her feel?

She shouldn't be thinking about sex *at all*.

But the images of what he'd done, and how he'd made her feel, and how much he seemed to enjoy what they did, rolled through her mind, an old-fashioned projector throwing slides onto her mental screen. She'd enjoyed what they did, she'd enjoyed *him*.

But she had to be sensible and see last night for what it was. She needed to be unemotional and clear-headed. Sex was a great stress reducer, an excellent way to get out of her head for a while. As a single, adult woman, she was entitled to pleasure and was allowed to have a fling. What she wasn't allowed to do was to imagine this was more than what it was: they were just two people who were attracted to each other. No more, no less.

She had to be smart and stop this madness in its tracks. And that meant no more hand jobs and heavy petting. No sex at all.

Gib was a complication she didn't need, and she didn't like feeling out of control. And, dammit, she knew it would only take one look from his marvellous eyes and she'd remember his mouth on hers, his hand running over her butt to haul her into him. One lift of that sexy mouth and she'd recall his talented mouth on her breasts, between her legs...

She'd just have to get the hell over herself.

A long time ago, she'd accepted that she was much better at creating relationships between the characters in her books than she was in real life. At least when she got things wrong in her manuscript, she had a delete button she could use to erase mistakes, and no one – especially her – got hurt in the process. This morning's suck-fest was a wake-up call that she wasn't good at the man/woman dynamic and that she should stay clear and keep her distance. She'd looked for love and validation in the wrong places and with the wrong men before, and she didn't want to repeat past mistakes. Couldn't repeat them. Wouldn't allow herself to.

No, this stopped. Today.

She just had to figure out how to get him out of this cottage.

Again.

This was starting to become a habit.

———————

'Asshole.'

Navy's voice sounded as clear as it would if he were next to him. Gib wiped the sweat off his forehead and checked his watch. He'd left the cottage forty minutes ago and he'd been running at pace, and he was six miles in, way past Oia. Because he wasn't paying attention, what he thought would be a five-mile run was likely going to end up being a twelve-mile-plus slog. It served him right for being a douchebag.

'I know. But you know how I am in the mornings before I have coffee.' It was a weak excuse and he despised himself for making it.

Navy, because he always called Gib on his bullshit, didn't give him an out. 'Actually, I called you an asshole for forgetting to pack condoms. Who *does* that?'

Yeah, not his finest moment.

'But you are a dick for lashing out at her. Wait, is asshole worse than being called a dick? I can never remember,' Navy said. 'You're an asshole-dick-bastard. There, all bases covered.'

Gib was just grateful Navy didn't quote Shakespeare, telling him *'thou art a boil, a plague sore'*. In his teens, Navy'd been hooked on Shakespeare, Tolkien and Chaucer and had peppered his friends with quotes, story plots and seventeenth-century insults. It had been a testament to Navy's good nature and popularity that he hadn't had his head shoved into a toilet.

'You aren't a kid, Gibson, so you're old enough to know you can't take out your bad moods on the people around you,' Navy told him, sounding just like Uncle Hugh, and to be honest, Gib's dad. And, yeah, a part of Gib felt like he was eleven again.

He squinted at the bright Aegean sea – wishing he'd remembered to bring his sunglasses – feeling even worse than he did earlier. If that was even possible.

'You owe her an apology, Gib.'

He'd figured that much out. 'I *know*.'

'Have you worked out why you lost your shit?' Navy asked him. Normally a question like that would make him break out in hives, but it was from Navy, and therefore, tolerable. *Just.*

And yes, he wasn't a total imbecilic or wholly unaware. A fraction of his sharp response was due to his normal early-morning surliness, the rest of it was a response to the flowers she'd picked and put into vases, her making breakfast and coffee, doing his laundry, *fussing*. His mom'd had hovering down to an art form and had been a bossy bee who wouldn't leave him alone. On the cottage's deck, he'd become reacquainted with his teenage frustration at being 'mothered'.

Confusingly, he had also liked it. He'd liked that Bea'd gone to the effort to make him as comfortable as possible. He'd enjoyed her bright smile, hearing her humming, the soft expression on her face – part embarrassment, part attraction. He'd even liked her making him breakfast, something he'd never expected her to do.

The crash of him hating what she did and enjoying it, too, had sent his irritation levels soaring; the combination of annoyance, memories, appreciation and attraction tipping him over the edge into terror. And he'd responded, because he was a man (and an asshole-dick-bastard), by lashing out.

Fuck. Apologising was going to *suck*.

'Gib? You still there?'

Gib touched his right ear pod in surprise. He'd forgotten he was talking to Navy. Reaching a crossroads, he turned around and started jogging back in the same direction he'd come from, breathing hard.

'This… What did you say her name was again?' Navy asked.

'Bea.'

'Tell me more about her. What does she look like, what does she do?'

These were questions he could answer. 'Brown hair, eyes that can be either blue or grey, with hints of lavender—'

Navy's laughter rolled across the miles and into his ear and Gib stopped speaking. What was so funny?

'Blue? Grey? Lavender? You're *fried*, dude.'

Gib chose to ignore his comment and ploughed on. 'She's Golly's assistant.'

'You're sleeping with a fifty-year-old single mom?' Navy demanded, suddenly serious.

What the hell was he going on about? 'Bea is in her late twenties, maybe early thirties, and she doesn't have kids.' He didn't think.

'Well, I *know* Golly's assistant. She's called Merle, she's super-efficient and practically runs the G&T agency. She's damn good at her job.'

Gib frowned, confused. 'That's what Bea told me. Though I think she might also dabble in writing.'

'What makes you think that?'

'Remember I asked you what the acronym meant? GNT—'

'GMC, for *chrissake*.'

Jeez, shoot him for not knowing the right acronym. He bet that if he asked Navy what ROI, CRM and KPI meant, he wouldn't be able to answer. No, he would. Navy had a photogenic memory.

'Goal, motivation, conflict,' Navy corrected him. He really didn't care.

'Anyway, I saw that acronym on a page in her notebook.' Gib went on to explain how she'd knocked over her coffee cup. 'I also read something about a series arc, rapids, someone falling off, and Pip reacting. I think she saw my kayak and it sparked an idea.'

'First thought? Maybe you should stop reading her personal shit.'

Fair point.

Navy stayed silent for so long that Gib thought he'd lost him. 'Are you sure you saw the word "Pip"?'

Her handwriting was crap, but it was only a three-letter word. 'Pretty sure. And Harriet, Henry, no— Shit. It was a strange name.'

'*Hettie?*'

'Yeah, I think that's what she wrote.'

'Holy, holy shit,' Navy said, excitement coating his words. 'I know who she is, cousin.'

Gib did too. The woman who'd turned his life inside out. The woman he still wanted to make love to, fucking *desperately*. He needed to stop in Oia and buy a box of condoms. Granted, he had less than an ice-cube's chance in hell of getting her naked, but millions believed miracles did happen.

If one came his way, he wanted to be prepared.

'I think your Bea is Parker Kane, Gib.'

Chapter Ten

'I'm sorry.'

Bea sat at the table on the deck, her specs on and her hair pulled up into a messy bun. She'd heard Gib come into the cottage and listened as he went into the bedroom and closed the door behind him. Heard the faint sounds of the shower and the buzz of an electric razor. The opening of the bedroom door, his big feet approaching her.

She'd kept her eyes on her screen, still too pissed off to look at him. 'Seriously, Bea, I was a prick. I'm sorry.'

Her parents had never apologised, neither had Gerry, and the sincerity in Gib's voice had her lifting her eyes to his face. His expression echoed the authenticity in his voice and she saw unease, and shame, in his eyes. Having never been on the receiving end of a proper, vocal apology – Golly either apologised via text or with an expensive present – she wasn't quite sure what to say.

'OK.'

He rubbed the back of his neck and for the first time she saw the man behind the imperturbable CEO, someone whose confidence wasn't, for a change, sky high. 'Do you want an explanation?' he muttered.

She tipped her head to the side and pulled her heels up to rest them on the edge of her chair. 'Would you give me one?'

He shrugged. 'Yeah.'

She rolled her hand, lifted her eyebrows and waited. He rocked on his heels, jammed his hands under his armpits and looked at the view. Gib flipped his sunglasses over his eyes and a few seconds later pushed them back onto his head. He looked down at his feet and rubbed the back of his neck. She knew he was hoping she'd take pity on him and let him off the hook.

No friggin' chance.

Bea wrapped her arms around her legs and waited.

Gib cleared his throat. 'I have this thing about privacy. Sharing this cottage with you isn't easy for me.'

She was tempted to tell him that he'd always had the option to shove off, but she was emotionally exhausted, and she didn't want to start another fight.

'I'm never at my best in the morning ... but that's not an excuse for me acting like a prick.' He dragged his hands over his face. 'If I give them the option to sleep over, my dates usually leave after sex, or when I leave to workout at five in the morning.'

God, she couldn't think of anything worse than being

booted out of his bed to do the walk of shame at that time of the morning.

'Don't frown at me, they knew that was going to happen,' he told her, with a touch of his previous asperity. 'Look, I'm just not used to having someone in my space. I'm not interested in a relationship, or any sort of commitment and I reacted badly. I felt uncomfortable with you cleaning up after me, doing my laundry, making the bed, and then rustling up breakfast. It's too domesticated for me.'

Bea opened her mouth to defend herself, to tell him that while he thought it OK to be a slob, she wasn't. But she pulled back her words, knowing she was latching onto an easy defence of her actions. He was a little untidy, but she hadn't given him a chance to clean up after himself. She'd swept in and done it for him, instinctively falling back into her old patterns of behaviour.

And yeah, she'd skipped out of bed this morning, buoyed by a fantastic orgasm and an even better night's sleep. She'd been raring to go, so she went for a swim, made breakfast, and made this table look like a prop from *Mamma Mia*. She'd offered him something to eat and handed him coffee. She'd been a heartbeat away from lying down and asking him to scratch her tummy…

She could see why a man who eschewed relationships would feel uncomfortable when the woman he'd made scream the previous night turned into Hannah Homemaker. But she wasn't prepared to let him totally off the hook. 'You were a jerk,' she told him.

His eyes didn't drop from hers. 'I know.'

She hauled in a deep breath. 'If I agree to not tidy up after you, and bring you coffee, will you try to pick up your stuff, make the bed, and stop annoying me?'

The misery faded in his eyes, as confidence rolled back in. 'Yeah. I'll make that deal.' He started towards her, and Bea knew he was about to kiss her. She couldn't think of anything she wanted more, but it wasn't going to happen. She wasn't ready to return to where they were before. Their argument earlier was his fault (and hers), but they couldn't go back and pretend nothing had happened. She didn't work that way.

She held up her hand and he stopped abruptly. 'We need a reset.'

He grimaced and did his hand-rubbing-his-neck gesture again. She'd learnt that he only did it when he was thinking about how to respond. 'So, you're not moving out?' he said, trying to inject a little humour into their conversation.

Bea decided she could meet him halfway. 'Nice try, but no.' She narrowed her eyes at him. 'But the pillows are going back up.'

'Aw, come on, Bea,' he cajoled, but she saw the understanding in his expression, acceptance in his eyes. 'I get it. I don't like it, but I get it.' He glanced at her laptop and gestured to the lounger. 'Would I bug you if I sat here, drank a cup of coffee and read my book?'

No, of course not. *Of course* she could work when the man who made her ovaries spin, her skin pebble, and her lady parts thrum sat just a yard from her, looking hot and sexy and oh-so-beddable.

Well, she could try.

'Sure, if *you* make *me* a cup of coffee. Milk and one sugar.' She dropped her legs and picked up her glasses, sliding them onto her nose. She'd give work an hour, and then she'd go up to the house and bug Cass and Nadia, or hang out with her godma and the Two Jacks.

Nothing surprised her more when Gib stopped next to her and bent down to drop a kiss on her head. 'I *am* sorry for this morning. Sexy glasses, by the way.'

Bea pushed away the urge to run after him and take him to bed.

Bad Bea. Keep your arse on this chair and put your fingers to the keyboard. Get to work. You can't, as the great Nora Roberts – or was it Jodi Picoult? – said, edit a blank page.

The next morning, Bea woke up to the dings of a couple of text messages. Swimming out of sleep, she reached for her phone, but couldn't move because a muscled arm was wrapped around her waist, holding her to a hard body. Her butt was nestled against Gib's groin and, judging by his massive erection, he was happy to have her there.

What happened to the pillows? She'd rebuilt her Great Wall Of Pillows last night and Gib, to his credit, didn't say anything about the soft barrier when he slid into bed. He'd just lifted an eyebrow, sighed and pulled back the covers.

She'd noticed he wore a pair of thin, exercise shorts and

a loose T-shirt. And seeing him covered up made her sad. A body like his should stay naked.

Right, she wasn't going there…

'Who the hell is texting incessantly so early?' Gib muttered, nestling his face into her neck. His stubble tickled her skin as he dropped an open-mouth kiss in the space where her jaw met her neck. His hand moved up her torso and clasped her left breast, his thumb brushing her nipple. Oh, man, that felt amazing…

'Judging by the sun, it's later than you think,' Bea told him, wiggling her butt into his hard dick. She turned her head to look at him over her shoulder. His eyes were still closed, and he had a small smile on his face. Looking relaxed and turned on suited him.

'What happened to my pillows, Caddell?' she asked, aiming for annoyance and missing it by a mile.

He lifted his head and squinted at the bed. 'Huh, no idea. I must've tossed them off while I was asleep. Sleepy me was looking for sleepy you.'

'Cute.'

Her phone dinged again, and she rolled away from him to reach it. He kept his hand on her, sneaking under the hem of her shirt to stroke her stomach, sliding his fingers under the band of her sleeping shorts. She looked at her phone, and the words danced in front of her. How was she supposed to make sense of Cass's messages when he was touching her like that?

'Cass needs me to run into Fira to pick up a few hundred

things for the party,' she told Gib, who was on his side, looking at her.

'Mmm, later.' He plucked her phone out of her hand and tossed it towards the bedside table, and she heard it crash into the bedside lamp. 'Right now, I have other plans for you.'

She smiled slowly. 'And those would be?'

'I'd very much like to make you scream, with my mouth and with my cock,' he stated, his drawl more pronounced. 'You up for that?'

In his eyes, in his urgent touch, Bea knew he was asking if she was ready, if she wanted him as much as he wanted her. She did. So much. Unable to find the words – strange, because words were her stock-in-trade – she simply nodded.

'I kinda need you to say it, Bea.'

She lifted his hand off her stomach and placed it on her breast. 'Make me scream, Gib. But if you don't have condoms, I might just lose it, right now.'

'I've got you covered, Bea-baby,' Gib murmured, his eyes glinting with satisfaction. Should she ask him not to call her that? Wasn't it the same as calling her a 'girl' as opposed to a woman? Why was she thinking about this, right now? She liked hearing Bea-baby coming from his mouth, it made her feel sexy, wanted, and a little cherished. *Stop thinking, dammit!*

He pulled away and Bea immediately missed his heat, his hands on her body, his mouth on her skin. Gib didn't drop her eyes from hers as he reached behind him to grab his T-shirt and pull it up and over his head. His chest was tanned, his nipples were flat discs and a light, soft triangle of hair veered into a trail over the hard muscles of his stomach. He was hard, fit and supremely masculine. He made her feel feminine and when he looked at her like that, like she was the last piece of chocolate cake on the planet, her knees softened and the moisture in her mouth dried up.

She'd never felt this way before, needy, lovely, desperate and excited. She had more chance of pushing the earth off its axis than walking away from him now. Oh, a part of her, the sensible, rational part of her, knew this was a mistake, that she was entering too deep waters, but she didn't care. He made her feel alive, more alive than she had in five years. It was a precious gift...

Bea placed her hand on his chest, her fingers drifting through the light hair on his pecs. So hard, so warm. She pushed her nose into his skin, inhaling his woodsy, sexy scent, part deodorant, part hot-man, and sighed. She was doing this, there was no backtracking now.

Gib swiped his thumb over her bottom lip. 'You're so fucking tempting,' he murmured.

'Be tempted, Gib.' Was that really her voice? Low, soft, her words coated with desire? Gib placed his hands on her hips, and his fingertips pushed into her. She placed her open mouth on his collarbone and her tongue slid over his skin.

She wanted him. She'd never wanted anyone as much as she did Gib.

His hand moved to her lower back, and he pulled her

closer to him, and her stomach connected with his erection, hard and thick. His eyes, hot and needy, slammed into hers before his mouth covered hers in a kiss that stopped her synapses from firing.

It was hot, wet, warm, desperate... Bea wound her arms around his back and pushed her breasts into his bare chest, needing to push past his skin and muscles, to find herself in the heart of him.

His hands slid up the back of her legs and underneath her shorts to rest on her bare butt cheeks. He pulled away from her, his eyes fever-bright. 'I think we need to shed some clothes.'

She helped him pull her shorts down, the heat of his hand a contrast to the cool air swirling around her bare thighs and bottom. 'I like being naked with you, Gib.'

'Back at you, baby.'

Gib handed her a deep, wet, demanding kiss, and she gripped his thick hair as he plundered her mouth. He approached sex as he did everything else, with complete confidence and skill. Her nipples pebbled and the space between her legs ached. She wanted more, immediately.

Gib yanked her shirt up and tossed it to the floor, before lifting her onto him. He jack-knifed into a sitting position, and it felt completely natural to wind her legs around his hips. This was where she wanted to be, in his arms, where she felt most at home. Her bare core pressed into him, the material of his shorts creating a delicious friction over his steel-hard erection.

She'd never felt both invigorated, turned on and sexy, as

well as safe, with anyone but Gib. He, this reticent man, knew exactly how to touch her, what she wanted, how she wanted him. Bea arched back and sighed when his teeth scraped over the cords of her neck, when his lips drifted over her collarbone. He pulled back to look at her, his eyes taking in her small breasts and pebbled nipples. She wished her breasts were bigger, fuller.

'You're perfect,' Gib murmured, alleviating her insecurities with his sexy growl. He lowered his head, pulled her nipple into her mouth and scraped his teeth over its sensitive flesh. So damn good. He switched to her other breast and Bea tipped her head back, floating on sensation.

But, as much as she loved his attention, she needed to touch him, to give him as much pleasure as he gave her. Bea slid off his body and moved off the bed. Standing, she brushed her hands over his chest, over his ridged stomach and knocked his hand away from the band of his shorts. She pulled them down his hips, and he sucked in a breath when her fingers danced up the length of his shaft. Gib was a big guy … everywhere. And she was grateful.

She smiled, enjoying the effect she had on him. Wanting to tease him, she ran her thumbnail from the tip down, loving the sounds of his harsh breathing.

Gib moved to the edge of the bed, swung his legs off, and looked up at her with burning eyes. 'Stand between my legs,' he ordered her, his voice rough with need. Bea did as he asked and he skimmed his hands up her sides, over her stomach. His thumb skated across her nipples, and she moved closer, needing his lips on her. Needing his lips everywhere. Bea speared her fingers into his soft hair, loving the way he trailed his mouth across his skin, and teased her before pulling her nipple against the roof of his mouth. She was already completely turned on, and she wanted him now, inside her, filling her, completing her.

'I haven't been able to stop thinking about you, about this,' she murmured when his mouth moved to her sternum, his lips streaking over her skin. She clasped his face in his hands, forcing him to look up at her. She couldn't believe that his light eyes could radiate such warmth…

Gib pulled Bea onto his lap. Her thighs straddled his and he yanked her close, and her core hit his hard, hot shaft and they both shuddered. Gib lifted his lips to grind against her and Bea saw stars behind her eyes. If he kept doing that, she'd come … right now.

As if knowing she was on the edge. Gib slowed down, his mouth skimming her shoulders, his hands running up and down her back, over her bare butt. Her hands did the same, taking in as much of him as she could, loving the muscles in his back, the bumps of his spine, and the feel of the slight scratch of his chest hair against her breasts. Gib lifted his mouth, covered hers and his tongue explored her mouth in a lazy, lovely kiss. The heat was there, but banked, needing just one spark for it to roar into a blazing inferno.

Gib, using just one arm and a whole lot of core strength, picked her up and laid her on her back on the bed. He stood between her legs and dragged his fingers down her, skating over her folds and skimming over her clitoris. Bea moaned and lifted her hips. 'Gib, please…' she pleaded. She needed him inside her, filling her, completing her…

'Not yet.'

Bea sucked in a harsh breath when Gib dropped to his knees and pushed her legs apart. His clever tongue stroked her, causing her to lift her hips and whimper.

'Please, Gib.' She wasn't the type to beg, but she wanted what only he could give her, as quickly as possible.

Gib's satisfied chuckle warmed her skin, and he slid a finger inside her, his thumb resting on her clitoris. Ribbons of colour and intensity shot through her, and she managed, just, to demand his kiss. Gib kissed her, sucking her into his mouth as he worked another finger into her, stretching her. But it wasn't enough, she needed him, all of him…

Bea sat up on her elbows, and her ragged breathing filled the room. 'Gib, come inside me, please.'

He looked up at her, his face tense, and nodded once, before looming over her, his tip probing her entrance. He muttered a curse and pulled back.

'What?' What was he waiting for?

'Condom,' Gib muttered.

'Quickly,' Bea retorted, her hands streaking over his back, his sides, down his stomach and fisting him. He groaned and jerked away from her to open the drawer of his bedside table. Pulling out a condom – thank God! – he ripped it open, and quickly covered himself before turning back to look at her. He picked a strand of hair off her face and tucked it behind her ear. 'Are you sure about this, Bea?'

Oh, yes. She lifted her hips and shuddered as he

positioned himself at her entrance. 'Very sure. I want you, so much.'

Gib's eyes held hers and although he didn't speak, she caught the longing on his face, knew how hard it was for him to slow things down, to make sure they were on the same page, reading from the same book. 'Make love to me, Gib. Please.'

Gib slid into her and buried himself deep, and Bea gasped, feeling herself stretch to take all of him. She hauled in a deep breath, and felt her body loosen, but the heavy and full sensation remained. In tune with her, he stopped and raised his eyebrows. 'OK?' he demanded.

'Very.'

Bea closed her eyes as sensations, tinged with pinks and blues and yellows, rolled over and through her, every wave lifting her higher.

'No, look at me, Bea, I want to watch you as you come,' Gib demanded.

She looked at him through half-closed eyes, thinking he looked like a warrior, his face a study in concentration. He was waiting for her, and only then he would let loose and fly. She wanted to see him lose control, to see him when his defences were down, when he was open and needy. Using all her strength, she pushed him onto his back and dragged her core across him, before pulling his cock back and slipping down to take him inside. He groaned and gripped her hips, biting his bottom lip in concentration.

She was so close, but she wanted him wild and free, she wanted to watch him lose control. She lifted herself, slid down slowly and then clenched her internal muscles. His eyes widened, and his mouth dropped open, as he struggled to hold onto his orgasm. She repeated the motion and he groaned. 'Bea, I can't … please … you've got to…'

She liked the turbulence in his eyes, wild with need. He was usually so controlled, a little remote. She rocked again, squeezed again and told him to let go. Gib tried to hold on, but then he sighed and bucked his hips, driving up into her, pounding her. She found his rhythm, and her climax built with all the speed of a bullet train. She saw him grimace, and his fingertips dug into her hips, and his face ended up in her neck and she felt, deep down inside her, his release. And as he fell apart, she followed … falling, tumbling, spinning…

Landing in his arms, against his neck … it was her new favourite place.

Later that morning, Gib found Bea in the kitchen of the villa, helping Cass pack away the shopping she'd picked up in Fira. He'd offered to join her, but as they were leaving, he received a call from Hugh who needed his urgent input on a joint venture with a famous Nashville music producer.

Bea told him to take his call and to find her later. Not having much choice, he watched her leave, uncharacteristically pissed at having to work. After his call finally wrapped up, ninety minutes later, he listened for Bea's rental and when he heard it return, he ambled over to the villa and headed for the back door leading into the kitchen.

He leaned against the doorframe and watched Bea help Nadia move groceries into the pantry. Golly, Reena and the Two Jacks sat around the kitchen table, eating fruit and cheese and drinking wine. He glanced at his watch, it was just twelve, but Golly and her friends evidently believed in the adage that it was five o'clock somewhere.

He stood there unnoticed by everyone but Bea, who sensed his presence and gave him a long, slow, knowing smile. He responded in the most male way possible, and he had to do multiplication tables in his head and recite the American presidents backwards to get his dick to stand down.

When things went back to normal, he tuned into a lively conversation between Golly and her friends. Bea winked at Gib – she really shouldn't do that – and looked at her godmother. 'Should I ask what you're wearing to your party, Godma? Have you chosen some weird outfit that's going to cause a stir?'

Golly lifted her nose. 'What I wear has nothing to do with you, Bea-darling.'

'Fair enough,' Bea replied, looking mellow. He knew he was at least eighty per cent responsible for her feeling relaxed and laid back, and that knowledge made him feel like he could move mountains. Weird, because he never usually felt so satisfied after sex. It was a biological urge and the effects rarely lasted. But this was Santorini, the island of sunshine, and he was bound to feel different here.

He just had to be careful that this romantic place didn't affect his common sense.

Bea dropped a kiss on Golly's cheek. 'Wear what you want, Gols. Hell, if you want to channel Wednesday Adams or Catwoman, go for it. It's your party.'

Golly narrowed her eyes. 'What's got into you?' Her eyes danced over to him, and she grinned. 'Well, good *morning*, Gib. I think that answers my question.'

Jesus.

Bea tapped her godmother's pink head. 'Golly, behave.' Her eyes found his, and she shrugged and mouthed, 'Sorry.'

He wasn't. About any of it.

Nadia smiled at him and asked if he wanted coffee, but he refused, thanking her. 'Actually, I've come to steal Bea away, I'm hoping to buy her lunch in Oia.'

Bea grinned at him. 'That sounds like a great idea.' She gestured to the shopping. 'Let me just finish up.'

'Sure.' He was super comfortable standing in the doorway, leaning against the frame, the sun on his back. Watching her.

Bea handed Nadia a huge basket of eggs and turned to Reena. 'Reen, you do know that you can't wear your jodhpurs to the party, right?' she asked, returning to their sartorial choices for tomorrow night's party.

Reena didn't blink. 'Not even my new black ones with a black T-shirt and black boots? I'll even polish them.'

Her tone was so bland that Gib didn't know whether she was messing with Bea or not. '*No*, Reena.'

Those bushy eyebrows pulled together. 'I'm not a complete idiot, child. Jacqui organised something for me to wear.'

Jacqui laid her exquisitely decorated fingernails – was that a miniature portrait of Golly on them? The mind boggled! – on her heart. 'A Fendi sheath, and you are going to look stunning, Reena.'

Reena looked horrified. 'A dress means I have to shave my legs, Jacqueline! I asked for a trouser suit, dammit!'

Gib sucked in his cheeks to keep from laughing. Hell, he'd never been so entertained by a random conversation before. Jacqui didn't drop her eyes from Reena's. 'Shall I get the strimmer out of the shed for you?'

Bea rolled her eyes at Gib.

Jacqui and Reena argued, Jack popped a piece of croissant in his mouth and wiped his carefully trimmed moustache with a linen serviette. 'And what are you wearing, Bea-darling?'

Bea sent him a quick, naughty glance. 'I've been frantic, so Jacqui kindly went shopping for me and sent me a few outfits. I finally decided on a white trouser suit with a Halston neckline and some sort of slit up the leg.'

Gib knew she was lying. He lifted an eyebrow at her, calling her out and her grin was wide. And naughty. She didn't want him to know what she was wearing…

That was … *hot*. It shouldn't be but it was.

'You're not going to be boring and stay in the cottage all alone, are you, Gibson?' Golly demanded.

He hated being put on the spot, but he'd known for a

few days, since he first kissed Bea, that he'd be attending Golly's party. He wanted to be anywhere Bea was, and if that meant him being at Golly's big bash, he'd put on his suit and socialise.

'I'll be there,' he told Golly and saw relief shoot across Bea's face. She wanted him there, with her. He shouldn't feel happy about that, as this was, at most, a brief fling. Nothing serious. Nothing to get excited about.

Reena interrupted Jacqui's lecture about how it was important for women to take pride in their appearance. 'How come Bea gets to wear a trouser suit and I don't?' she demanded.

'For the love of God, Reena, you are making my headache worse,' Jacqui whimpered. 'Nadia, do you have any painkillers?'

'You can't mix painkillers and booze, Jacqui,' Nadia told her, sounding uncharacteristically bossy. Now that she felt secure around Golly and Bea, her maternal side was starting to emerge.

'Pfft! Take a few pills, and have another drink, Jacqui,' Golly told her friend. Gib thought abstaining, a few glasses of water and a nap might be a better idea, but what did he know?

Golly pushed away from the table and Bea raised her head to see her put her hands together in front of her chest as if she intended to pray. 'I'm going to meditate before my big day of adulation tomorrow. *Namaste*.'

Golly drifted away singing Frank Sinatra's 'My Way' off-key. Gib looked at Bea, who met his gaze, laughter and 'do you see what I have to deal with?' in her eyes.

'Ready to go?' he asked, holding out his hand. She nodded and slipped hers into his, and behind them, he heard a collective sigh, followed by a couple of '*aws*'.

He looked down at Bea, who looked unfazed. 'I think they know about us,' he deadpanned.

She faked her surprise, her eyes wide and her gasp unnaturally loud. 'Really? What makes you think that?'

Gib laughed and tugged her toward his Jeep, resisting the urge to take her back to bed. They'd made love twice this morning and then indulged in some heavy petting in the shower afterwards. She had to be sore, and he desperately needed food.

They'd have lunch, and then they could come back for an afternoon *non*-nap.

Chapter Eleven

After lunch at one of her favourite restaurants, Bea and Gib wandered through the twisty alleys of Oia and stopped when they approached a bookshop. Gib scanned the books on the long trestle table outside the store. The books were all second-hand, a mixture of English and other languages, including, obviously, Greek. Bea dragged her fingers across the spines of a row of romances, thinking she shouldn't buy any as she had at least fifty on her TBR pile on her Kindle, and paperbacks she'd ordered and not read at home. But the urge to splurge was strong.

She glanced at Gib and her heart nearly stopped when she recognised the book in his hand, the second of her *Urban Explorer* books. She looked down and saw the first and the third book on the table. *Shit.*

'What have you got there?' she asked, internally wincing at her squeakier-than-normal voice. She took the book from him, turned it over and pretended to read the back-cover copy. 'I think this is a little young for you,' she told him, handing it back.

'Haha,' he said, picking up book number one in the series. 'This is the author Navy has his eye on. I want to see what he thinks is so special about her.'

Firstly, Bea still found it a little shocking that Navy Caddell liked her books enough to want to represent her. Secondly, and for the love of God, Bea couldn't cope with Gib reading her books. What if he hated them? What if he thought her premise silly, her characters unbelievable? Would he think her books were boring? Would he see himself in Pip?

'It's a kid's book, Gibson.'

'So are JK Rowling's and those are awesome,' he told her, handing over some cash. He nodded at the paperback in her hand. 'Want me to get that for you?'

She looked at the book and shook her head. 'No. I'm good.' She bit the inside of her cheek and sent another look at the three-book set. 'I wouldn't waste your money.'

'Spending money on books is never a waste,' he told her. True. 'Besides, I don't think this purchase is going to put me into debt.'

Bea scratched her cheek and wished she didn't feel so jittery. How was she supposed to live with him, sleep with him, knowing that at some point – maybe even while he was staying in the cottage! – he was going to read her work? How was she supposed to act, relax, not ask him what he thought? And if he hated them, how would she react? She'd had bad reviews before, as every writer does, but it was different when you were looking at them on Goodreads, where you could skip the one- and two-star reviews.

But someone, other than Golly, critiquing her work to her face? That was a whole new level of torture. Gib squeezed her hand, and she looked up at him. Expensive sunglasses covered his eyes and his stubble glinted in the sun. He pulled his hand from hers to skim his thumb over her cheek. 'Are you OK?'

She nodded and pushed her hair behind her ears. 'Sure. Why?'

'You seem far away, a little distracted.'

How was he able to read her so well, after so little time? 'I'm fine.'

He didn't say anything, just cupped her cheek in his big hand. After a few beats, he dropped his head to skim his mouth across hers. Bea wrapped his shirt around her fist, enjoying the slow, hot, sexy kiss. Then Gib pulled back but left his hand curled around her neck. 'If we keep that up, we might be arrested for lewd behaviour.'

She smoothed his crumpled shirt and nodded. She expected him to suggest that they go back to the cottage, so she was surprised when he asked her to show him something of Oia she loved. 'Like what?' she asked, looking around.

He lifted one shoulder. 'Anything. Your favourite ice cream, a store, something you enjoy.'

She thought for a moment, before asking him whether he was up for a bit of a walk. He patted his stomach. 'Sure. I need to walk off that moussaka. I can't get enough of it.'

He'd also eaten a starter of dolmades and finished with *karidopita*, a pie-ish dessert of fresh, chopped walnuts in a syrupy base made of breadcrumbs. The guy could, as Bea discovered, eat. His food bill had to be enormous.

She looked down at his footwear. Luckily, he was, like her, wearing trainers with a decent tread. 'OK, then I'll show you one of my favourite places in Oia.' She gestured to the caldera. 'It's way down there.'

'Sounds good.' He lifted his shopping bag containing the books. 'Let me run this back to the car first. I'll meet you back here in five minutes, OK?'

Gib seemed to know exactly where they were; a feat given the twisty, narrow alleys in the town. When he returned, she led him towards Oia Castle, which was little more than a ruin. They walked down the two-hundred-plus steps to Amoudi Port and Bea smiled when Gib stopped to take in the picturesque port with its seafood restaurants and colourful, bobbing wooden boats.

They wandered through restaurants spilling onto either side of the road and when they came out the other side, Bea told Gib to look back at what she thought was one of the best views on the island, Amoudi in the foreground and Oia at the top of the cliffs. Gib took a series of photos on his phone. 'Oh, this is great, Bea.'

She grinned. 'We're not there yet.'

'There's more?'

'Oh, yeah.' She continued leading him down the path away from Amoudi Port and wasn't surprised when he asked her whether the path was safe, as there seemed to be an abundance of warning signs about falling rocks.

'I haven't been taken out by a rock yet,' she told him. They stood aside to let another couple pass them and then continued down the path. Ten minutes later, she stopped them at a tiny cove.

She gestured to the view of the caldera and pointed to the towns further along the edge of the crater. 'That's Fira, and Imerovigli is further along.' She pointed to the small island in front of them. 'On that island is the church of Agios Nikolaus, it's a tiny chapel carved into the rock. It's my favourite place on Santorini. You can lie on the rocks and there's a high platform jutting out from the church you can jump from.'

He looked around and grinned. 'I *remember* this place. My dad brought me here and I did that jump … must have been twenty or thirty times that summer.'

She could believe it and could easily imagine him diving or jumping from the platform. It was something Pip would do.

'Have you done it?' he asked, slinging an arm around her shoulder.

'Lots of times, but when I was younger,' she told him.

He pushed his sunglasses into his hair, and his grin made him look ten years younger. 'Let's do it,' he suggested.

She shook her head, gesturing to her sundress. 'I'm wearing very lacy, very revealing lingerie,' she told him. 'And the water is too cold for me, even for a quick swim.'

'It's not cold. And even if it was, cold water is good for you.'

Yeah, so was kale and she avoided that, too. Gib grabbed the back of his shirt to pull it off his back. He dropped it to the rocks and placed his wallet, phone and sunglasses on top of it. Bea watched as he toed off his socks and trainers and opened the button to his shorts, pulled down the zip and pushed them down his hips. He wore black briefs and that space between her legs heated as she took in his spectacular body. He dumped his clothes on top of his trainers and his mouth curved into a smile. 'I'm gonna go be eleven again. Be back soon.'

With a quick kiss, he was in the sea. Bea sat down on a flat rock and pulled his sunglasses onto her face. Before long, Gib was on the islet and he disappeared, and she assumed he was inspecting the chapel. Ten minutes later, she heard a piercing whistle and looked up to see him on the platform. Laughing, she watched as he dived into the stunning blue water. He surfaced, shook his head and trod water for five minutes or so, looking up at far Oia above them.

Then he fast-crawled back to where she was sitting and hoisted himself onto her rock. She squealed when he rubbed his wet head against her chest and pushed him away. 'Arrgh, that's cold.'

'But so worth it,' Gib told her, grinning. 'That was the most fun I've had in a year. In quite a few years.'

It was the most personal thing she'd heard him say since she'd met him. 'You should come to Santorini more often.'

'I should get out of the office more often,' he countered, stretching out his long legs and tipping his face up to the sun. 'Any chance of getting my sunglasses back?'

'None,' Bea replied.

'Thought so.'

She pulled her sundress further up her thighs to get some sun on her legs. 'Is your work really that demanding?'

He lifted a shoulder and rolled his head to look at her. 'My uncle would say that I make it harder than it needs to be. He's always on at me for being too much of a control freak, and for not giving our highly paid managers enough responsibility. He'd like to see me let go a little.'

'So, why don't you?' she asked.

'Because I am a control freak,' he admitted. 'And a workaholic. Work is my mistress and my number one priority.'

There was a warning in his words, one she needed to take in. 'There's this concept called work-life balance,' she said. 'Are you familiar with it?'

He banged his hand against his ear. 'I must have water in my ears, I didn't hear a word you said.'

And that was his way of telling her, as gently as he could, that the subject was closed. A silent reminder that he didn't like to talk about himself. OK, then, they could just sit in the sun and listen to the sea roll against the rocks. Easy enough to do.

Five minutes later, Gib lay down, the back of his damp head resting on Bea's thigh. 'I could take a nap,' he told her, sounding lazy.

She finger-combed his hair off his forehead, happy to sit here, not saying anything, with him. 'Are you looking forward to the party tomorrow night, Bea-baby?'

'Yes, but more for Golly than for me. She loves parties, loves the attention.'

'Really? I would never have guessed.'

She smiled at his dry comment. 'I know she's over-the-top, but I adore her. She was there for me, as a child and an adult, when many people weren't.'

He lifted his arm behind his head to grip her thigh, his fingers lightly digging into her skin. 'Your parents?'

'Fairly bloody useless. I lived with my dad, and I only saw my mum a couple of times a year. As per their custodial agreement, she got me for six weeks in the summer holiday but having me underfoot was inconvenient for her, so she shipped me off to Golly, which was *very* convenient for me. I spent many summers here on Santorini.'

'Lucky you.'

She had been. 'Where did you spend your long summer holidays?' she asked. It was a fairly innocuous question, one she hoped he wouldn't object to.

'Here and there.' He opened his eyes and tipped his head back to look at her. 'I loved making love to you this morning, Bea.'

She stared at him, confused by his abrupt change of subject. How could he be so frank and open about sex, and how much he wanted her, but so reticent about himself?

'Bring your mouth down here, I need to taste you.'

230

She bent down and settled her mouth on his, tasting the salt on his lips, loving the heat of his tongue. Their kiss quickly turned desperate, and Gib gently pushed her up and away from him. He sat up and lifted her – how did he do that so easily? – onto his lap. She sat astride him, her panties against his damp briefs, his cock swelling between them. His hand snuck up the back of her skirt and palmed her butt. 'You're so fucking sexy,' he muttered, the tips of his fingers sliding under the band of her panties.

In his arms, she felt sexy, wanton, freaking incredible. She held his face in his hands and kissed him, her tongue tangling with his. He might not talk about himself, or give anything away, but what did that matter when he kissed her like this, when he made her feel like she was lit from the inside.

She rocked her hips, loving the friction against her clit, but Gib grabbed her hair and gently pulled her head back. '*Bea-baby*, if you do that, the people on the path are going to get more than they bargained for.'

She cocked her head and heard laughter drifting over to them. Damn, tourists! She scrambled off his lap, tossed his shorts in his direction and he pulled them over his lap, hiding his erection. At that moment an older, fit couple came into sight and called out a cheery greeting.

Bea stood up and walked up to the path, distracting them by feeding them facts about the islet and the tiny chapel while Gib pulled on his shorts, shoes and T-shirt. When he joined her, Bea noticed he'd raked his hair off his face.

He snatched his sunglasses back and put them on before taking her hand and sending the older couple a shit-eating grin. 'I don't mean to be rude, but my wife is ovulating and we're trying to get pregnant, so we need to be off.'

The couple's mouths dropped open in shock and Bea stared at his back as he led her down the path. She let him lead her out of earshot of the couple before punching his bicep.

He turned and grinned and her heart stopped at the laughter in his eyes. 'OK, so you're not my wife, and I definitely don't want you to fall pregnant, but I do want to take you to bed.'

She drilled a finger into his chest. 'How much time have you been spending with my godmother? That sounded like something *she* would say.'

'Yeah, yeah. All I'm interested in is whether we're going back to bed or not.'

'What do you think?' she asked, trying to be coy.

He brushed his thumb over her tight nipple. 'I think this tells me I have a good chance of you saying yes.'

Bea sighed. He wasn't wrong.

On the night of Golly's party, many of her guests, especially those who flew in that day or late the previous night, gathered on the esplanade to watch the sunset. Cass dispatched a couple of waiters to the area to keep the guests lubricated with champagne as they eagerly waited for the

Santorini spectacle to unfold. Glasses clinked together as laughter filled the air, mingling with expensive scents, the native herbs on the island and the smell of the sea.

As the sun began its fall, casting a warm glow across the landscape, the sky bloomed with vibrant pinks, oranges and purples. No one spoke as it painted its masterpiece across the sky: it was as if everyone understood that speech would destroy the ambience and experience, and that this was the universe's way of paying homage to one of its most excellent creatures: Golly.

Standing apart from the guests, Bea watched as the sun dipped below the horizon, dousing the sea in hues of fiery orange and molten gold. With each passing moment, the sky seemed to pulse with passion. It was bright and bold, an exact match for Golly's strong and vibrant personality. Had she sent a memo upstairs, demanding an incredible sunset? Bea's lips quirked upward. Honestly, she wouldn't put it past her godma...

Reena came to stand next to her and nudged her in the ribs with her elbow. She wore Jacqui's sheath, and the small rips of toilet paper dotting her legs and the big patch of coarse hair on her right shin suggested that shaving wasn't something she did well. Or often.

And instead of heels she wore bright green Crocs. Bea smiled at her. 'Hi, Reen.'

'Bea-darling,' Reena replied, in her husky voice. 'Golly is loving all the adulation and is totally up her own arse at the moment.'

She could always rely on Reena to call a spade a spade.

Reena ran her hand over her short grey hair. 'And I bet she forgot to tell you that Lou won't be here tonight. She called sometime this afternoon with some excuse.'

Bea placed her hand on her heart. She'd been on high alert, expecting to see her mother, but Reena's assurance allowed her anxiety to drain away. 'Thanks for letting me know, Reen. I can relax now.'

'With your godmother around?' With a snort of disbelief and a pat on her shoulder, Reena headed back to the villa.

Bea pulled her eyes off the sunset and scanned the guests for Gib. He stood at the back, and a little apart from everyone, and as if sensing her gaze on him, turned his head. Their eyes clashed and held, and Bea wasn't surprised when he crossed the flagstones to stand next to her. He took her hand, palm to palm, their fingers intertwined, and Bea placed her temple on his bicep as she turned her gaze back to the darkening sky. It seemed right to share this surprisingly quiet, completely perfect moment with Gib, to allow herself to be lost in the beauty of the sunset and the magic of this much-loved island. A little overwhelmed by nature's magnificence, she knew this memory would never fade.

The sky turned navy, then indigo and the fairy lights in the pergola flicked on, as did the lights illuminating the path back to the villa's courtyard. The deepening sky raised the volume of the guests, and their laughter and chatter danced on the evening air.

'Everything OK?' Gib asked, his hand lightly resting on her lower back.

She nodded. Now that she knew Lou wouldn't be around to spoil the evening, it was better than OK, it was perfect. She and Cass had done their last-minute checks earlier. Long trestle tables had been stretched across the courtyard, draped in crisp white linens and adorned with sparkling candelabras and delicate floral arrangements. Each place-setting was a work of art, with gleaming silverware, crystal glassware, and personalised menus showcasing the culinary delights to come.

As she and Gib joined the procession moving from the esplanade to the villa, conversations between the guests washed over them.

'Darling, it's so good to see you!' Kiss, kiss. *'I meant to call you about missing the opening night of your exhibition...'*

'I'm glad to run into you, Angus. Can you spare a half hour tomorrow to talk about a project I'm launching? I think you'd like to invest...'

'Have you met Kylie? She's just completed a run in the West End, sweetie. So talented.'

Live music from a jazz quartet drifted through the evening air, and laughter added another element to the celebratory atmosphere.

When they reached the courtyard, Gib excused himself and Bea sipped her champagne, her eyes on Golly, who stood in a group with Jack and a well-known author. Golly wore a scarlet dress with a feathered bolero jacket, in acid green, for warmth. The colour combination shouldn't have worked, but because Golly was Golly and didn't care what anyone thought, she pulled it off. She was in her element,

Bea mused, entertaining the great and good at her home, all the focus of the attention on her.

Bea smiled as Cass approached her, looking elegantly competent in her black shirt and trousers, carrying her iPad. Black hightops back on her feet. Bea knew Cass had an earpiece in her ear and a small microphone attached to her dress, making it easier for her to bark quiet orders to the staff. They were lucky to have Cass coordinating this event, and lucky to have Nadia in the kitchen. Even luckier that Cass and Nadia had agreed to stay in Santorini for the rest of the week – switching from event and catering whizzes to house and cooking elves. Cass joined her and Bea surprised herself, and Cass, by threading her arm through hers. 'It's going well, isn't it?' she murmured.

'*Rather*. And I haven't had any surprises from Golly yet,' Cass told her. 'No strippers have arrived, and the circus hasn't pitched their tent.'

The night was still young. Bea squeezed her arm. 'Have the belly dancers, fire-eaters and fire-stick-swinging people arrived?'

'The fire dancers?' Cass smiled. 'Yes, and the fireworks crew are ready to roll at midnight. I've got everything under control, Bea.'

'And I'm so grateful,' Bea muttered, tossing back half of her champagne.

Cass pulled her out of the mêlée and behind the bar. Telling her to stay put, she walked away and returned a minute later with two shot glasses, one of which she handed to Bea.

'Tequila?' she asked, sniffing the contents.

'Tequila,' Cass confirmed. 'Cheers.'

Bea pulled a face as the liquor slid over her tongue and down her throat. Actually, it was better than the gut rot she remembered from her university days. It was quite palatable. And warming.

Cass nodded to where Golly was being dipped by Jack, whose cheeks were red with exertion, his waistcoat button straining.

'Oh, God, he'd better not drop her,' Bea said, hand on her throat.

'I bet if he did, Golly would knee him in the balls,' Cass retorted. Jack placed Golly on her feet and Bea smiled at her sparkling eyes and the way Jack gently straightened her tiara. It was different from the one she'd worn earlier in the week, rubies instead of sapphires, and, like the other one, Bea hadn't seen it before. Had Golly commissioned it for the occasion? Highly possible.

'She feels young again, and people and entertaining invigorates her,' Cass said. 'She loves this, the adulation and the attention. She's amazing. I want to be just like her when I grow up.'

Bea grinned. 'Join the club.'

Cass smiled at her. 'Can I make an observation, sweetie?'

Bea nodded.

'I've noticed that you spend a lot of time looking around, seeing how you can make things better, how you can make people more comfortable, happier.'

Bea's mouth dropped open. 'You noticed that?'

'Since it's what *I* do for a living, yeah. Take the night off, Bea, I've got this. Switch off for a little bit.' Cass squeezed her hand. 'Go out there, and dance with that gorgeous man who can't keep his eyes off you. Sneak away for some hot sex and get a little tipsy. Make this night one of the best of your life.'

Bea considered her suggestion. It was a stunning night, she was wearing a short, gold cocktail dress that almost made Gib swallow his tongue earlier and a pair of pretty but horribly uncomfortable thin-heeled shoes. Gib was out there somewhere, looking for her, at her, someone who'd help her have a fabulous night.

Bea leaned forward and gave Cass a quick hug. 'I am so glad you're here, Cass. You and Nadia.'

Cass flashed her a smile and held up her finger as she listened to someone on her earpiece. Cass lifted her microphone to her mouth. 'I'll be with you in five,'

Seeing Cass's slight frown, Bea's panic metre revved straight into the red zone. 'What's wrong? What's happened? Oh God, Golly's done something over the top, hasn't she?'

Cass laughed. 'That was my wife, who has a five-minute break and wanted to know if I was up for a quick snog.'

Bea's heart returned to normal. 'Oh. Right, good. Yes, go! Go snog your wife.'

'I will, thank you.' Cass grinned, and was starting to walk away when she suddenly turned back 'But maybe you should know that Golly *has* coloured outside the lines,' she said with a wince.

Bea knew it! She *bloody* knew it! 'What has she done?' she asked, wondering if she really wanted to know.

'Do you know that there are mobile S&M dungeons, complete with leather-dressed doms who'll ease you into that world if you're keen to explore it? Golly thought it would be fun—'

Cass's words sank in, and Bea blanched. Where the hell had they set up a mobile dungeon? Could she make them leave? What the hell was Golly thinking? How much did hiring them cost? Was supplying BDSM services in Greece illegal?

Oh, God, she could feel a panic attack coming on.

Cass doubled over, laughing. 'I'm *joking*, Bea! God, your *face!*'

Bea forced her heart back down her throat and growled at Cass. 'That's not even remotely funny! You don't understand that she's capable of doing something just like that!'

'Then her hiring a psychic isn't such a bad thing, is it?' Cass asked, laughing. 'Said psychic is in the morning room at the villa, and I'm to start spreading the word that she'll do a reading for any guest who wants one. Golly's already had one and is raving about her!'

'Fabulous,' Bea muttered, rubbing the back of her neck, and still trying to get her breath back. 'So, what did she tell her? That she's going to retire? That one day, a long time in the future, when God and the devil are done arguing over her, that she's going to die?'

Cass shook her head. 'We're all going to die, sweetie. We need help on how to *live*.'

Bea swayed in Gib's arms, her cheek on his chest. His hand was curled around hers, his other arm around her waist. A piece of paper wouldn't fit between them and that was the way she liked it.

God, he smelt amazing … clean, and crisp, of green apples and limes, of the sea. 'What cologne do you wear?' she asked, feeling lazy and lovely and turned on.

He pulled back to look down at her. 'Sorry?'

'You smell so good. I want to buy a bottle so that I can sniff it and remember this moment in the future.' She smiled, riding that delicious high from just enough champagne and an overdose of lust and need. 'Does that sound creepy?'

He dropped her hand to show her the inch of space between his thumb and index finger. 'A little.'

She swatted his shoulder with the back of her hand, and he recaptured her hand and kissed the tips of her fingers, sending sexy shivers down her hand and up her arm. 'Is this moment that good, *Bea-darling*?'

She liked the way her godma's pet name for her rolled off his tongue. His stubble was thicker tonight, his hair a little messy. He wore the same stone-coloured suit trousers from earlier that week, but tonight he'd left the jacket behind and wore a collared, powder-blue dress shirt he'd left unbuttoned at the neck. The shirt beneath her fingers was crisp cotton, the body beneath as fine.

'It is. It's a stunning night. Golly is, so far, behaving herself, and I pigged out at supper.'

Nadia had served her variations of Golly's favourite dishes – seafood platters, paella and lamb stew, aubergine and parmesan bake for the vegetarians and vegans – and everybody had tucked in with enthusiasm. Drinks flowed, and the jazz quartet played Golly's favourite songs. Laughter rolled and people flirted, and whenever he could, Gib put his big hand on Bea's bare thigh.

He topped off her wine glass and sneaked spoonfuls of luscious tiramisu cheesecake off her plate when he thought she wasn't looking. He'd engaged in a few conversations with the people who shared their table, acquaintances to her, strangers to him, quietly charming, effortlessly engaging. But she soon noticed that if she wasn't a part of a conversation, he'd adroitly end his, and focus his attention on her. It was as if his only reason for being there was to give her the majority of his attention. For that alone, she utterly adored him.

'Do you like parties?' she asked, playing with the hair skimming his collar.

'They aren't my favourite way to spend time. They are necessary sometimes, though, so I make an effort. But I far prefer smaller dinners, with people I get on with and enjoy. Nothing beats a barbecue with beer and old, good friends.'

Wow. Information!

'Who do you invite to your barbecues?' She really

wanted to ask who he'd invite as his date, but even she wasn't that gauche. Besides, she knew he wouldn't answer.

'Ah, Navy, I guess. He's not only my cousin, he's my best friend. I also have a few good friends from college, and one or two I've met through work. Plus their wives and kids.'

'And would you cook? Or would you hire someone to grill your meat for you?'

He looked horrified at her suggestion. 'Of course I'd cook!'

Whoops. She swallowed her giggle. 'And where would all this happen? On the balcony of your Upper West Side flat?' she teased.

He pinched her lightly. 'I have a house in Nashville. That's where Caddell is headquartered.'

Bea frowned. They were an international company with offices all over the world and she expected their head offices to be somewhere more cosmopolitan. 'Why aren't you based in LA or New York? Even London?'

He'd answered five, or six, questions in a row and she was on a roll. She hoped he wouldn't clam up now.

'That would be because my father and his brother, my Uncle Hugh, grew up in Nashville. We have offices in those cities, of course, and in Hong Kong and Sydney, but Hugh and Navy live in Nashville. I tend to travel a lot, but Nashville is home.'

Huh. Tennessee. It didn't fit him … or did it? He had that rangy, loose-limbed southern gentlemen-stroke-surfer vibe.

'So, I heard Golly hired a psychic. You going to get a

reading from her?' That was the worst attempt at changing the subject she'd ever heard.

She narrowed her eyes at him. 'Closing me down, Gib?'

He fed her a soft, lovely kiss and pulled back before it gathered any heat. Her stomach rolled over and her toes curled up. Good to know they were still alive as she'd thought her heels shut down the blood to them hours ago.

She wanted to kiss him, but she was content to keep talking to him as well. The man was fascinating. The band segued into another song with a faster beat, but neither of them reacted.

'So Navy is your best bud, you live in Nashville—'

He shrugged, then looked away. When his eyes clashed with hers again, she knew he was done talking. He stroked his thumb across her cheek and his half smile kicked her libido up. 'It's a gorgeous evening and I'm holding a sexy, sexy woman in my arms. Why the interrogation?'

It was called *conversation*, but she wasn't going to argue with him. Bea knew he was trying to put some emotional distance between them and sighed. Look, she *knew* this wasn't going anywhere, it was a fling at best, but that didn't mean they couldn't be friends.

Before she could speak, he bent down and brushed his lips across hers, his hand sliding down her back, his fingers coming to rest just about her butt. He did that a lot, used their attraction to distract her. And it worked.

Every. Single. Time.

'Did I tell you that you look sensational?'

'Not in so many words, but you did bunch my dress up

and take me up against the wall shortly before we walked over here, so I figured you liked the way I look.'

His smile was the perfect mixture of sweet and sexy. 'I did, I do. But as much as I like your dress, I also like your ragged denim shorts, your messy hair when you sit in front of your computer, and your cute sundresses. But you look your best when you're naked and under me.'

It was the nicest thing any man had ever said to her, and she smiled at him. Judging by the way his eyes widened, her smile was sultrier and more seductive than she'd meant it to be. Maybe she could flirt, just a little. But she was done with words, she needed action. 'Will you kiss me, Gib? Please?'

He didn't hesitate and a second later, maybe less, his mouth covered hers and Bea forgot they only had a week left, and that his home was on another continent. All she needed, wanted, was Gib's mouth on hers, his hands on her body. His attention, for as long as she had it, on her.

Tonight, the future could take care of itself.

Chapter Twelve

Golly wrapped up her too long, but very funny speech by thanking Cass and Nadia, and Bea, for all their effort in arranging her party and then exhorted her guests to visit the psychic, and to enjoy the entertainment. She'd ordered a lot of booze, she told them, and they'd better bloody drink it!

Judging by the approving roar, Bea assumed Golly's guests were more than happy to obey her order.

'On that note...' Gib said, leaving Bea, Jack and Jacqui to head for the bar to get them a round of drinks. The waiters were run off their feet and, as part of the family, Gib could slide behind the bar and pour the drinks himself.

As the applause died away, Bea released a relieved sigh. 'That wasn't too bad,' she said, flicking imaginary sweat from her forehead. 'Golly was reasonably restrained. I can, sort of, relax.'

Jack rubbed his hand up and down her arm. 'You look tired, darling. Are you OK?' he asked, concerned.

OK? She was sharing her bed and her body with Gib, who was also reading her books. He didn't know she was Parker Kane. He was leaving the island, and her life, in a week or so. She liked him, more than she'd ever expected to. She needed a new agent and even though Gib had mentioned Navy was interested, she wasn't sure whether he, or anyone else, could be trusted to keep her real identity a secret. She'd also started to wonder if Golly was right, and that it was time to step out from behind her pseudonym. Her mum's affair with Gerry happened five years ago, would anyone even remember? Care?

'I'm fine.'

Jack and Jacqui wore identical expressions of disbelief.

'That was quite a kiss you and Gib shared on the dancefloor earlier,' Jacqui said, mischief in her eyes.

She couldn't talk her way out of this one, so Bea decided to act as nonchalantly as possible. 'He's quite a man.'

Jack, always protective, frowned. 'Just be careful, OK? We don't want to see you hurt again.'

'He's just a fling, Jack,' Bea assured him. But, question of the day, if she was just using him for a good time, as a way to get out of her head, then why was she feeling so off balance, so squirrelly? Whenever he was around, her heart turned into a rocket and zoomed around her body. Her stomach took on the consistency of a jellyfish and her breath hitched, her skin buzzed.

Her reaction to Gib was terribly inconvenient. It could

be because she was out of practice, and her reaction to him was just her hormones, excited at the idea of a fun time. Fancying him could be a way of distracting her from her professional dilemmas. It didn't mean she was falling for him. Not after six days. That wasn't possible. She was far too cautious.

What could she say to change the subject? Right, she remembered something she'd been meaning to ask Jack. 'Isn't it a pity about Golly's Art Deco couch?' Seeing his blank expression, Bea frowned. 'The one that was in the cottage?'

'What about it?' he asked, obviously confused.

'Golly burnt it. She said it was riddled with woodworm.'

He sent her an *are-you-insane* look. 'My dear Bea, what are you talking about? I checked Golly's furniture six months ago and none of it had woodworm. And the couch is in my warehouse at the moment. She sent it to me a few weeks ago, saying she wanted it recovered. God knows why, I only recovered it two years ago and the material was not only a bitch to find but completely fabulous.'

Bea narrowed her eyes, smelling a rat or two. 'Have you stripped it of its fabric yet?'

'No, I'm waiting for Golly to choose a new fabric. She said she would, but only when she got back to London.'

The interfering witch! 'I wouldn't hold your breath, Jack,' Bea drily suggested.

'What do you mean?' Jacqui asked, equally bewildered.

'My godma is playing matchmaker. She removed the

couch from the cottage, to make sure Gib and I *had* to share the bed.'

Jacqui glanced from her to Gib and back again. 'Frankly darling, you could do worse. To be fair, you *have*.'

Yeah, yeah, Gerry was a cockroach. Tell her something she didn't know! Anyway, that wasn't the point.

'Golly has no right to manipulate my sex life!'

Jack sent her a pitying look. 'But, darling, at least now you *have* a sex life.'

She did. A freakin' hot, look-at-me-and-I-melt one. A 'sex in the sunshine, in the shower, on the deck' sex life, one that most women craved. Bea looked down at her feet and smiled. Gib was a fantastic lover, generous, assertive, and demanding.

But she was only in this position because bloody Golly had forced them to share a cottage and a bed. Bea was both grateful – what woman wouldn't be? – and annoyed by Golly's interference. Apart from a couple of conversations about how it was time to get back on the dating horse, and that lack of orgasms caused wrinkles, Golly generally stayed off the subject of Bea's love life.

Bea'd never, not once, expected her to go to these lengths to push her and Gib together! And hell, gratitude and annoyance were uncomfortable bedfellows. But the thing with Golly was, if you gave her an inch, she took your whole arm. Sometimes a kidney. And half of your spine.

She definitely needed to be reined in! Where was she? They needed to have a word. Or six hundred. Bea looked around and spotted her on the other side of the dancefloor, talking to a tall man with a shock of white hair. He looked vaguely familiar, but Bea couldn't be arsed to work out who he was.

'Tell Gib I'll be right back,' she told the Two Jacks. 'And if I murder your friend, tell everyone I had a justifiable cause!'

Bea slipped around people, and stepped up to Golly's side and gripped her forearm. 'Sorry to disturb you, but can I have a minute?'

'*Bea-darling*!' Golly cried, her eyes glassy from too much wine. Well, Bea hoped that was all she'd had. Again, it was another of those 'don't ask unless you really, *really* want to know the answer' questions. 'Do you remember Llewellyn Baker?'

Bea smiled at Golly's friend. 'Would you excuse us? I need to talk to Golly.'

'You're her goddaughter, am I right?' Llewellyn took her hand and lifted it to his lips. Some men managed the old-fashioned action with aplomb, but he wasn't one of them. It took a lot of effort to not yank her hand from his damp fingers.

'Sort of,' Bea replied, half turning her back to him. She widened her eyes at Golly, and she finally took the hint.

'Lew, darling, fuck off,' Golly told him. When he was out of earshot, she cocked her head to the side. 'Now what is so important?'

'He's a sleazeball,' Bea told her. 'He made the hair on the back of my neck rise.'

'He has a title,' Golly shot back, taking a whisky from a

waiter with flashing dark eyes. 'Thank you, darling. Keep them coming.'

'Then he's an aristocratic sleazeball.'

Golly wrinkled her nose. 'You're not wrong, I recall he was very handsy with his staff when he was an MP. The PM had to talk to him about it a few times. He should've been fired, but that was a long time ago, and thank God there are different rules today.'

'Right,' said Bea. Unfortunately, the issue of legislating against matchmaking old ladies had yet to be given the attention it deserved. 'I'm *very* cross with you!'

Golly didn't look remotely fazed. 'For ordering the psychic? I wanted to hire some male strippers, but Reena said you'd be furious.'

'She'd be right. And no, hiring a psychic is fine, and she's very popular. She's booked up for the rest of the night and has bookings for tomorrow and Sunday.'

'I know, I booked the two o'clock slot.'

'I thought you saw her earlier?' Bea asked, perplexed. 'And what do you want to know? You've been everywhere and done everything, as you keep telling me.'

'Not for me, for *you*.'

Oh, *hell* to the no!

'I'm not seeing your psychic, Golly.'

'Why not?' Golly asked, genuinely perplexed. 'Why wouldn't you want to know what your future holds?'

'I'm hoping my future will be the same as it is right now. Writing, reading...' Bea folded her arms and tapped her foot, instantly irritated when Golly stuck her finger in her mouth and mimicked gagging.

Bea knew she was going to regret her next question but couldn't stop it leaving her mouth. 'And what is wrong with my life?'

'It's more boring than watching bowls,' Golly retorted. 'You don't see anybody, you don't date anybody, the only person you ever *really* talk to is me…'

'I talk to other people,' Bea protested. 'I've been remarkably social this weekend.'

'When I say talk, I mean open up. We're not meant to be alone, Beatrice, we need friends, and you, more than most, need someone to confide in.'

She'd talked to Gib and opened up to him a little. *Huh.* So that was weird. She didn't second-guess herself with him, talking came naturally. He knew more about her than most. More, in some ways, than Golly did.

'And, child, I'm happy you are having your engine revved. I was worried your guava had closed up.'

And that, ladies and gentlemen, was why Bea never touched that particular fruit.

Bea looked around, hoping that no one had overheard Golly's observation. Her lady parts weren't something she wanted to be discussed in public. Or anywhere. *Ever.* 'Will you please keep your voice down? And stop commenting on my sex life!'

'You haven't had a sex life up until this week.'

Gaaaah!

Golly grinned, placed her palms together and bowed.

'When blue-moon events happen, they will be spoken about.'

'Oh, *shut up*!'

Golly laughed, delighted she'd managed to rile Bea. She sipped her drink and raised one perfectly pencilled-in eyebrow. 'What did you come to talk to me about, Bea-darling?'

Bea closed her eyes, trying to remember why she'd stormed across here. Oh! Right. The bed situation. Man, this was going to be fun.

It was her turn to act, just a little. 'I'm *so* sorry to hear about your couch, Golly.'

Confusion. Excellent. Exactly what she was aiming for. 'What couch?'

'The delightful Art Deco one that was in the cottage? Jack was just telling me his assistant made a mistake and instead of ripping the fabric off another couch, he ripped the fabric off yours and binned it,' Bea lied, without blinking. After all, she'd been trained by the best.

Golly's red lips dropped open, utterly dismayed. '*No!* I love that couch. It took us years to source that fabric, it was printed in the thirties and inspired by Sonia Delaunay's designs. You *have* to be mistaken, Bea-darling, Jack would've told me.' She looked around for Jack, a little frantic.

Got you!

Bea placed her fists on her hips. 'So you didn't burn the couch because it had woodworm?'

Golly's mouth snapped closed, and she wrinkled her nose. It was her classic 'I'm busted' look. 'Um…'

'Um … you lied to me?' Bea said. 'Um … you had the couch removed from the cottage to ensure that Gib and I shared a bed? Um … you're a matchmaking, interfering old hag?'

Golly sniffed and lifted her nose. 'Matchmaking and interfering I'll agree with, but I object to you calling me a hag!' She gestured to her outfit, a scarlet wraparound ballgown that highlighted her incredible cleavage. On what planet was it fair that Bea's seventy-year-old godmother had better boobs than her?

'What were you thinking, Golly?' she quietly asked.

'I thought I'd give you and Gib a little push. He's a lovely boy, and you're a lovely girl and you both need a bit of fun.' Golly's smile turned wicked. 'And judging by what I saw on the dancefloor, pushing you together seems to have worked. So, how did it happen? Did he barge in on you in the shower? Did you see him in a towel? Did you find yourself spooning in the night?'

Yes, yes, and yes. But that wasn't the point!

'You've read, and edited, far too many romances!' Bea cried. 'We're both in our thirties and we're perfectly capable of managing our own affairs!'

'Him, *sure*. You? Not so much,' Golly said, dismissing her statement with a languid wave of her hand.

Bea released a low growl, her irritation levels soaring. 'Golly, stop interfering. And let me make something very clear, I am never, repeat never, getting involved again!'

Golly looked genuinely perplexed. 'Who's talking about involvement? Not me! I just want you to have great sex for as long as you can get it.'

Well, Bea was certainly getting that.

Before she could find an adequate response, or *any* response, Golly patted her cheek. 'As per usual, you are putting the horse before the cart, Bea-darling. You're creating obstacles where there are none, and dreaming up complex, probably-won't-happen scenarios. Has he asked you to date him, move in with him or marry him?'

Her question shocked Bea to her core. 'No, of course not!' They'd met a week ago, for the love of all that was holy. And, in Golly's case, what wasn't holy.

'Exactly. Live one day at a time, dammit.' Golly patted her cheek, a little harder than it needed to be. 'Now, you are being incredibly boring, darling, and I refuse to be bored at my own party.'

'I … you…'

'And when you see your handsome lover, tell him he owes me a dance. I'm desperate to get my hands on his tight arse.'

Dear God. Bea did a quick mental calculation to see how much money she had in her current and savings accounts. She might, if she had a nice judge, be able to scrounge up enough money to post bail.

Gib, about to walk behind the bar, turned to look for Bea – he couldn't keep his eyes off her – and saw her in an animated conversation with Golly. Her back was to him, but he immediately noticed her shoulders were up around her ears.

Great, one step forward, a hundred back.

The barman lifted his hand. 'It's quietened down so you don't need to serve yourself. Thanks for doing that by the way. So, what can I get you?'

He had been about to order another glass of wine for Bea, but decided she needed something stronger, so he ordered two tequilas, and two beers. While he waited for the drinks, he watched her approach him, her expression suggesting she was *pissed*.

What the fuck had happened now? Bea caught his eye, jerked her head, veered left and stomped down a path. OK, he'd follow. Picking up the two shot glasses and shaking his head at the bartender's offer of lemon slices, he hooked the two beer bottles in his fingers and followed Bea. He walked for a little while without catching up to her, and then she disappeared. He was about to call her name when a hand shot out from the path and gripped his arm. The glasses holding the tequila wobbled and the liquid ran down his hand.

'In here,' Bea shout-whispered.

'In here' was a narrow slit between the bougainvillaea hedges, and Gib had to turn sideways so as not to hook his shirt or pants on the spiky thorns. When he was inside the grassy circle holding a bench and a dry fountain, Bea carefully rearranged the long branches of the hedge to cover the entrance. If you didn't know it was here, you'd walk right past the hideaway.

And that was, he realised, the point.

'Is that tequila?' Bea demanded.

Before he could answer, she snagged a glass from his hand and threw it back. *OK, then*. He offered her the other, but she shook her head, taking a bottle of beer instead.

'What's got you so riled?' he asked, swallowing the other shot. He took the glass from her and placed the shot glasses on the grass beneath the wooden slats of the wrought iron bench. He sat down and stretched out his legs, prepared to listen to Bea's explanation. He liked listening to anything she had to say; she was endlessly entertaining and always interesting.

'My bloody godmother!'

Yeah, he'd gathered that much. 'What's she done now?' he asked.

Despite holding her beer bottle, she managed to slap her hands on her hips. He very much approved of the way her gold dress showed off her long legs and hugged the curves of her body. He hoped he'd get to pull it off her later. He needed Bea, in the most biblical way possible, naked and screaming.

'Did you know she was matchmaking by making us share the cottage?' Bea demanded. She waggled her finger between them. 'She arranged to have the couch taken out of the cottage to nudge us into sharing a bed.'

She was only just realising that now? He hadn't believed

one word of that story Golly spun them about the bed and the lack of hotel rooms and him needing to stay in the cottage. Oia was less than two kilometres away for God's sake! 'It was pretty obvious.'

'Then why didn't you say something to her?'

He took a sip of beer, enjoying its crisp taste as it slid over his tongue and down his throat. 'Why would I say something to her? When someone arranges for me to share a beautiful woman's bed, why would I say no?'

Bea blinked, her jaw dropping a little. 'You think I'm beautiful?' she asked. He'd heard other women ask the same question as a way to fish for compliments, but Bea didn't do coy. She genuinely looked surprised.

He tipped his head to the side. 'Something shines deep within you, Bea, a light that makes people look twice. Then again.'

She placed her hand on her throat. 'Oh. That's a lovely thing to say.'

He held back his smile and lifted his bottle to her in a small toast. She wasn't comfortable with compliments, and he wondered why.

Bea shuffled from foot to foot in her heels. He knew she'd love to kick them off and go barefoot, and wondered why she didn't. 'I've lost my train of thought ... what were we talking about?'

'Your godmother,' he helpfully replied, enjoying her adorable confusion.

Bea frowned. 'Right, *her*. She's an interfering old hag. Do you remember her telling us that the couch from the cottage had woodworm and she had to burn it?'

Vaguely.

'Well, it's not a pile of ashes, it's sitting in Jack's warehouse!' Bea resumed her pacing. She winced slightly with every step. 'Woodworm was just an excuse to get it out of the cottage so that we'd be forced to share the bed.'

A decision he thoroughly approved of. He patted the bench next to him. 'Come and sit down.'

'She's got no right to interfere in my life,' Bea muttered. 'I can sort myself out, I don't need her to do it for me.'

There it was, the essence of what was bugging her. He suspected it was also linked to Golly pushing her to find a new agent, to step out from behind her pseudonym. He'd started reading the first book in her series yesterday, and caught her watching him, the side of her bottom lip pulled between her teeth. She obviously wanted to know what he thought but couldn't ask him. As far as he could tell, and he wasn't an expert, the book was fabulous. Fast, funny and, most importantly, she didn't talk down to young readers. He'd expected to be bored, but found himself entertained.

He really wanted to know why she hid behind her pseudonym, why she was so desperate to stay anonymous. They were good books, and she should take pride in them.

And yes, he was conscious of the irony of wanting to get to know her motivations and backstory, while not giving away any of his own. In fact, he'd told her more than he'd told any woman, ever, about his past, home life and family.

But that was all she was going to get from him. He

wondered if she, or anyone, would understand that he couldn't, physically, form the words to explain the cause of his reticence. As a teenager, a psychologist suggested he had a very mild form of alexithymia, or, in normal people's terms, difficulty experiencing, identifying and expressing emotions. He'd researched the condition and discovered it was often caused by traumatic situations, and he reckoned his mom's insane prying, his parents' death and his guilt over the fleeting relief he experienced on hearing they were dead might've pushed him into a slight dose of alexithymia-tinged PTSD.

At the core of it, keeping his emotions locked away was a hard habit to break.

He looked up at her, saw her wince again and decided enough was enough. 'Bea-baby, take a load off.'

Bea sat down next to him, rolling the beer bottle between her hands. 'Drink your beer,' he told her, bending down to pick up her foot.

'What are you doing?' she demanded, frowning.

He turned to face her, her foot in his hand. 'Shift back.'

When she did, he looked at her shoe, trying to ignore the soft, fragrant skin under his hands, and found the tiny buckle above her heel. His big fingers couldn't pull it apart, so he pulled the strap down and eased off her shoe, dropping it to the grass.

His fingers dug into a pressure point on her instep and she groaned, in part agony, part ecstasy. Her eyes brightened with that sexy combo of lust and need, and his cock hardened at the pleasure-pain expression on her face.

Yeah, he'd never needed a bed more.

'So good,' Bea murmured.

She'd used the same phrase last night, her voice thick with want. God, he craved her. More than he needed to keep breathing. This woman tied him up in knots, and he needed to loosen one or two. Making love to her was the only option. In a day or two, these weird feelings would fade, and perspective would stroll back in. If it didn't, he was in deep shit.

'I presume you gave Golly a mouthful for her attempt at matchmaking?' he asked, pushing those uncomfortable thoughts away.

Her eyes flew open, and irritation flashed. 'I told her we were old enough to sort ourselves out,' she told him. She swung her other leg onto his lap, silently requesting that he rub her other foot as well. Because her dress was so short, he caught a flash of her panties. He thought they were red, or a deep pink. He sighed. He loved women's lingerie, loved taking it off even more...

'I know I am, but she thinks you need help. Why?'

Bea scrunched up her nose, something she did when she was thinking. Golly did it too. 'Ah. That might be because I haven't dated much lately. She's worried I'm a dried-up, born-again virgin.'

He looked at her, unable to resist pressing her foot against his hard cock. He needed to do something about it before it split his pants. An exaggeration, maybe, but he was straining-his-underwear hard. 'You are definitely not dried up, Bea-baby.'

She swallowed, her eyes turning darker, obviously remembering his mouth on her, the way she came on his tongue and then on his fingers. 'But she's right, sort of. I haven't dated much, or at all, since my split with my ex.'

The pain in her eyes told him how committed she'd been to the relationship, how much it hurt when it ended. 'How long were you together?'

'A few years,' she admitted.

Huh, talking about her ex was an excellent way to make the blood drain out of his cock. Good to know.

'Why did you split up?' he asked, conscious of the burning sensation in his gut. Was that jealousy? He couldn't be sure since it wasn't an emotion he was familiar with. He didn't get jealous, firstly because he never cared enough, and secondly because he thought it was a waste of time and energy. But Bea made him feel new things … *strange* things.

She also had him asking questions, questions he'd refuse to answer if they were directed at him.

'Let me think … maybe because he was a man-child, a serial cheat, a terrible partner and someone who couldn't hold down a job.'

He relaxed at her description of her ex. He was a fully functioning adult, he had a decent job, and he only slept with one woman at a time. He had no idea what type of husband he'd be, but since he believed in equal effort from both parties, he didn't think he'd be awful at it. Not that he intended to check himself into that institution, he didn't have the time or the energy. Or the courage.

'Is that all?' he teased her, wanting her to lose the

pinched skin between her eyebrows. 'Don't you think your expectations are a bit high?'

She pushed her big toe into his ribs and handed him a reluctant grin. 'Anyway, Golly thinks I should be out there sowing my wild oats. She's disappointed at how staid and boring I am.'

He bent his head to kiss her sexy big toe. He lifted his eyes to hers, still holding her foot. 'You're anything but boring, Bea. That being said, I am happy to help you sow some of those oats for as long as I am in Santorini.'

That was sensible, right? He couldn't promise her anything more. This was a holiday fling, a way to have a little fun.

'So we're having an affair, Gib?' Bea quietly asked.

She didn't play games and he liked that. 'I think fling is a better word,' he corrected her. 'I'm single, and as I've said a few times, I intend to remain that way.'

Bea swung her legs off his thighs and placed her feet on the grass. She gripped the edge of the bench and turned her head sideways to meet his eyes. 'I'd love to keep having a fling with you, Gib. As long as Golly hasn't forced or manipulated you into it.'

Nobody forced him to do anything, ever. Not in business and not in his private life. 'This is between you and me, and our attraction. Let's leave your godmother, and anything and everything else out of it, OK?'

She grinned. 'Gladly.' She pushed her toes into the grass and shifted down the bench to move closer to him. Her thigh rested gently against his, and her small shoulder pushed into his arm.

'Sex with you is, God ... *amazing*. I can't stop thinking about it,' she said, and her husky voice shot blood back into his cock. Harder than before, he shifted, trying to get comfortable.

How would it feel to take her here? Now? Her back to his front, her hands gripping the back of the bench, her lovely butt in the air and his thick cock buried deep inside her.

He wanted her. In every way a man could want a woman.

His fascination with her should've worn off a little by now, but it burned as bright as it did when he first saw her standing by the car, the wind plastering her dress to her body. The body he now knew intimately.

Bea waved a hand in front of his face. 'Earth to Gib?'

'Sorry, I was miles away, thinking about fucking you.' Would she object to the word? To his blunt way of talking?

She stilled, and the air between them started to shimmer. 'That's pretty direct.'

'Do you have a problem with me telling you what I want?'

'No, it saves time.' She pulled her bottom lip between her teeth. 'In case you were wondering, I'm happy to leave and head back to the cottage. We can come back to watch the fireworks at midnight.'

Leaving to return to the cottage was a good idea, sensible. But fuck being sensible.

'I couldn't possibly wait that long.' But, because he didn't want any misunderstandings, he issued another reminder. To her, but mostly to himself. 'I need to say this again... I don't do relationships, I don't do commitment. I don't talk. I'm going back home next week. I can't give you more than another week.'

'So very direct,' Bea murmured, placing her hand high on his thigh, her nails digging in. Gib swallowed his moan. He'd never been so turned on, and so quickly, by anyone before. Why this woman? Why was he so crazy attracted to her?

'Where and when?' she asked him.

The blood rushed from his head. 'Here. And *now*.'

She was going to say no, of course she was.

'We're in the middle of a party, Gib,' she pointed out, but not sounding shocked. 'Guests will walk past us. We might get caught.'

The thought of the danger ramped up his excitement. He'd never been one of those people who liked getting it on in cars, alleys or semi-public places, and he'd never understood how the thrill of getting caught heightened pleasure. He did now. He glanced at the covered entrance to this hideaway, and it looked impenetrable. If they were quiet, nobody would know...

Gib rose to his feet and moved to stand in front of her. She sent a nervous glance at the entrance of the hedge, and he sighed, disappointed.

'If you want to, we can go back to the cottage,' he told her. Because, really, he was lucky to have her any way he could get her, and he was adult enough to wait the five minutes it would take them to get back to the cottage. Two minutes if they sprinted.

Instead of answering him, she tipped her head back to look up at him and grinned. His cock strained against the zipper of his pants, and she ran a finger down it, slowly and deliberately.

Gib's eyes didn't leave her face, but he didn't push. Like before, he felt the need to give her control of the moment, of what happened next. But it took all he had not to kiss her. He wanted to taste her mouth, to nuzzle his nose into her long neck, and make a long and leisurely exploration of her body, then do it again later. Tomorrow, next week, next mon—

No! This was about sex, about getting each other off and living in the moment.

'Got a condom handy?' she asked. He reached into his pants pocket, pulled out a condom and handed it to her. She put it on the bench and, dropping her eyes, pulled his soft leather belt apart. She undid the clasp on his pants and slowly pulled down the zip, and lightning buzzed through him as her knuckles brushed his hard cock. She looked up, her gaze slamming into his.

Bea sent him a slow, naughty smile and in that instant, he hopped aboard Hurricane Bea, eager to spin and be spun. Bea pulled down his boxer briefs and slid her hand behind his shaft to pull him free. Her thumb drifted across his broad head and ran down the thick vein running up the side of his cock. He was at the perfect height, and he wanted her to take him in her mouth, to taste him in the most elemental way.

'You smell like sunshine and sex, a wild, wild wind,' she murmured against his skin, her words drifting up to him. She nuzzled her nose against him, sucking the skin of his shaft between her lips.

Taking him into her mouth, she let him rest against her tongue before starting to suck. He groaned, loving every moment of this, trying not to grind himself into her mouth. She was a little clumsy, charmingly unpracticed. But he wouldn't swap her enthusiasm for skill. Her kissing him wasn't a chore, a tick on the list ... her appreciative murmurs reassured him she was loving the act, enjoying him. She worked her tongue, then her lips around his tip, licking him like an ice cream cone, and he knew he couldn't hold on much longer.

About to blow – so not cool, as he rarely lacked control – Gib pulled back. A couple of things happened at once then, or in quick succession. He yanked her to her feet and reached for the condom. Ripping it open with his teeth, he pushed his pants and briefs down, sat his bare ass down on the bench, and quickly, competently, rolled on the condom. He reached for Bea, pulled her onto his thighs, shoved her dress up her hips and palmed her bare ass, his thumb sliding under the thin cord of her thong.

'Sexy panties, Bea-baby.'

Bea wrapped her legs around him, trying to rub her clit against his cock, desperate for contact. Gib, panting heavily, pushed his hand between them, his thumb dragging through her wet warmth, and pulled her panties to one side.

'You are so fucking gorgeous,' he told her. He gripped the back of her neck, pulled her head down and sighed when her mouth landed on his. His cock pushed inside her at the same time as his tongue entered her mouth.

There were no words to describe the rush of heat, the hit of need. For the first time in his life, he was fully, emotionally, in the moment, driven to give her everything to make this experience unforgettable for her. He wanted the memory of him to slide into her mind every time her mind drifted to sex. He filled her completely, stretching her.

'Are you OK?' he demanded, needing to know whether his size was too much, or if she was uncomfortable.

'I'm amazing,' she panted, her eyes wild. 'Don't you dare stop.'

Amazing worked for him. He rocked, she moaned, he panted, she pushed. Heat and light, sensation overwhelmed him and everything, but her warmth and scent and incredible body, faded away as he fucked her on this bench, rudely, passionately, *thoroughly*. Gib had no idea how long it took her to come, a minute, maybe less, but she flooded him, her body vibrating and her inner walls clenching his cock. Bea buried her face in his neck, sobbing with relief, need and a desire for more.

He wasn't done with her, not yet.

'Again,' he told her, pumping into her. 'Come again.'

'I can't,' she sobbed.

'You can.' He shoved his hand between them, found her

clit and rubbed and Bea arched her back, moaning his name.

'You don't have to, I'm good with one,' she murmured.

'Fuck that,' he replied against her mouth, flicking her clit gently before stroking her again. When she was close, he slapped his hand over her mouth, muffling her muted shout, trying not to groan as she tightened against him. She fell apart on his cock and his fingers, and he moved his hands to her hips, his fingers digging in as he pistoned into her. Sensation rocketed from his balls and up his spine, and he came on a low, drawn-out groan, feeling like he'd run a marathon. She held on as their shivers subsided, as they gradually gathered their shattered wits and the present faded back in.

Placing his hand under her butt to support her, Gib withdrew and he stood up. He held her as her legs dropped to the ground, not letting her go until she was steady on her feet. Unembarrassed, he pulled off the condom and tied it off before shoving it into the pocket of the pants he pulled on. He zipped them up, smiling as Bea adjusted her panties and smoothed down her short dress, looking thoroughly disorientated. Anyone with sexual experience would instantly realise she'd just had a mind-blowing orgasm.

She had that dozy, what-the-hell-was-that expression on her face. And he'd put it there, making him feel like a sex god. Smiling, he buckled his belt.

'How are you doing, Bea-baby?' he asked, as she swayed on her feet.

'Good,' she replied, pushing a hand into her hair. She

handed him a shaky grin, and then her hand. It disappeared into his, and he was once again assailed by the feeling of how right she felt. Whether it was her hand in his, his cock in her, or simply standing here, smiling at each other in a secret garden hideaway.

'I want to drop to my knees and prostrate myself before Golly for manipulating us into sharing that bed,' he told her.

She laughed, and the sound rushed through him, hot and bright. 'Please, *please* don't. She already thinks she's ridiculously brilliant and needs no encouragement.'

She pushed her tongue into her cheek, her expression mischievous. 'Shall we head back to the cottage and do that again, but in a bed?'

Along with the invention of the wheel, contraceptives, the internet and email, that sounded like the best idea ever.

They didn't make it back to watch the fireworks.

Chapter Thirteen

T he next morning, hung over from sex – and the bottle of champagne they'd shared when they got back to the cottage – and still in bed, Bea placed a video call to Cass, who immediately answered. Bea could see she was in the courtyard, helping the cleaning staff clear the tables and pack away unused glasses.

'Thank you for a marvellous, marvellous evening.'

Cass, looking exhausted, grinned at her. 'It was good, *right*?'

Cass was normally so self-confident, and Bea smiled at her need for reassurance. Didn't everyone need to be praised now and again? *She* certainly did. 'It was truly brilliant, Cass.'

She should get up and go and give Cass and Nadia a hand, she was sure they could use the help, but this bed was super comfortable, and she was hoping Gib would bring her a cup of coffee.

As if hearing her mental SOS, he appeared in the doorway, a mug in his hand. Oh, bliss. She took the cup and his quick kiss, and he pulled back to look at Cassie. 'You and Nadia did a fantastic job, Cass. Maybe we can talk about you catering some of the Caddell International functions in the future. Are you and Nadia prepared to travel?'

Joy flashed across her face. 'Anytime and anywhere.' Cass nodded enthusiastically. Bea smiled when she saw the heat in Cass's cheeks. She was chuffed by his compliment, and she had a right to be.

Telling Cass to hold on, she looked up at Gib, who looked far too fine for someone who'd had so little sleep. He wore chino shorts, an open neck shirt and trainers. She pouted, she'd been hoping he'd come back to bed. Gib's grin suggested that he knew what she was thinking, and he told her he was on his own video call and would be done soon. *Yay.* Bea lifted her mug to her lips. How wonderful it was to be in Santorini on a warm, stunning autumn day, surrounded by people she loved. And a man she liked a lot and, if she wasn't careful, could come to love…

Bea looked down into her mug, blindsided by her thoughts. Why was she going there? She knew there couldn't be anything between her and Gib! They lived on separate continents, and he had a life in Nashville and hers was in London.

And let's not forget that he didn't want more from her. This was just a fling, a step out of time. So why was she even letting her mind drift off into uncharted waters?

He had no part to play in her future. And after their sojourn in Santorini was over, she wouldn't see him again. Her heart sank at the thought.

'Bea?'

Bea remembered Cass was still on the phone, and she spent the next five minutes catching up on last night's highlights – which included the psychic hooking up with one of the fire dancers. The amount of booze the guests drank was staggering, and the bill would match the GDP of a small country. Cass said Nadia was making breakfast, and did she and Gib want to wander up?

Bea said they might or might not, she needed to shower and see what Gib's plans were.

After her shower, Bea pulled on a pair of lacy briefs, and Gib's shirt from last night, held together with a single button. She didn't want to get dressed, she wanted Gib to get undressed.

Feeling buoyant, and self-confident, she walked into the lounge and saw him sitting at her desk on the deck, his back to her. His shirt was tight against his wide back, his head bent.

No sounds emanated from his laptop … which meant he must be done with his call. *Excellent.* They only had a week left, and she wanted all his attention on her. Opening the button holding his shirt together, she walked up to him and plastered her bare chest against his back, wrapping her arms around his neck.

She bit his ear gently. 'I'm suffering from you-in-me withdrawal symptoms,' she said, sliding around to his front and onto his lap. She picked up his hand and put it on her bare breast. 'Want to stop working and do me instead? And afterwards, we can go down to the villa. Nadia is making pancakes. I *love* pancakes.'

Bea heard muffled laughter, then a snort and a cough, neither sound emanating from Gib. Simultaneously hot and cold, an odd sensation, she turned her head and looked at his laptop ... and into the face of a blond man, his jaw heavy with stubble, dark blue eyes fixed on a point above his laptop camera.

Oh, shit. Oh, fuck. She'd just flashed Gib's literary agent cousin.

Gib pulled his shirt closed. 'I thought you were done, nobody was talking,' Bea shout-whispered, her face on fire.

Laughter rumbled through Gib. 'Navy has a law degree and is trying to help me decipher some legalese for a deal we are about to sign. Unfortunately, it's not something that can wait until I get back to the office. We were concentrating, that's why we were quiet.

'Bea, Navy. Navy, Bea,' he added.

'Hey, Bea. It's nice to meet you.'

Bea closed her eyes and waved at the screen. She tried to get up but Gib's arm around her waist and his hand on her thigh kept her pinned in place. 'I'm so embarrassed right now,' she muttered.

'Don't be, I didn't see much,' Navy assured her.

Judging by his immensely cheerful tone, he'd seen enough, so Bea kept her eyes shut. She'd *never* be able to look him in the eye.

'It's nice to meet the fabulous Parker Kane, although I didn't expect her to be half-naked,' Navy said, still laughing.

Gib tensed, and Bea's eyes flew open, and she caught Gib making a slashing motion across his neck. Had Gib's cousin really linked her with Parker Kane or was she finally losing her mind?

'Navy, you *fucker*,' Gib muttered and slammed his computer closed.

———————

Bea scrambled off Gib's lap and wrapped his shirt around her, wishing the world would stop rocking. '*What* did he just say?'

Gib grimaced, stood up, and ran his hands through his hair.

'*You know who I am?*'

He pointed to his laptop. 'That wasn't how I wanted you to find out. I wanted you to tell me yourself.'

She was struggling for air and couldn't make head or tail of his statement. She pulled in a few deep breaths, but her heart didn't stop racing, and neither did the world stop spinning. 'That's pretty rich considering you won't tell me anything.'

He winced and she knew her arrow had hit its target. She stomped into the cottage and sat down on the edge of the divan, barely aware of the rough fabric on her exposed butt cheeks and the springs poking into her skin. 'Have you told anyone?'

How much damage control did she need to do?

Gib pulled the coffee table close to her and sat on it, his knees brushing hers. She slammed hers together to keep from touching him. He knew her biggest secret, and she thought she might shatter. 'No, I wouldn't do that to you, and neither would Navy.'

'I don't know Navy at all. I barely know *you*.'

'That's not fair, Bea, you do know me.'

Oh, bullshit. 'I know you live in Nashville, that your parents died, and that you don't do relationships. *Whoop de doo*.'

She dragged her fingers across her forehead. They'd moved off the subject. 'How did you find out I'm Parker Kane?'

He rested his forearms on his knees and let his hands dangle between his legs. 'That day you spilt your coffee, I picked up your notebook and read a few lines. You'd circled an acronym, GMC, and left a note to send out a newsletter.

'I sent Navy a text, asked him what the acronym meant —' He saw her narrowed eyed stare and shrugged. 'I was curious. He explained they were terms used by writers and wannabe writers.'

Shit. 'That's still a leap to identifying me as Parker Kane.'

He rubbed his jaw. 'After our fight, I was talking to Navy, telling him what happened between us.' Oh, stunning. Now his cousin knew she'd acted like an overzealous fifties housewife. *Excellent.*

'I mentioned to him that in addition to the acronym, I'd read something about a Pip and rapids. Navy told me I should stop reading your private stuff—'

'Good of him.'

'But he also connected the dots, and suggested you're Parker Kane. After reading book one, I know you are, too. I hear you, I hear your voice in the words on the page.'

Bea pulled her knees onto the divan and rested her forehead between them. A part of her was happy he knew – she wanted him to know – and a part of her was terrified he, or Navy, would out her. Because the only way to keep a secret was not to divulge it in the first place.

Gib's hand skimmed across her hair. 'Can you tell me why you feel the need to hide behind your pseudonym, Bea? You're a great writer, and you're doing so well that my cousin wants to rep you, and he's a picky bastard. Why aren't you out there, taking the credit you deserve?'

She lifted her concrete-block-heavy head. 'How can you ask me to open up to you, when you can't do the same for me?'

'Because you are so much better at it than me, Bea-baby,' he murmured. He held her gaze, his eyes brimming with sincerity and begging her to trust him. The hell of it was that she did. She knew he wouldn't tell her secret. Hell, he'd known for days, but he'd kept his curiosity at bay. He'd been waiting for her to tell him.

And she'd wanted to. It had taken all she had not to ask him whether he liked what he was reading. And damn her for wanting to tell him about the rest, about *everything*.

Because she suspected he was the only person, apart from Golly, she could trust.

He got her, on levels she never thought were possible. She respected his opinions, loved his sharp mind, adored his body. Yeah, he was closed off, he kept his thoughts and emotions under tight control, but he wasn't cold, or heartless. Someone caused him to keep his deepest feelings to himself, someone hurt him deeply enough for him to question being honest and open, to make him afraid of showing his softer side. Bea would like to track that person down and shove a fork in their throat.

She scooted back on the divan, and grimaced when she teetered on the edge of the dip. She stood up, and took the chair, and Gib moved to the short side of the coffee table, to face her again.

'Since you know I'm Parker Kane, I might as well tell you why I can't be Parker Kane.'

Gib frowned. Right, that was clear as mud.

He stood and went into the kitchen to grab two bottles of water from the fridge. After cracking the top for her and handing it over, he sat again, his expression pensive as he waited for her to open up. She liked that he didn't badger her to talk, that he was content to let her take her time.

But it was hard, it always had been. As much as she loved Golly, her godmother wasn't a sympathetic soul. She'd had friends at schools, but lost contact with them a short while after she and Gerry started dating. As for her ex…

Well, Gerry wasn't interested in any subject beyond himself.

'I told you I was raised by my dad, but that's wrong. I raised *him*. I was an incredibly adult child, and I took on adult responsibilities … cooking meals, paying bills.' She hauled in a breath, knowing the next bit would be hard. 'Because of him, I sometimes still feel it's my fault when people disappoint me. I'm compelled to make people happy, frequently to my own detriment. I'm overly responsible and have always felt the need to hold up the sky.' What had she forgotten? Right, the big one. 'And I *hate* being criticised, even a little bit. It takes me straight back to my childhood. As a child, I made adult choices with adult consequences, but I was criticised when things went wrong.

That's as much as I can say about my dad. It wasn't fun, and holidays with Golly kept me sane.'

Gib picked up her hand and placed a kiss in her palm, before returning her hand to her lap. That little action and his lack of judgement encouraged her to continue.

'My mum messed me up in other ways. Being a mother wasn't something Lou was prepared to do or be. She was a journalist, covering social events, and she landed a job writing a weekly column for a tabloid newspaper. How, I don't know, because her writing sucks.'

Did she sound bitter? She *was* bitter. Bea often wondered if her mother's editors and readers realised how often Lou recycled phrases, ideas and thoughts. She was convinced Lou hadn't had an original thought since 2001.

'Go on,' Gib encouraged, opening his water and draining half the bottle in one long swallow.

'Lou rarely made an effort to see me, and ten years ago, her columns changed. She became more outspoken, and more outrageous in her views. Her work hit a nerve, because she started getting lots of reactions, both good and bad, to her opinion pieces.' She wondered how to explain what her mother did next. 'Have you ever seen those "*Am I an asshole*?" threads online?'

He nodded. 'I'm familiar with the concept.'

'Well, Lou started writing a monthly column called, '*Am I wrong*?'. She'd take a hot topic, and twist it up, spin it around, mock it, and cause mayhem. She became a household name, mostly for being a jerk.'

Bea waited until Gib looked at her and he sighed. 'There's more, I take it?' he said, sounding resigned.

'So much more…' Bea took a swallow of water, anger and humiliation blazing through her. She picked up the end of his shirt and twisted it around her clenched fist.

'You don't have to tell me, Bea,' Gib said, his words calming some of her internal heat and frustration.

Another sip of water, another sigh. 'I picked up a contract for my first three *Urban Explorer* books. Professionally, I was flying, personally, my world was collapsing. The day after I got the offer, I caught my ex cheating, in my bed. During the fight that ensued, his fist flew past my ear and landed on the fridge door behind me, denting it. Instantly, I knew the next time he raised his hand, it would connect with my face or my body. It was the wake-up call I desperately needed. I threw him out and changed the locks.'

'Good for you,' Gib murmured.

'I told him to text me his new address, so I knew where to send his clothes and possessions, and when he sent it I found out … well, that he'd moved in with my mother.'

'*Fuck.*'

The memories were a knife sliding between her ribs. 'Not only did he move in with her, but he also moved into her bed, and they were often photographed together. I kept a very low profile, so it took a while for the press to work out she was dating her daughter's ex. Then she penned one of her '*Am I wrong*?' columns, saying she was in a relationship with her daughter's ex and was it wrong when her daughter kicked him out and ended their relationship?'

Gib ran his hand over his face. '*Christ.*'

Yeah. 'The press were relentless, desperate for a reaction from me. That's when my publishers suggested I consider using a pseudonym. My mother still doesn't know I'm Parker Kane.'

Gib shook his head and Bea saw anger in his eyes. 'That was a truly shitty thing for them to do. I'm so sorry, Bea. Can I rearrange his face for you?'

His offer made her feel a little warm and fuzzy. 'Not surprisingly, she and Gerry didn't last long. Partly because they're both cretins, partly because I genuinely believe you can't build your happiness on someone else's sadness.'

She looked past his shoulder. 'She still writes the column, it's still popular.' She pulled her lip between her teeth. 'I'm scared of being linked to her, scared of the public criticism and scrutiny.'

Bea couldn't allow Parker Kane to be tainted by her association with Lou. 'I still keep a really low profile, and I never tell anyone Lou is my mother,' she said, hoping Gib would read between the lines and reassure her, again, that her secret was safe.

'Navy and I won't tell anyone, Bea. But you should. If she wasn't a columnist, would you step out from behind your pen name?' he asked.

'Yes, I guess.'

'Then you're allowing her to affect your life, to have a say in your career.'

He didn't get it. 'But what if she does a review? Criticises my books?' she demanded, sounding a little shrill.

Gib shrugged. 'It'll send a whole lot of people to your books, they'll read them because they'll want to know what the fuss is about and then they'll realise she's wrong. And you make bank.'

She'd never thought of it like that, but still wasn't sure she could do it. 'I don't want anything to do with her,' she stubbornly insisted. 'Freezing her out works for me.'

'I think you've built this up in your head, making more of it than it needs to be. The anticipation is always worse than the deed, Bea.'

No, she was pretty sure she knew what would happen. If it came out that Lou was Parker Kane's mother, social media would explode. She'd be painted with the same brush as Lou and her career, and brand, would take an enormous hit. She was still convinced it was better to stay as far away from her mother as she possibly could

'Could it be that you're allowing your fear of being criticised to dictate your actions?'

Maybe. But it worked for her.

But did it really? She wasn't sure about anything anymore. God, she was tired. She'd emotionally vomited all over Gib, and she now felt empty and exhausted. She just wanted to go back to bed, sleep, and not think.

Bea pulled in a deep breath and finished her water. 'Cass said that Nadia is serving breakfast up at the villa if you're hungry,' she stated, deliberately changing the subject.

'Aren't you hungry?' he asked her, pushing a heavy strand of hair behind her ear and trailing his fingers down her jaw.

She shook her head. 'I think I'm going to take an aspirin and go back to bed.'

He gently held her chin and forced her to look at him. 'Don't shut me out now, Bea.'

'Why not, Gib? You do it to me all the time.'

Leaving him white faced and without a comeback, she stood up, walked back into the bedroom, threw back a couple of aspirins and climbed under the covers. Today could carry on without her.

Bea's parting shot was a punch to his gut.

Gib looked at the closed bedroom door and scrubbed his

hands over his face. She wasn't wrong. She'd told him pretty much everything and he'd given her nothing, hadn't trusted her with anything but the basics.

But how was he supposed to change a habit of a lifetime and start bleeding words and feelings? Keeping his own counsel was as innate to him as breathing. Even if he managed to find the courage to talk to her, he didn't know if he was *physically* able to talk to her, if the words would come.

Gib stood up and walked onto the deck, wrapping his hands around the balustrade so tightly his hands turned white.

This wasn't supposed to get so complicated, but he had to admit this thing between them wasn't superficial. They'd tried hard to keep it light and fluffy, but somehow, when they weren't paying attention, they'd slipped into something deeper, something – *goddammit* – meaningful.

He liked her, more than he'd liked a woman in a long, long time. Was that due to him being able to take the time, spending many hours with her instead of rushing through dinner dates as he usually did? Maybe the reason he'd caught feelings was because he was on vacation, and didn't have the excuse to run off to work, or check a report and take a meeting.

Caught feelings…

It was such a trite phrase, but it was disturbingly accurate. He just wasn't sure what they were and what the hell he was going to do with them and what they meant.

Finding out she was Parker Kane the other day had been

a revelation, and he appreciated her talent. He'd read the first book, and was three quarters of the way through the second. He thought, mistakenly, that he'd skim through it, but he'd found himself lost in the story, thoroughly enjoying the depth of her characters, their banter and the pace.

If any of his business rivals heard he was reading a kids book on vacation he'd be booted out of boardrooms all over the world, but she was – and he wasn't just saying this because he was fascinated by the woman – a damn good writer. If you could hook a jaded thirty-five-year-old and make him forget that the woman he was sleeping with was the books' author, then she was something special.

It wasn't a surprise that Navy wanted to act as her agent. It was a no-brainer.

Gib had no doubt that Navy would keep her identity a secret and had no need to remind him to do so. Navy's integrity ran deep and wide, and he'd never out her. Neither would Gib. But damn, he wished she would step out from behind her name and into the spotlight. She deserved to be seen, deserved to be lauded, deserved to…

Be loved.

But he couldn't give her what she needed. She'd been let down by her father, had a witch for a mother, and while he had no doubt Golly loved her, Golly was programmed to put herself first. Bea deserved someone standing in her corner, ready to catch her when she fell, someone to bolster her when she was down, to remind her of how wonderful, sexy and lovely she was.

He couldn't be that person. And not only because he

was an emotional virgin, terrified of feeling anything at all, unable to verbalise his emotions but also because he was a busy, busy guy.

Being the CEO of Caddell International meant he spent a good part of the year in planes, and cars, bouncing between their various satellite offices all over the world. He owed it to Hugh to be the best he could be and to do that he needed to be hands-on, to be at the coal face. He couldn't run Caddell International and also be an involved, supportive partner.

The two didn't mix. He'd get frustrated and she'd be disappointed, he'd feel guilty, and she'd get pissed. Long-distance relationships were hard work, even when you were emotionally able to invest in one.

Bottom line, Bea deserved … well, she deserved *everything*.

But he wasn't the guy to give it to her.

Chapter Fourteen

O n the following Friday, Bea heard Gib walking into the cottage, and wished she'd taken him up on his offer to teach her to kayak. Anything, even testing her useless coordination and using muscles she rarely exercised, would've been more fun than the time she'd spent at her desk.

She'd accomplished next to nothing for most of the morning. She'd tried various plots for book ten, and none of them worked. Frustrated, she'd flipped over to brainstorming her spin-off series and every idea was either clichéd or boring as mud.

She'd spent the morning treading water, and was sinking under the weight of imposter syndrome, self-doubt and writer's block.

And yes, she was resentful that she'd chosen to sit in front of her computer instead of spending the little time she and Gib had left with him. Her arse was numb, and she was grumpy. What a bitching waste of her time…

Gib stepped onto the deck, his grin wide. With his messy hair and heavy stubble, his shirt open and his shorts hanging low, he looked like he'd had a great time on the water. She was glad one of them had enjoyed their morning.

Waah, waah, waah… God, she was annoying herself.

Gib placed one hand on the back on her chair, the other on her desk and bent his head low to brush his mouth across hers. 'Your morning wasn't productive,' he stated.

He knew her so well, already, and could read her like, well, a book. 'Horrible,' she admitted. 'I made no progress at all.'

'Maybe you need to step away,' he suggested, placing his butt on the desk and stretching out his long legs. He was tanned, and she smiled, remembering the blond-haired boy who'd raced through the villa, did wheelies on his bike, and annoyed her.

His board shorts hung off his hips, showing off a strip of white, sun-deprived skin. She drew her finger across it, slowly. He captured her hand and held it against his semi, his eyes turning darker and warmer, a sure indication that he was turned on. Oh, and the hardening of his erection was a good clue, too.

'Come to bed, I'll inspire you.'

She laughed. Her morning was about to improve. She was about to stand when the notification of an incoming email flashed on her screen, one she couldn't, or didn't want to ignore.

'Let me just read this quickly, it's from my editor. It's probs just an email saying she loved book nine and wants a few revisions. I won't be long.'

'Take your time,' Gib said, but he didn't release her right hand from the bulge in his pants. It took Bea more time than she liked to click on the email using her left hand, but she didn't complain.

If this was an email from anyone but Merle, she'd blow it off. She skimmed through the words, but they didn't make any sense.

Her last paragraph penetrated Bea's confusion.

Frankly, this MS would require a massive rewrite to get it to the desired standard, and given the amount of work that would entail, I believe it might be better to move on from this WIP. I recommend setting this story aside and starting fresh, incorporating all the essential elements you need to effectively capture the essence, action and wit of your previous books.

Bea slapped her hands on either side of her laptop, turning ice cold as the words danced in front of her eyes. Was she reading Merle's words correctly? She was demanding an entire rewrite? On the book Bea had thought was good, maybe even great?

'Bea, what is it?'

What? How? How could she have gone so badly off track? What happened? What was so bad about this manuscript that Merle wanted her to start again? *Jesus.* The sense of failure, hot and acidic, crept across her soul, melting it inch by painful inch.

She'd always hated criticism, but this was more. This was *failure*, on an epic scale. Professional failure, and a dagger to her heart. Merle must think she was such an idiot, uncaring and ridiculous, or arrogant and careless. Apart from Golly, there was no one whose opinion she valued more. Her editor made her books better, took a slightly rough stone and polished it to brilliance. But apparently she'd handed Merle a piece of coal.

How the hell did she come back from this?

Gib's hand on her shoulder gently shaking her forced her to look at him. 'Stop biting your lip, Bea, it's bleeding.'

She swiped the back of her hand across her lip, and looked down, seeing the blood smear on her hand.

'What's happened?' Gib demanded, his eyes darting from her face to the laptop screen. 'Has someone died? What's the problem?'

She shook her head, wanting to double over from the cramps knotting her stomach. Acid flared and crept up her throat.

'Bea! *What?*'

Was Gib starting to panic? She looked at him, feeling a million miles away. 'My editor hates my book and wants me to rewrite it. To start again.'

His taut body slumped, and he released a long, audible stream of air. '*OK.* I thought it was something really bad.'

He did not say that! No *fucking* way. 'This is the worst

thing that can happen to me. I have to *rewrite* a book. What part of that do you not understand?' she yelled, sounding like the shrew he'd accused her of being when they first met. 'I messed up so badly that none of my work is redeemable, Gib! Nothing! What kind of writer does that make me?'

'A normal one? Surely everyone messes up, Bea.'

'Not on a scale like this, they don't!' she retorted, furious because he wasn't getting it. This might not be career suicide, but it was a self-inflicted wound. 'Merle must think I'm a total idiot, like I've lost my mind or something.'

Bea paced, her arms hugging her chest. The problem with talking to non-authors about your industry was that they just didn't get it. They didn't understand that writing a book was like birthing a baby, and then holding it up to the world and asking whether your kid was pretty. As much as she tried to keep it impersonal, to divorce herself from her writing, she couldn't because her characters were a part of her, ripped from her soul. How could you not take criticism personally when writing was all you knew how to do, what you loved?

She didn't like criticism at the best of times, it always made her feel like she wasn't doing enough, being enough, adult enough, but criticism from her editor killed her. And being asked to rewrite a book was criticism on steroids.

Gib sighed, pushed his hand through his hair and guessed that sex was now off the table.

He caught the glitter of tears, and the depth of her pain in her eyes. Her quick-to-smile mouth was tight with tension, and her shoulders were up around her ears. Right, this was a lot more serious than he thought. Her world had been rocked, and he wanted to understand how and why.

This from the guy who never asked questions, who kept a hefty emotional distance between himself and the women he slept with. But Bea wasn't just another woman, she was someone who'd slid under his skin, who'd breached a wall, maybe two. She was dangerous…

He knew he needed to find the willpower to walk away from her before whatever the hell was bubbling between them spilled over and scorched them.

But that was for later. Right now he needed to work out how to handle, and comfort, Bea. Because, God, she needed it. Taking a chance, he walked over to her and pulled her into him, criss-crossing his big arms over her back and plastering her to his chest. She stood board still, her arms at her sides, refusing to engage.

That was OK, she just needed to know he was here for her.

'I've got you, Bea-baby,' he murmured, his lips in her hair.

Bea slumped and he held her up as her hands lifted to grip his shirt. When a wet patch of his shirt stuck to his chest, he realised she was silently sobbing. Not knowing what to do, or say, he pushed his fingers into her hair and cradled her head to his chest. If crying would release some of her tension, he was all for it.

She'd cried a little the other day, but this time she cried noiselessly, endlessly, and every intake of breath sounded painful. He didn't understand how an email could cause so much hurt. Because these weren't ordinary tears, the normal ups and downs of a professional relationship. This was visceral, a hurt that sliced through muscle and chipped bones, that ripped apart lives and scorched souls.

'Can you talk about it?' he asked, after five minutes had passed.

She shook her head, her refusal unsurprising. Some things went too deep for conversation. Stepping back from her, he wiped away her tears with his thumbs before placing his lips on her hot forehead. Remembering what she'd said about her childhood, how she hated criticism, he thought she might need a little perspective.

'How long has this Merle person been an editor?' Gib asked, stepping away from her.

She threw her hands up in the air, annoyed. 'What's that got to do with anything?' Anger was acceptable, it was far better than despair. Or self-pity. Anger was alive and active, and healthier.

His eyes didn't leave hers. 'Humour me.'

'I'm having a crisis and you're asking me inane questions? I don't know … fifteen … seventeen years? Can we go back to what's important?' she snarled. 'FYI, that's my incipient nervous breakdown.'

He ignored her statement. She was a lot stronger than

she thought and needed to be reminded of that. 'And in all that time, after editing hundreds and hundreds of books, do you think you're the first person Merle has asked to rewrite one?'

She stared at him, his words sinking in. 'No, probably not, but—'

'But people go off track, they mess up. They get bogged down and don't see the wood for the trees. They get tunnel vision.'

Maybe it would help if he told her about some of his failures. Ordinarily, he wouldn't bother, but Bea needed to understand she wasn't the only person who'd messed up. 'About seven years ago, Hugh asked me to oversee a deal for him. We were looking at buying out a music label and I was confident, cocky, and didn't consider all the implications of that deal. My mistake cost the company a million dollars.'

Her eyes widened. 'A million? Holy crap, that's a lot of money. What happened?'

He didn't bother telling her that a million dollars was peanuts in the grand scheme of things. 'My uncle gave me a loud and long – what's that word you English use? – bollocking, and told me to get my shit together. Then he gave me the opportunity to do another deal.'

'And you made the million back,' she muttered. 'I'm sorry, but it's not the same and you don't understand.'

Failure was failure, and however you did it, it still stung.

'No, I lost money on that one, too. Not so much, but we

still took a bath. I learned something from those deals, though.'

'Why are you telling me this?' Bea demanded. He knew she wanted him to walk away, to allow her the space to give into her despair, to crawl into the corner and weep. He wasn't going to let that happen.

'Because you learn from failures, Bea, you learn from criticism. It makes you better, and stronger. Failing is not the issue, how you react to it is. And you always learn more from failure than you do from success.'

'Yeah, I'm learning that my instincts about being a fluke are dead on. I've written eight books, maybe that's all I have in me! My well is empty and I can't make words anymore.' She ran her hands over her face. 'I'm an eight-book wonder. I could, maybe, live on my royalties for a little while, but then I'd have to get a job!'

'So, I guess coming out as Parker Kane is the least of your problems, now?'

She glared at him, and Gib rolled his eyes. Right, too soon. But it was time for her to snap out of her woe-is-me attitude.

Gib gripped her shoulders and bent his knees so his eyes were level with hers. 'Snap out of your self-pity, Beatrice, and step back from your emotion. Start thinking and stop reacting.'

Her eyes widened at his sharp tone. 'You're not hearing me, Gib! I don't know if I can do this anymore. Even before I got this email, I was doubting myself, couldn't find my creativity. I need to write this book, am contracted to give them something, but where do I go from here?'

He went into problem-solving mode, something he was an expert at. 'You still have the choice about how to react. Is your editor prepared to work with you, to help you get it right?'

She glanced down at the email, shook her head and wiped her eyes. She read the email again and shrugged. 'Merle said she'll help me in any way she can.'

Then he didn't see the problem. 'Then you take her help and rewrite the book. And you do it better than before.'

'You make it sound so easy,' she complained. 'You don't understand … writing is hard work. Hemingway called it bleeding over the typewriter, and to lose that number of words feels like a death.'

A tad dramatic, but he'd let it go. 'All work is hard, and rebounding from a mistake is harder still. This is just a bump, Bea.'

'A bump? It's a bloody mountain!'

Stubborn, too. Gib slid his hands into the back pockets of his shorts. 'The other day, you told me that you were heavily criticised as a child. Are you reacting to this like a child, or like a professional? Can you step back and read that email without judging yourself? Can you try and read it without becoming triggered, and defensive? Can you pretend that email is directed to someone else, and put some space between you and it?'

'This isn't a business deal, Gib, it's my life!' she retorted, rocking on her heels.

'OK, then what are your options?' he asked, striving for patience. 'Break it down.'

She bit her lip. 'Do the rewrite or buy myself out of my contract. I'd have to rework my entire writing life if I do that.'

That sounded drastic and melodramatic. 'You *are* going to rewrite the book, Bea. That isn't up for debate.' He wasn't going to let her give up, just as Hugh had never allowed him to. Quitting wasn't an option.

'And while you get cracking on writing another kickass *Urban Explorer* adventure, you'll start to realise that this is a way to grow, to learn, and to prove to yourself that you aren't that kid who can't take criticism anymore.'

Gib ran a hand over her head, his finger down her jaw. 'And let's be honest, Bea-baby, you can't give up writing to find a job. You'd hate it, and it would steal your soul. And there isn't a boss in the world who'd let you amble into work in yoga pants and messy hair, a makeup free face and wearing your most comfortable slippers.'

She pulled her bottom lip between her teeth and let it go when he tapped her chin. Hopefully, his talking this through with her, logically and unemotionally, had given her some perspective. She looked calmer, her tears had tried up, and she'd stopped rubbing the spot between her ribs. Had their chat made her feel stronger, tougher, a fraction more resilient?

Honestly, he thought it went quite well. For someone who never usually engaged, who stayed uninvolved, he'd willingly walked into an emotional situation and tried to help. He'd offered some good advice, some genuine encouragement.

Navy would be proud of him for getting his hands emotionally dirty.

But he felt a little drained himself and, honestly, could murder a beer. 'Let's get out of here. We'll go for a walk, hit the beach and a taverna. You need some time to digest this.'

She looked grateful for the reprieve, and he wasn't surprised. He knew from experience how good it felt to bury your head in the sand for a while. The problem was that you had to yank it out at some point and carry on.

'That sounds good. I think I'd like that.'

Gib followed Bea into the bedroom, watched as she pulled a bikini from the chest of drawers and started to walk into the bathroom to change. He hooked his finger into the band of her shorts and stopped her in her tracks. 'After everything we've done together, you still can't change in front of me?' he asked, smiling.

Heat flooded her cheeks. He'd explored every inch of her – with the lights on! – and she had no secrets from him, but she still felt bashful. She looked away, her cheeks brightening.

'God, you're adorable,' he said, laughing. 'I love your body, Bea, and there's no need to hide it from me.'

He wanted her to feel beautiful, and lovely, and adored, so he hooked his hand around her butt and lifted her to her toes, and he bent his head to kiss her mouth. He kept their kiss light, but he sensed Bea wanted more.

'I want to make love to you in the sunshine,' she softly murmured.

Her tongue slipped into his mouth, and he pulled back, his hand brushing her hair off her forehead. 'You've had an emotional morning, Bea, and I don't want to be the plaster you slap on your weeping wound.'

She bit her lip, considering his words. 'I'm not going to pretend I'm not upset, Gib, and confused and feeling emotionally battered. But your touch burns everything away.' Her smile seemed a little forced when she added, 'Has anyone ever told you you're pretty good in the sack?'

He lifted an arrogant eyebrow. 'Only pretty good?'

She sighed dramatically. 'OK, shockingly good. Why wouldn't I want to be on the receiving end of all that skill?'

'Are you sure?'

She nodded and he wrapped his big hand around her neck and lifted her chin with his thumb. 'If we get naked, I don't want you to think about anything else but me, Beatrice.'

'As soon as you kiss me, all I'll think about is you and the pleasure you give me.'

Gib's last rational thought was that it would be a long, lovely, pleasure-filled while before they made it to the beach.

Bea lay on a lounger on the beach and watched Gib swim out to sea. His stroke was long and sure, powerful and controlled, elegant. It was a pretty good description of the way he made love.

She'd lied a little this afternoon, she did use him as an emotional Band-Aid, as a way to get out of her head. When he touched her, nothing else mattered, she was totally, completely in the moment, lost in the pleasure he gave her, as mindful as she ever got.

But now that she was alone, the morning events came rolling back in and she sucked in a breath, caught between mortification and frustration.

Where did she go so wrong? How did she not realise that she'd gone so badly off track? Had she been so involved in the story that she forgot the framework, neglected to pull all the threads together in the revision process? Or had she got lazy and complacent, thinking she was smarter and more experienced than she really was? Had she thought she could coast?

Maybe a lot of getting lost in the story, a little arrogance.

She picked up her towel and wrapped it around her shoulders, bending her knees. A man played with his toddler in the shallows, picking her up every time the waves rolled close to her feet, laughing when she squealed.

Bea felt calmer now and being away from the cottage afforded her enough emotional distance to think logically. Gib was right: her only real option was to rewrite the book. She had time – she'd submitted that first draft a couple of months before it was due – and maybe that was the problem, maybe she'd rushed it, and hadn't given it the time and energy it deserved. With the next one she would take it slower, be more present.

She'd reacted badly earlier, immaturely, caught up in the criticism and the emotion it pulled to the surface. Of course she couldn't throw in the towel, couldn't give up because of one setback. What she could do was be a professional, suck up the criticism – God, it was hard, and it felt like steel wool scrubbing her soul – and tell Merle she respected her opinion. Which she did, of course she *did*.

When she got back to London next week, they could set up a video call to rip her submission apart to see where she'd gone wrong – everywhere? She'd need to take a couple of homoeopathic anti-anxiety pills, but she'd grit her teeth and get through it. And when the writing equivalent of a waterboarding was over, they could brainstorm ideas for the rewrite.

And maybe that was why she hadn't been able to make any progress with book ten? Maybe it was because she knew, subconsciously, that book nine was problematic?

OK, she now had a plan of action, and she felt calmer. And as Gib had said, she'd learn from this, and become a better writer. Be stronger and tougher and more resilient. Unlike other authors, she hadn't gone through the rejection-after-rejection grind. She was the goddaughter of an agent and had the inside track. Golly wouldn't have tried to sell anything she didn't believe in, but her initial success surprised both of them. Instead of the rejections she'd been warned to expect – a fact of life in publishing – her series went to auction, with six publishers clamouring for her *Urban Explorers*. The highest bidder got the deal, and she got a substantial advance. Books one to eight had undergone what she thought were normal revisions, in that they hadn't been hard or taxing.

This was her first proper publishing setback. And she'd fallen apart at the first bump. And she would probably still be on the floor sobbing if Gib hadn't been there to give her some direct, challenging and supremely logical advice. *Everyone messes up. It's how you react to it that counts. You don't throw in the towel.* It stung, but it hurt because it was true. And she could either wring her hands or be productive. She chose the latter. Because, as Gib said, ultimately, *you learn more from failure than you do from success.*

She watched Gib emerge from the water, looking far better than Daniel Craig did when he walked out of the sea in that Bond film. They'd turned a corner this morning, and she felt so close to him, emotionally connected.

Yes, yes, she knew that this was supposed to be a fling, that it was only sex-based, but something more bubbled under the surface. He looked at her like she was special, as if he could, maybe, love her, like he couldn't think of a way to let her go. She wasn't imagining it, was she? Seeing more than she should?

No.

It was in the way he touched her, in his sweet kisses, when she caught him watching her when they were on opposite sides of the room. Chemistry and tension hummed between them, sparkly and lovely and undeniable.

She didn't know what would happen when they left Santorini, but not seeing him again wasn't an option. He, this, was too special to walk away from.

Gib sat down on the lounger beside her and shook his head, spraying wet drops over her. She slapped his shoulder and pushed him away, laughing. 'You jerk! Why do you keep tormenting me with cold water?'

He leaned back on his hands and tipped his face to the sun. 'You've got some colour back in your face, some light in your eyes. Feeling better?' he asked.

She traced her fingers over his shoulder. 'I am, thank you. Thank you for being there for me, for talking me through it.'

'Sure. So, what are you going to do?'

'Have a meeting with my editor, work out what went wrong, write it again.' It would be hard, but not insurmountable.

'Good,' Gib murmured, his eyes still closed.

He now knew everything about her, knew her fears and insecurities, her secrets, her past and her plans for the immediate present. He knew her better than anyone, and she liked that he did. Since he knew everything about her – from her childhood to her being Parker Kane to today's embarrassing fiasco – surely she had the right to ask questions, to dig a little?

She was an open book, and he could be too. Would be. 'Tell me what it was like when your parents died, Gib.'

She was watching his face and saw his eyes tighten

briefly. But he kept his lids down and his head tipped to the sun. 'Shit.'

Well, obviously. 'Obviously, you were devastated. How did you cope with that? Did Hugh come and get you straight away?'

'Yes.'

God, pulling a dinosaur's teeth would be easier than this. 'Was the funeral big? Do you remember it or did you tune it out? They say that happens.'

He sat up slowly and turned to face her. 'What's with all the questions?'

'Well, we've never spoken about your past, and what you went through.' About *anything* really.

His face, degree by degree, shut down. 'I'm sorry, but why would you think that's something I'd discuss with you?'

She jerked back, his words a hard slap. 'Gib, come on. What's the big deal? Why won't you let me in?'

'Why should I?'

Holy crap, this wasn't going the way she expected it to. 'Gib, I've opened myself up to you, you know everything about me. You know more about me than my ex does, and we were together for five years.'

His expression turned remote. 'You gave it to me, I didn't ask for it.'

Bea rubbed her hand over her mouth, trying to make sense of what he was saying. So she was expected to be vulnerable, open, and show him all her cards, but he could keep his locked down? What the fuck?

She pushed her hand through her hair, trying to work out what to say, how to act. 'I'm not sure what to say to that,' she admitted, her voice hoarse. 'I thought we'd turned a corner, that we had something…'

Gib looked out to sea. 'I'm not saying that we don't, but I'm not saying that we're going to create a life together either. It's far too soon for that, and…'

And what? She wanted to grab him and wrench the words out of him.

'And if you expect me to bare my soul to you, to talk about my feelings, my parents and my past, it's not going to happen, Bea. It's not who I am.'

No, that was bullshit. 'No, it's who you've conditioned yourself to be.'

He lifted one shoulder in a shrug that could mean 'whatever' or that he agreed. The knot was back, tighter than before, acid flaming in her stomach. He was being end-of-the-world serious; he was *not* going to talk to her.

Bea dropped her legs and stared at the pebbles beneath her feet. She could say it was fine, could keep taking whatever he'd give her and push her resentment away. Or she could walk away, telling him she wanted everything or nothing at all. She knew so little about him and had no idea what made him tick.

She was the only one standing in the storm, emotionally battered and whipped. He was somewhere else. Safe, and keeping himself dry.

Had meeting her changed him at all? Had she taught him anything? What was he risking? As far as she could tell, nothing. She was all in, and he stood on the edges of the maelstrom, watching her twist, unwilling to join her.

Bea realised she had another choice to make, and it was a big one. She could compromise or she could be brave and stand up for herself by demanding more. But if she did that, she could lose him…

Before she could decide, Gib spoke, his deep voice low and quiet. 'This is just a fling, Bea. It's not supposed to be this serious.'

Was he blaming her? It sounded like it. 'And that's *my* fault?'

'I didn't say that,' he countered. She knew he was irritated, she could see it in his eyes and his tight mouth. Well, tough. She was beyond irritated, she was really pissed off.

Hurt, too. And that hurt would probably deepen and spread, but right now she was as mad as a raging river in full flood. What the hell was wrong with this man? Would it hurt him to give her *something*? Anything?

'Look, Bea, we've only known each other for less than two weeks…'

Yeah, she knew what was coming next. 'I'm not at a point where I feel comfortable sharing my inner world with you.'

And wasn't that another verbal slap. What was wrong with her that he didn't feel like he could trust her? No, wait, hold on … why was she somehow at fault for him being unable to open up? This was *his* issue, not hers. She wasn't in the wrong here, she wasn't the one who was emotionally fucked up. OK, she was, but not as badly as him.

Bea pulled her shirt over her bikini top. She stood and stepped into her pretty, short floral skirt. Instead of her habitual flip flops, she'd worn a pair of beaded sandals, thinking that she and Gib would go out for a drink, maybe supper later.

This day had been long enough, though, too much had happened, and she needed some space, some distance. For the first time since last Sunday, she didn't want to be around him. Now she was desperate for the privacy he claimed he wanted.

She didn't know how she was going to share a bed with him tonight, but that was for later. Right now, she just wanted to go back to the villa.

'Bea—'

She didn't want to hear his excuses, to listen to his justifications. Nothing he said would make her feel better, so it was better he said nothing at all. 'It's been a hell of a day, Gib. Will you drive me home now?'

He placed a hand on her arm, and she looked down at it, wishing he didn't make her body sing. But, like his unwillingness to talk, it was something she needed to live with. Or not live with. She had to work that out.

'We can talk about this, Bea.'

'*Bullshit!* You can't, or won't talk to me. I do all the talking, I open myself up to you, lay it all out, and you dip in and out, skimming the surface. I don't know if I can do that anymore.'

His mouth tightened. 'Are you saying we're done?'

Oh, God she didn't *know*! 'I'm saying that I don't want to talk anymore. I'm saying that it's been a long day and I want to go home. Will you take me home, or should I call a taxi?'

He stared at her, obviously frustrated.

'I'll take you.' He picked up his shirt, dragged it over his head, and placed his sunglasses on his face. Picking up his keys, phone and wallet, he placed a hand on her back to steer her to the car.

She sidestepped and moved away from him. She didn't need his guidance, just like he didn't need her questions.

Chapter Fifteen

G ib walked from the en suite into the bedroom, sighing when he saw Bea with her back to him, her palms under her cheek, pretending to be asleep. She lay on the very edge of the bed, as far away as she could get from him. Great, the Great Wall was back up, without the pillows, but still insurmountable. He walked over to the credenza, placed his phone on top of his state-of-the-art charger and looked out of the window, the full moon hanging over the sea. This wasn't how he'd thought today would end.

Bea didn't say anything to him on the drive back to the villa, and when he placed his hand on her thigh, as he normally did, she pulled her leg out of his reach. He knew she wasn't happy with his response on the beach today, but what did she expect? That because she'd opened up to him, he could reciprocate?

Didn't she know that if he could he would?

But keeping himself closed off, safe from ridicule and judgement, was a habit he couldn't seem to break. God, she was so much stronger than him. She'd survived being a child forced to take on adult responsibilities, simply rolling up her sleeves and getting it done. He didn't, not for one moment, doubt that Bea would rewrite her book, and do it spectacularly, because she knew how to bounce back, she'd been doing it all her life. She might say she was scared of criticism, of being judged, but, as far as he could see, she was pretty well-adjusted.

When they arrived back at the villa, she told him, quietly and with dignity, that she was going to spend some time with Golly and that she'd see him later. It was a quiet, dignified dismissal and he wasn't surprised by her late return earlier.

'Good night?' he'd asked her.

She'd nodded, unable to meet his eyes. 'Yes. You?'

'Quiet.' He nodded to the bedroom, needing to know. 'Are you sleeping with me tonight?'

Her eyes slammed into his, bottomless pools of emotion, and for the first time since he'd met her, unreadable. 'I'm sleeping in the bed, yes.'

Her 'not with you' was a silent shout.

He couldn't deny it any longer, he'd fallen for her. And that was a surprise because he never allowed himself to do anything other than skim along the surface, to take pleasure where he could and then bow out. But while he loved making love to Bea – and making love *was* what they did –

he was equally content to have her feet in his lap as she talked about anything. And nothing.

She *got* him. And he her. And he was fucking up something that could be amazing because he was a secretive son of a bitch. People thought he was so strong, a hardass, tough, business warrior but he knew he had no emotional resilience. He wasn't even brave enough to get into the game. Bea'd fought a couple of tough rounds, and taken more than a few emotional punches, but she was still fighting, putting herself out there.

He was outside of the ring, watching, too much of a wuss to take a punch.

But how do you change something that is so deeply ingrained in you? How do you take a leap? Fuck, how do you even take that first step?

He rubbed his heart, feeling it beating deep inside his chest, conscious of the nagging ache. None of this was supposed to happen.

It was supposed to be a holiday, a time for him to recover from burnout, to re-centre and rest. But he'd run into Bea, and she'd flipped his world. She made him think, remember and feel.

He turned to walk over to his side of the bed and climbed under the covers. He reached out to touch her slim back. 'Bea?'

'Yes?'

He couldn't lie in this bed without touching her. 'Can I hold you?'

In the moonlight, he saw her shake her head. His heart

sank, but then she reached back and, still facing the wall, placed her hand behind her on the bed, a silent but powerful invitation to take her hand.

He'd take anything he could get so he threaded his fingers through hers and held on tight.

———

The next morning Bea rolled onto her back when she heard Gib leave the bed. It was ridiculously early, a little past dawn. The sky was a cheerful pink, a happy pink, and Bea wished she felt the same way.

It was Saturday, and Gib was supposed to leave the island tomorrow. She so regretted opening that email from Merle and having that meltdown in front of him. If she'd ignored it, maybe she and Gib would've had a fantastic day on the beach, a romantic dinner, and would've spent last night and today chasing pleasure, and making memories.

But yesterday on the beach, when he told her he couldn't talk to her or open up, he extinguished the fire between them, as easily as he would the flame on a candle. If she didn't feel so much for him, if she wasn't fathoms deep in love with him, she might've been able to carry on sleeping with him, to take what pleasure she could and then wave him goodbye.

But, as much as she wanted her hands on him, she couldn't make love with him knowing her feelings ran so much deeper than his. Sex wasn't enough, she needed more. Mostly, she needed him to trust her...

If he couldn't allow her access to his heart, she couldn't allow him access to her body. And no, she wasn't playing games, she wasn't trying to punish him, she simply knew the pleasure wouldn't be worth the ensuing pain. When her orgasms faded, when her breathing settled down, he would still be unable to open up, to trust her enough to be vulnerable.

To love her. Because what was love without trust?

She watched as he pulled on a running vest and swapped his sleeping shorts for running shorts. He sat down on the edge of the bed and pulled on socks, his broad back tight with tension.

They couldn't keep ignoring each other , she wasn't that strong. 'I think I'm going to—'

'If you're going to give me the cold shoulder—'

Gib turned around to look at her, Bea scooted up the bed, and pushed her hand into her tangled hair.

He gestured for her to speak. Bea twisted the sheet in her fingers, looking past him to the lightening sky over the sea. 'I think I'm going to move into the villa tonight.'

He turned back to pull his other shoe onto his foot and bent low to tie the laces. Standing, he placed his hands on his hips, a classic warrior pose, and faced her. 'Don't bother. I'm planning to leave today.'

Although his words weren't unexpected, pain's talons ripped through her soul. 'You're leaving?'

He shrugged, his face in shadows. 'If you're going to ignore me, I might as well.'

Her instinct was to apologise, to make things right, but

she was better than that. She *had* to be. 'I'm not keeping my distance because I want to, Gib! *You* won't talk to *me*.'

'I do talk to you, of course I do. You're just pissed because I won't talk to you about my past, about my feelings and shit. I don't have to do that, Bea. It's not a rule.'

His feelings and *shit*. His dismissive tone was nails on a chalkboard. 'No, of course it's not. But you know everything about me, and I know nothing about you. Do you know how vulnerable that makes me feel?'

'It was your choice to tell me your shit!'

That was the second time he'd used the swear word as a euphemism for her feelings. 'It was my choice, I'll give you that. It's also my choice to slam on the brakes.'

He scowled at her. 'Are you thinking that if you withhold sex, I'll cave? Newsflash, I've been having sex for more than half my life, and nobody has cracked me yet. You're not that – *fuck*…'

'Special?' she filled in the missed word hanging between them.

He linked his hands behind his head. 'Why do women always do this? Why do you start off saying it's a fling, that it means nothing, then change course halfway through? Why couldn't we have had this, and maybe, when I made it to London, we could've hooked up again? Why can it never be simple?'

His voice was rough with frustration, but she heard the undernote of confusion.

'I can't speak for anyone else, Gib, but having you drop

in and out of my life isn't good enough for me. I want more.'

'What does more even mean?' he demanded, putting his hands on the bed and leaning forward. The muscles in his arms bunched, and the veins on his arms lifted. He looked tough, dangerous and demanding but so very hot.

'What are you asking from me? Do you want a commitment? A ring? Babies? A future? Good God, we've only known each other for two weeks. Nobody makes crazy decisions like that in so short a time!'

Cass and Nadia did…

She shook her head. 'I'm not that needy, Gib, and you're the one who's looking too far into the future.'

'Then what the hell is your problem?'

Her problem. Yet again, she was being blamed for something she didn't do, for something she wanted, for putting her needs first. Well, to hell with that. This was her heart, her life and if she didn't protect it, who would? She had to write her own story, she refused to hand over that power to anyone else.

'My problem is that you think sex and a couple of laughs is enough. That it's fine for me to be emotionally vulnerable but not you. That it's OK for me to feel exposed, one giant nerve ending, but for you to be closed down and shut off. You think it's quite fine for there to be a different set of rules for me. If you didn't want me probing and poking around in your head, then you should've stayed out of mine!'

He rubbed his jaw with his palm and covered his mouth with his hand.

'I don't think it's OK for me to confide in you and you not to do the same. I don't want a sex and surface-based relationship where we exchange a few text messages, and you drop in and out of my life. I've had a bad relationship before, Gib. My ex used me, and if I agreed to what you suggested earlier, you flying in and out of my life, I'd be allowing you to use me, too.'

'That's not fair!'

She lifted one shoulder to her ear. 'You'd get what you needed from me – great sex, a couple of laughs, some superficial conversation – and then you'd return to your eighty-hour work weeks until you could spare the time to see me again.'

Not happening.

'I deserve more than that, Gib. My parents put their needs before mine, and so did my ex. This time I'm putting my needs first. I want a guy, I *deserve* a guy who's there a good portion of the time, someone to share my life with, to give me good advice when I need it, to hold me when my world is falling apart. But I also deserve to be with a guy who trusts me enough, who thinks I'm strong enough, to hold up *his* sky when it's about to fall on him. A guy who will talk to me, seek my advice when he needs it, who needs my support. I want someone in the storm with me, not standing outside of it, safe. Bottom line, I'm not prepared to settle for imbalance anymore, Gibson.'

He slowly stood up, his eyes tumultuous. 'I can't give you that, Bea.'

'I know.'

She threw back the covers and walked around the bed to where he stood. Surprising him, she wound her arms around his waist and placed her forehead on his chest. His hands stayed at his side, and he was board-stiff. She hugged him tight and stood on his toes to kiss his cheek.

'Thank you for the best almost two weeks, Gib.' She remembered the boy he'd been and dredged up a smile. 'You were definitely more fun this time around.'

'And, this time, there's nothing easy about leaving you,' he softly said.

Bea nodded. Holding her head up high, she walked into the bathroom and closed the door behind her.

And then she started to cry.

While tears ran down her face, and pain soaked into her skin, Bea held onto the thought that when she was done crying, when the pain became a little more manageable, she'd start picking up the pieces of her life and start fitting them together. Some pieces wouldn't fit and would have to be turfed, others could be reshaped.

A new Bea would, hopefully, emerge, better and stronger than before. She'd done this before – recovered, started over, walked down a new path, and regrown her heart. She could do it again. She had to. She had no choice.

She'd gather the pieces of her sliced and diced heart and tack them back together again. It would be smaller than before, but tougher. In time, months or years, so would she.

She hoped.

Late Sunday afternoon, Bea sat on the wall of the esplanade and watched the sun go down. Was it less vibrant tonight? The yellows weren't as rich, the pinks and purples a little faded, the orange and reds wishy-washy. To be fair, everything seemed muted on the island since Gib left yesterday. The sun had lost a lot of its warmth, the wind was colder and brisker, and the sea choppier. It was like Gib had taken all the colour and intensity with him.

It had only been a day, but she missed him. God, so much. But although she was walking around with a hole in her soul, she knew she'd made the right decision. She couldn't settle for less than what she needed, and she couldn't put his needs above her own. If he'd been willing to compromise, to try and work on his reticence, if he'd even *suggested* he was willing to try, she might've backed down a little, but she hadn't meant enough to him to even make that much of an effort.

Her fault for falling in love with him. So stupid.

In between bouts of tears, she'd spent a lot of time thinking about her life, and deciding what she could, and should, take responsibility for. Had her father stepped up to the plate and not been a self-involved git, she wouldn't have rearranged her world to make people comfortable at the expense of her happiness. She was done with that. She was worthy of more.

While she was thinking about useless creatures, she thought she might as well work through any lingering issues she had with Gerry and her mum.

Surprisingly, she didn't find any. She wasn't, in any

way, responsible for Gerry ending up in her mother's bed. In no way, shape or form did she push Lou and Gerry together. And Lou chose Gerry over her *daughter*, and also used their sick love triangle for publicity. She didn't miss either of them, and her life was better without their toxic presence.

Neither of them deserved another atom of her energy. Ever.

Bea stretched her arms and rolled her head, feeling the muscles in her neck stretch and lengthen. The sunset was fading, and the temperature dropping. She should think about eating a proper meal; she'd done nothing but drink coffee since she'd watched Gib drive off in his rental, taking her heart with him…

No, she wasn't going to think about him anymore. She was heading back to London tomorrow, she, Reena and Golly were on the same mid-morning flight. She'd be in her flat by lunchtime, and she could get stuck into work in the afternoon.

She imagined herself in her two-bedroomed flat. Her double bed just squeezed into the bigger of the two bedrooms, and her desk into the small study, which looked out onto a frankly ugly steel and glass building.

The weather would be grim, rainy and cold, and the days would be considerably shorter. She didn't want to go back to London. She wanted to stay here a little longer, and not only because she wanted to cement her memories of Gib. This was her happy place, where she felt she could breathe. But the lovely days of Autumn were over, the days were growing colder and Santorini in winter was as miserable as wet, dreary London.

Bea felt a blanket on her shoulders and looked up to see Golly standing behind her. She managed to smile at her godmother, and murmured her thanks.

'Working out the world's problems, Bea-darling?'

'Just mine.' Bea patted the wall and Golly sat, crossed her legs and pulled a cigarillo and a lighter from her pocket. She lit up and pulled in a long drag. The smell of the cigar was deeply comforting.

After a few minutes of comfortable silence, Bea spoke. 'I think I want to step out from behind Parker Kane.'

Golly, damn her, didn't even look a little surprised. 'I thought you would. The best way to do that is to hire a PR person to manage that for you.'

'Do you know someone?' Stupid question, of course she did. Golly knew *everyone*.

'Yep.' Golly crossed one leg over the other. 'What prompted this decision?'

She shrugged. 'I'm just finished with things that don't serve me anymore. I think I'd like to do book signings, go to conferences, be a little more public. Yes, I'll be linked to Lou initially, but maybe the PR people can negate that.'

'I'm sure they could.'

'Also, I'm cutting Lou out of my life. I won't have *any* contact with her from now on.' Bea watched a speedboat skim across the caldera, lights blazing.

She wanted to *live* her life.

She wanted to stop hibernating, she wanted to make

new friends. Maybe, in time, if she could get past her feelings for Gib, even start dating. For the last five years she'd lived a small, quiet life, and now she wanted heat, laughter and passion. She wanted to *feel*, even if those feelings hurt. At least then she could say she was living rather than existing.

'Bout bloody time, Pip said in her head.

'Merle wants a rewrite of book nine. My manuscript wasn't … great,' she said, still a little embarrassed.

'She copied me in on the email.' Golly shrugged, not fazed. 'It happens. Do the rewrite and, for God's sake, get it right this time.'

Bea just managed to stop herself from making a sarcastic reply, something along the lines of 'yeah, because that wasn't an option I'd considered'.

'Oh, and you're fired, Golly. Making that call to the PR people will be your last act as my agent,' she stated.

Golly grinned, showing the smudge of red lipstick on her incisor. 'Fan-bloody-tastic.' Bea saw the relief in her eyes and watched as tension seeped out of her. *Shit*. She should've done this years ago and allowed Golly the freedom to enjoy her retirement.

'I'm sorry if representing me was a drag, Gols,' she said, her voice quiet. 'Thank you for guiding and supporting me.'

'If you cry, I *will* pinch you,' Golly muttered, but Bea caught the tears in her eyes. Golly hated feeling vulnerable and growled and griped when emotions got the better of her. Just like Gib did.

Golly stubbed out her cigarillo on the wall. 'Navy

Caddell would be a good agent for you,' she stated and lifted her palm when Bea started to protest. 'Navy is young, hungry and passionate about your work. His agency is new, he's only repping a handful of people, and he is said to be brilliant at forecasting trends. Editorially, he's not bad, either.' Golly leaned forward, brown eyes shrewd. 'He's got the family drive and ambition, and he'll take you further than most.'

Bea wrinkled her nose. That might be true, but could she work with Gib's cousin and best friend? Navy would be the link to what she couldn't have.

Besides, the man had seen her boobs, for God's sake!

'Now, what the fuck are you going to do about that boy, Bea-darling?'

Bea released a heavy sigh. 'There's nothing to *do*, Golly. It was only ever going to be a fling, and he told me not to expect anything more.'

Golly threw her head back and stared at the sky. 'Dear God, give me strength.'

'You don't believe in love and monogamy and happy-ever-afters, Golly,' Bea pointed out. 'You're strictly a happy-for-this-moment type.'

Golly looked at her. 'But that's me, Bea. I like variety and adventure, the thrill of falling for someone, the tension and the passion. But you, boring creature that you are, need a forever person, someone to grow old with. And the two of you could be very happy together. You should run after him.'

Now those were words she'd never expected to hear

from her treat-'em-mean, keep-'em-keen godmother. 'A), I absolutely will not, and B, the last thing Gib wants is a committed relationship. We only met two weeks ago, there's *nothing* to *make* work.'

'Apart from the fact that you two could power North America with all the energy buzzing between you. I knew you two would hit it off.'

'How?' Bea asked. 'We could've looked at each other and wanted to hurl. And was it really necessary to make us share a bed?'

Golly tapped the side of her nose. 'Call it instinct, but I knew he would be good to you and for you. I don't want you to be alone anymore, Bea-darling.'

'He can't give me what I *need*, Golly. And after putting my needs aside for my dad, Gerry and even for Lou, I won't do that again. I have to live in the world the way it is, not the way I want it to be. I can't make Lou less of a witch, I can't change the past, I won't ever understand my father. And I can't make Gib love me. All I can do is control my reaction to whatever happens to me.'

She let out a breath.

'So I'm letting Gib go. I'm sorry he can't be with me, but I can't force him to love me, to give me what I need. I can only be grateful for the time we spent together.'

Golly picked up her phone, lighter and pack of cigarillos from the wall next to her and sighed. 'There's no getting away from it, your generation makes everything far too complicated with your desire to understand your emotions and all that self-improvement bullshit. Just shag the boy, and keep shagging him until you get sick of shagging him and want to shag someone else.'

Ah, to live in Golly's uncomplicated world.

Golly patted her knee. 'In the morning I'll call a PR Agency on your behalf, but now I'm going to have a couple of G&T's and then a lovely bottle of Bordeaux.'

'Golly, you smoke and drink far too much,' Bea quietly reminded her. 'And despite you being an enormous pain my arse, I want you around for as long as possible.'

'Another issue I have with your generation is that you have access to far too much information, and it's made you scared and tissue-paper soft. Listen, I died once when I was five, and my mother told me to just walk it off.'

Bea rolled her eyes at her majestic embellishment. 'Ten-four, dinosaur.'

'So damn cheeky.' Golly looked around, frowning. 'Now where's my fucking phone?'

Bea sighed. 'You're holding it, Gols.'

Chapter Sixteen

G ib walked into his and Navy's favourite place in Nashville, feeling like death warmed up. The last place he wanted to be was in a bar, and he looked around hoping Navy had managed to secure a booth. No such luck; his cousin sat at the end of the hand-crafted bar, a beer in front of him. In his faded jeans and loose T-shirt, Navy looked relaxed.

In comparison, Gib felt like day-old roadkill. He'd come straight from the airport after spending two days in New York and a week in Hong Kong, with a stop off in Berlin on his return, all the while trying to talk himself out of making a detour to London to see Bea. But nothing had changed, and she'd made her feelings clear… She wanted more, he couldn't give it to her, and they were at a stalemate.

He dug his index finger and thumb into the corners of his eyes, trying to rub away the gritty feeling.

He'd managed about two hours of sleep on the ten-hour

flight, in which he'd dreamed of walking through his house in Nashville with Bea, her commenting on the white walls and stark furniture. He told her she could paint the place lime green with pink spots, as long as she stayed. She could do anything she wanted as long as she slept in the same bed as him.

Maybe his subconscious was telling him he only wanted one bed for the two of them for the rest of their lives. But you didn't plan the rest of your life after knowing someone for less than two weeks. That was a dumbass move, right? Even if he could open up to her – and be emotionally vulnerable – the next few months of his life would be insanely busy, and he'd be bouncing between Hong Kong, LA, and New York, and didn't know when next he'd be in London. Or even in Nashville. Even if he *could* give her an emotional commitment, what else could he offer her? Long stretches alone, with him stumbling in after fourteen- or sixteen-hour days. Sex, and him leaving early to catch a plane to go wherever Caddell needed him next. None of that was fair on Bea.

But memories of her were the mental equivalent of a chipped tooth. He couldn't stop going there.

He was a cautious guy, someone who didn't jump into situations easily or quickly, yet in just a few days he'd slept with a woman, heard her secrets, opened up a little, fallen deeper than he'd planned, had some soul-shocking conversations and split up with her.

They'd gone from zero to one hundred in just a few seconds. Their relationship was Formula One fast.

'Gib!'

He lifted his head at Navy calling his name and wondered how long he'd been stood by the door, thinking. Shrugging out of his jacket, he pulled down his tie and ordered a whisky from the barman before clasping Navy's lifted hand and giving him a quick shoulder bump.

'You OK?' Navy asked as he sat down. It had only taken Navy a few seconds to clock something was wrong.

'Yes, no. I don't know.'

'Right. I feel so much closer to you now.' Navy lifted his beer bottle to his mouth. 'Is this about Bea?'

There was no point in denying it, Navy would nag until he talked the problem through. He might as well just get it over with. 'Yes.'

'So many words…'

Gib narrowed his eyes at his sarcasm. 'We were sleeping together, it's now over.'

'You've slept with many women before, but I've never seen you looking like this. What did you do?'

'Why do you think it was my fault?' Gib demanded and signalled for another whisky. The first went down well, and he had a pleasantly warm sensation in his gut. Nice, because he hadn't felt warm since he left the island.

'Because you're you,' Navy replied. 'Let me guess, she wanted more, and you told her you couldn't give it to her.'

Gib stared at him. 'That's pretty specific.'

'But true. You only get this morose when you find a girl you like, then you sabotage it.'

'Bullshit.'

Navy started to tick items off his fingers. 'Jenny, senior year of high school. You were mad about her, but you called it quits. Hayley, final year of college. You guys slept together for a year, but she bailed because you refused to call her your girlfriend or introduce her to my dad. Hannah, six years ago. She saw through your can't-commit crap straight away and called it over after a month. She wanted a family and wasn't prepared to wait for you to get with the programme.'

Gib shook his head. 'I'm not sure whether I should be impressed or creeped out by how much you've remembered about my love life.'

Navy tapped his bottle with his index finger. 'I remember the ones you fell for.'

'I haven't fallen for Bea.' Such bullshit, but he needed to put it out there. Maybe if he said it out loud, he would start believing his own spin.

He dropped his head and rubbed his forehead with his fingers. Jesus, this was hard. He'd never met anyone as amazing as her. She got him on levels no one had ever before, and he understood her. And let's not forget that being in her arms, naked or clothed, was where he most wanted to be.

But he wanted her on *his* terms, not hers. Just like he'd wanted the others.

'She wants a proper, messy, emotional, honest relationship,' Gib quietly stated, without lifting his head. 'I want to keep it … sanitised, I guess.'

'Because of your mom?'

Gib jerked his head up, shocked by Navy's quiet words. It was the first time in nearly twenty years that Navy had mentioned Gib's mother. He swallowed, trying to force the lump in his throat down. 'Why mention my mom?' He hesitated. 'What do you know?'

Navy's broad shoulders lifted.

'Before my folks divorced, I remember my parents talking about yours, specifically your mom. They said she needed to lighten up and get a life.'

They hadn't been wrong. He shifted in his chair. It felt wrong to discuss his dead mother like this. Then again, Navy was his brother in every way that counted.

'I want to talk to you about it, but the words just won't come out of my mouth,' he admitted, wrapping his hand around the glass the bartender put in front of him. His sigh came from the deepest parts of him. 'Bea knows there are things I'm keeping back, she thinks I don't trust her, or that she's not important enough to me to share my past with her. But, Jesus, if I can't even talk to *you* about my parents, how can I talk to her?'

Navy gently tapped the edge of his bottle against the bar. 'Then maybe it's time to get a professional involved, bud.'

Fuck, he couldn't think of anything worse. 'I tried that, remember?'

'You were sixteen and grieving, and you have distance now,' Navy pointed out. 'I also think you need to ProCon it.'

ProCon was a tool Hugh had taught them both. When

329

faced with a difficult decision, they should make a list of the pros and cons and see which column won. Navy pointed his bottle at him. 'Give me the pros for moving on from Bea, not going to therapy, to keeping life the same as it was before you went to Greece.'

'Do we have to do this now?' Gib asked, conscious of a tiny whine in his voice.

'*Now*. Go.'

OK, *shit*. 'Pros for staying single… It's easy, and it's what I know.' He thought some more. 'I can work without guilt, I don't have to think about a partner and her needs. My time won't be split, and I can devote myself to Caddell.'

Navy made a production of yawning. Yeah, message received: he was boring. 'Cons?'

There was only one he could think of, and it was huge. He picked up a coaster, rolled it between his fingers and spun it around. He scratched his cheek and pushed his hand through his hair.

'Stop fiddling and give a con, Gibson. And don't bullshit me, I know you have one.'

Fuck, he was going to make him say it. '*Iwon'thaveBeainmylife.*'

Navy, the fucker, put his hand behind his ear and leaned forward. 'Sorry, what was that?'

Bastard. 'I won't have Bea in my life.'

Satisfaction glinted in his eyes. 'And how big a problem is that for you?' Navy quietly asked.

He forced himself to lift his eyes up and look at Navy. 'Fucking big,' he reluctantly admitted.

'Big enough for you to do something about it?'

The ten-billion-dollar question. 'Yeah, big enough for me to do something about it.'

Navy used the bar counter as a makeshift drum. '*Excellent*. Because, as Tolkien said, "I would rather spend one lifetime with you than face all the ages of this world alone."'

'Oh, *fuck off*. Seriously, I *will* put your head down a toilet.'

———

Six weeks after her birthday bash, Golly decided she needed a Santorini reunion party and bought tickets for her, Reena, Bea, the Two Jacks, Cassie and Nadia to fly to Fira. They arrived late on Friday night, and spent Saturday relaxing, with Nadia offering to make pizzas in the wood-fired oven on the esplanade for supper. It was a bit cold for outdoor entertaining, but they huddled around the huge blaze in the fire pit, drinking red wine and catching up.

Due to Bea's insane schedule these past few weeks – after coming out as Parker Kane she'd run from print interviews to podcast interviews, to book signings – she'd barely had time to eat, and she'd lost a bit of weight.

No, that was a bit dramatic. She'd had time, everybody did, but she didn't *feel* like eating. Her tastebuds hadn't worked properly since Gib had left Santorini. But it was lovely to see Cass and Nadia again; she'd spoken to them, but hadn't seen them. They'd been in New York, and Bea wanted to ask if they'd been working for Gib, but even saying his name hurt.

She missed him. So damn much.

A Santorini reunion without Gib was a ridiculous notion. It was like a puzzle with a gaping hole in the middle. Oh, wait, that was *her* life.

'Golly says that the press attention has died down, Bea-darling,' Jack said, a whisky in his hand. He sat next to Reena, who was studying a racing form.

'It was a bit mad when the press releases first went out.' Bea leant against one of the pergola's pillars. There'd been a few mentions of Lou and Gerry's affair, but nothing dramatic.

Golly, and Gib, were right when they said her imagination would be worse than reality.

'And you have a new agent?' Cass asked. 'Gib's cousin? Is he as sexy as Gib?'

Nobody could *ever* be as sexy as Gib. 'He's not my type,' Bea told Cass.

Cass snorted. 'I looked him up online. Masculine and ripped is every heterosexual woman's type.'

Not hers. 'Why did you go with Navy Caddell, Bea?' Jacqui quietly asked.

'I had meetings with a few agents, but I didn't gel with any of them,' Bea explained. 'Then Navy video-called me, told me nobody would be better for me than him, and I would be a fool not to sign with him.'

And he said it all in a lazy drawl, and with this twinkle in his eye.

Cass's eyes widened. 'And what did you say to that?'

'I didn't have a chance to say much. He told me he loved my books, and he has ideas for my spin-off series.'

She didn't tell them that to get her to take his call he'd sent her a basket of luxury goods – champagne, expensive chocolates and high-end, including Creed, toiletries. In amongst the goodies was a printed list with the heading: A Writer's Guide to Video Calls with Their Agent. There was just one bullet point on the list.

Are you suitably dressed?

On the back of the list, she found a jotted note from Navy.

Gib said I wasn't to mention it, but I disagreed. We could wait until we're wrinkled to laugh about it, or we could start now. Let's talk.

And with that, her embarrassment faded away. She'd had a few calls with Navy since signing with him a week ago, but she'd yet to find the courage to ask how Gib was, where he was and, crucially, was he missing her?

And Navy, damn him, didn't volunteer any information, either.

'Bea-darling, I'm a bit chilly. I think I left my green silk pashmina in the cottage earlier, do you think you could run down and get it for me?' Golly half turned to look at her.

She didn't remember seeing a pashmina in the cottage, but she was so tired – physically, mentally, and emotionally – and the small things didn't always register. She'd go look for it, as she could do with five minutes alone.

She walked towards the cottage, her movement

sluggish. Her heart and head ached, and she wanted Gib's arms around her, telling her it would be OK. Because as long as he wasn't in her life, nothing was OK. All right, mildly dramatic, but she didn't think she'd ever feel whole again. She'd thought she could do this, be without him. She'd taken the high ground, without realising how incredibly lonely it was. So what if he couldn't open up, if she couldn't mean as much to him as he did to her? He liked her, respected her, was thoughtful and considerate and so very good in bed. Maybe a little of something was better than a lot of nothing.

It had to be. She needed him and would take anything she could get, and her pride could go to hell. She pulled her phone from the back pocket of her jeans and dialled, holding her breath as she waited for him to answer.

'Bea-baby.'

She closed her eyes, letting his voice roll over her and fill the empty spots inside her. But only being with him could fill the massive, Gib-sized hole in her heart.

'We're at Golly's Folly and everyone important is here, but you're not and—' Should she say this? Why not? She was so damn sick of pretending that being apart wasn't ripping her apart. 'And I miss you. I wish you were here.'

He waited a beat, before speaking again. 'Why do you want me there?'

He was going to make her explain? Well, OK, then. 'Because I'm miserable without you.'

She stopped and rubbed her fingers across her forehead. Too much? Too soon? 'Sorry,' she said when he didn't reply.

'I didn't mean to dump that on you, but it's been a long day.'

Six weeks that felt like six thousand.

'Look, I really want to keep talking to you,' Gib replied, 'but I need to do something first. So fetch whatever Golly's asked for, and I'll speak to you in five minutes, maybe even less.'

He disconnected and Bea stared at her phone. *Crap*. It was Saturday morning in the States, and he was probably working. And something, or someone else, needed his attention. It was a reminder, one she didn't need, that his work always came first.

There wasn't much space for her in his life, and she knew she'd never be more important than his work. But she didn't think she cared anymore. She just wanted to be with him. In any way she could. If he gave her the smallest hint he'd welcome a visit from her, she'd go to Fira and catch the first flight out.

Bea bit down on her lip, wishing she could stay in the cottage, curl up in the bed she and Gib had shared. But that would upset Golly, who'd paid a hefty amount to get them back to Santorini for their brief reunion. She'd grab the pashmina, go back, eat as much pizza as she could, and stay an hour, maybe two, then bolt.

She looked down at her phone, it had been three minutes since Gib said he'd call her back…

Bea walked into the dark cottage, not bothering to switch on a light as she could see well enough by the light of the moon. She couldn't see the pashmina anywhere. Wait, didn't Gib say something about fetching something for Golly? He *did*. She frowned. How did he know…

'Took you long enough to twig.'

She looked down at her phone, checking they weren't still connected. Nope. Joy, wild and fast and free, clobbered her, in the best way possible. Her heart triple-timed when she saw him leaning against the doorframe to the bedroom, arms folded, and one ankle crossed over the other.

'You're here.' He wore dark jeans, trendy trainers on his big feet, and a white T-shirt under a navy jacket. He'd cut his hair, and his stubble was neatly trimmed. He looked… God, he looked *fantastic*.

'Yep. And you're too far away' He walked over to her and, without warning, he bent his knees, put his shoulder to her stomach and lifted her up and over his shoulder. Bea squealed and then laughed.

Gib. Was. *Here.*

Gib walked through to the bedroom and dumped her on the big bed. He loomed over her, curled his hand around the back of her neck and rested his forehead against hers. 'That was, bar none, the longest six weeks of my life. I can't be apart from you for that long ever again, Bea-baby.'

She had to kiss him, right now, so she lifted her mouth to his, her body sighing when he gathered her close. She fell into the kiss, completely forgetting Golly's request, that Nadia was making pizza.

She pulled back a long while later. 'Did Golly even need a pashmina?'

He laughed. 'I wanted an excuse to get you here alone

and, as always, she was happy to engage in a little subterfuge.'

She would think about Golly's involvement later. All that was important was that Gib was here. Joy, relief, and contentment flooded her system. All was well with her world. In his arms was where she wanted to be, his mouth the only one she wanted to kiss. With him, her heart puzzle was no longer missing its most important piece.

Gib tasted of coffee and mints and smelt like citrus and sea-scented air. Powerful and gentle, his tongue twisted around hers, every stroke telling her how much he missed this, how much he missed *her*. It was a *you-are-mine* kiss, a *missed-you-so-much* kiss and Bea understood she wasn't the only one who'd been utterly miserable.

They might not have known each other long, but that was all the time her heart, and hopefully his, needed to know they were meant to be together. How, she didn't know. But they were smart people, they'd figure it out.

Gib pulled back and moved his mouth to her ear. 'I want you so goddamn much, but if we carry on, we might set this bed alight.'

Bea pushed her hand under his jacket and placed her hand over his heart. 'I'm willing to take that risk.'

Gib smiled, his thumb drifting over her bottom lip. 'I can't think of anything I'd like to do more, but—'

'If you're about to tell me that you can't stay, I swear I will … I will … I'll *scream*.'

He grinned. 'Oh, you're going to scream, but not

because I'm leaving,' he promised her, lust in his eyes. 'I was going to say that we need to talk.'

'Oh.' She wrinkled her nose, unsure. He might want her, but that didn't mean he wanted her full time, or on a permanent basis. Maybe he was going to remind her that they couldn't be anything more than bed-buddies, or friends-with-benefits or some other horseshit.

'I still need more,' she blurted. 'I'm not going to push you away again, but it's only fair that you know.'

Instead of replying, Gib pulled her upright and sat down next to her on the bed.

'This isn't working, Bea-baby.'

Bea felt like she'd just been kicked off the Burj Khalifa skyscraper. Man, this landing was going to hurt. The ground rushed up to meet her and she tensed, bracing for the collision.

Gib's thumb rubbed the top of her hand. 'We need to find a way to be together, to see more of each other. I'm useless without you.'

Her downward dive was halted by his words, and she hovered there, inches from the ground, trying to make sense of what he'd said.

'I know you want me to open up, to be emotionally accessible, to talk about my past...' He looked up at the ceiling. 'I'm trying, Bea.'

She frowned. 'I don't understand.'

'Look, I had a very complicated relationship with my mom, and with my dad, I guess. She wanted everything from me, all the time. With her, I felt like I was an experiment. She was a professor of psychology in Berlin before she married my dad, and there were no boundaries in our family. She was relentless in wanting to know everything about me, all the time. As a kid, I learned to shut down, and to protect my thoughts and my privacy.'

She could see him struggling to find the right words and she put her hand on his cheek. 'Gib…'

'I've been working with a therapist, in person and online trying to get past that, to break that habit,' Gib told her, his voice ragged. 'I want to talk to you about it, tell you what happened, how it shaped me, but I don't know how. Not yet, anyway.'

Just the fact that he was trying, that he'd gone to the effort of doing that made her heart sing. Maybe he was only doing it for her, but she knew getting professional help would benefit Gib in the long run. How could it not?

'I so appreciate that, Gib. Thank you. I know it can't be easy.'

He winced. 'Setting my hair on fire would be more fun,' he told her. Then he shrugged. 'But if it can help me work through some shit, make our relationship richer, bring us closer, then I'm up for it. There's nothing I wouldn't do for you, Bea-baby.'

Her heart did a zoom around her body. God, this man. He was *everything*.

He pushed his hand into her hair. 'I've decided to cut down on my travelling and to trust my expensive, very smart VPs a little more. You can work anywhere, and to an extent, so can I. I know London is home for you, and Golly is, mostly, there, but maybe we can split our time between London and Nashville. And spend our summers here, on Santorini. Maybe you can travel with me occasionally.'

Bea held up her hand, palm facing him. 'Whoa, hold on. I'm trying to make sense of this… Are you saying that you *want* us to be together?'

'This weekend, getting everyone here, was my idea. I wanted to surprise you.' He raked a shaking hand through his hair. 'And, yes, I want us to be together. I've been fucking *desolate* without you.'

Bea saw the anguish in his eyes and noticed that he looked drawn and gaunt, and not half as confident as he usually did. He looked like he said he felt: dejected. It was weird to see him so expressive. Before, he always seemed to be in complete command of himself and his emotions.

He didn't look like the successful businessman, the charismatic CEO she met on the road two months ago. He looked like a man who was in love, someone who had no place to put his love. He wanted her and that made her feel feminine and fantastic, powerful and potent. But would it last? She was just a normal, rather average woman who spent most of her time in the make-believe world populated by an unruly gang of pre-teens, someone who was only adventurous when she tossed black letters onto a white screen. He was hero material, she was the woman who went to work in yoga pants and slippers, her hair in a messy bun, glasses on her nose.

'OK, I'm dying here,' Gib said, his voice shaking. 'I've just told you that I'm crazy about you, but you're just sitting there looking like I smacked you with a two-by-four. Have you changed your mind about me and what you want?'

The two-by-four comment was a pretty accurate analogy, actually. She did feel like he'd knocked her off her feet.

'Acceptable responses are... "*I missed you too*", or "*I want to be with you, too*". The perfect response would be "*I'm crazy in love with you, too*".'

Her mouth fell open again. 'Are you? In love with me?' she asked, needing to make sure her ears were working properly, and her imagination wasn't playing tricks on her.

'Yeah.'

'Why?'

His eyes filled with emotion. 'Why do I love you? How could I *not* love you, Bea? You're real and strong, and smart and imaginative and you have a heart as big as the sky. I want to spend the rest of my life with you, waking up with you and going to sleep with you, having children with you. You're ... you're... This is going to sound stupid, but you fill in the blanks.'

'*I* fill in the blanks?'

'I have money, success, whatever the hell that is, and I love my job. I thought that was enough until I met you. Then I realised there were all these missing things in my life – love and acceptance and trust – and you gave them back to me.'

'Oh.'

'That's all you can say?' Gib muttered, running his hand down his face. 'God, I need a drink.'

Bea blinked back her tears and handed him a watery smile. 'I need *you*,' she told him softly.

His eyes narrowed, his entire focus on her. 'Are you going to expand on that?'

She bit the inside of her lip, trying to find the right words. 'Do you remember that first sunset we watched, the night of the cocktail party?'

He shrugged. 'Sort of. I mean, I had my eyes on you most of the time, but I remember it was good.'

Bea smiled. 'It was this riot of pinks and purples and golds and reds, streaky and stunning, probably the best sunset I've seen, and I've seen a lot of sunsets on this island.' She tipped her head. 'You don't know where I'm going with this, do you?'

'Haven't a freaking clue,' he admitted.

'You dropped into my life like that sunset, tossing colour across the sky. Everything with you is bolder and brighter. Food tastes better, music is sweeter, and my words come easier. When you're in my life, it's in technicolour, and when you're not, it's like those old sepia movies, the music scratchy and the words stilted.'

He looked at her for a long time, and Bea held his stare, letting him see every emotion in her eyes. 'Pretty words, Bea, and I appreciate them. But not the ones I most want to hear.'

She didn't move, didn't blink. 'I love you. Please can we be together?'

Gib responded by cupping her face and sliding his lips across hers. 'Yes. Let's do that.'

She held his wrists, thrilled his were the eyes she'd look into for the rest of her life. 'Glad that's sorted,' she told him. '*Now* can we set this bed on fire?'

He kissed her again before pulling back to frown at her. 'Are you seriously asking me to pass up the opportunity to eat Nadia's wood-fired pizza?'

She grinned at him and lifted her sweater and shirt up and over her head. His eyes fell to her chest, and he dragged a finger over her lace-covered nipple. 'Fuck food. We can live off love, sex and fresh air.'

He lifted her onto his lap and held her close. 'God, I do love you, Bea-baby. We're going to be so damn happy.'

'I already am,' she told him, kissing his jaw. 'I can't wait to share *my* bed with you again, Gib.'

'Bea, I can't wait to share *everything* with you.'

Epilogue

Standing on the now almost empty beach, Gib watched Bea in the shallows, their three-year-old daughter Molly-Cate standing between her legs. Their eight-year-old son, Bhodi, did a duck dive into the clear Aegean water and popped up a minute later. He was, Bea and Gib were convinced, part fish, part seal.

Bodhi ran out of the water and shook himself, spraying water over Bea and his little sister. Bea pretended to swat him, but Mary-Cate actually did, her small hand connecting with his thigh. Bodhi simply picked her up, tossed her over his shoulder – he'd seen Gib do the same with Bea often enough to learn the technique – and jogged down the beach with his sister bouncing on his shoulder.

His son was the spitting image of him at the same age, and he recalled those halcyon days when he'd first visited Greece. If he told his younger self that he would go on to marry the solemn little girl he was made to share a room with, pre-teen Gib would've laughed in his face. Ten years after re-meeting Bea, he couldn't conceive of a life without her at the centre of it.

His world turned because of her.

It had taken some time for him to tell her about his childhood, but she eventually heard all of it. Bea, because she was Bea and wonderful, was empathetic and a good listener, but she didn't analyse the subject to death.

Bea caught his eye and waved. He walked down to her, kissed her mouth and swung his baby girl, who'd escaped from her brother, into his arms. Because she was a Daddy's girl, she immediately pushed her face into his neck. Bea took his free hand and squeezed. 'You were looking quite solemn, darling. Something on your mind?'

'I was just thinking about the wild boy and the book-reading girl we were.'

She laughed. 'Young me would be disgusted at the thought of marrying you! You didn't read.'

'And you read too much,' he countered, dropping a kiss on her forehead. 'Thank God for Golly's matchmaking.'

Bea grinned. 'Please don't tell her that,' she begged. 'She's impossible enough as it is. God, you'd think she's the first person in the world to turn eighty.'

'What's she done now?' he asked, as they walked along the beach. Bea was, yet again, and with Cass and Nadia's help, planning an epic birthday party.

'She's scatty and demanding and keeps changing her mind. One minute she wants a blowout party, the next she wants to hire a yacht. She wants only vegan food, then only seafood. If she invites this person, she has to invite that person.'

'Threaten her with afternoon tea at The Savoy, Bea-darling. You once told her that's how we'd celebrate her eightieth.'

'Golly's fucking impossible,' Mary-Cate said, in her piping, but oh-so-clear voice.

Bea pointed at him at the same time he pointed at her, each laughingly blaming the other for their daughter's bad language. 'We really have to clean up our act,' she told him and went on to lecture Mary-Cate about using adult words.

Bea – the love of his life – was more like her godmother than he'd expected. Being in love, maybe even being with him, flicked a switch in her, and she morphed into a bold, confident, occasionally crazy person. Someone he loved with every fibre of his being. For the past ten years, they'd spent every summer at Golly's Folly with her family and his flying in and out depending on their schedules.

Whether they were in London, Nashville or at Golly's Folly, she left scraps of paper all over the house – *Pip has his first crush on an older woman. Learn to play poker. Hugh likes it. Get Bodhi's hair cut* —her version of a to-do list. He'd learned not to speak to her when she was in author land, as she never remembered a damn thing he said. He instructed the housekeeper they'd hired to fill the fridge with healthy snack options because Bea would live on doughnuts and canned cheese if given the choice.

Best of all, she loved him. And God, he loved her. She

was everything he wanted and, possibly, far more than he deserved. She was the beat of his heart…

Bea turned, and said heart stuttered as he noticed her hand on her lower belly. Baby number three was on the way, and he couldn't bloody wait. His woman, his children, they'd created the family he'd never had.

Bea rested her temple against his bicep as they walked hand in hand down the beach. 'Do you know about Admiral Edward Russell's Cocktail party?'

He shook his head, used to her rapid change of subjects. 'Who's he and when was that?'

'In 1694, he was the First Lord of the Admiralty and was heavily involved in the Glorious Revolution.' No idea what that was, but if he asked, he'd get a history lesson and it would take an age for her to get back to her original point. Not that he minded listening to her…

'Anyway, this admiral held a party at his Covent Garden home. He emptied one of his fountains and filled it with brandy and wine and lemons and sugar. Basically, he made an enormous cocktail, and it took his guests a week to drink the fountain dry.'

Gib winced, immediately connecting the dots. 'Golly's latest idea?'

'She's going to have the courtyard fountain drained, scrubbed, disinfected and re-lined, and has commissioned a mixologist to create a cocktail in her honour.'

Oh, *God.*

Bea covered their daughter's ears with her hands. 'She's calling it Golly's Fucking Folly.'

Of course she was. Because nothing else would make any sense.

Acknowledgments

To my lovely readers, thank you for sharing your precious time with Bea, Gib and Golly! (She'd haunt me if I left her out!) I hope you loved reading *One Bed* as much as I loved writing it.

Twenty-five years ago, before we had children, Vaughan and I were lucky enough to have a Greek island holiday, and Santorini was a highlight of that trip. It's still the best holiday we ever had. I'll never forget the warm, stunning sea, the hot sun, eating grilled octopus and drinking retsina in beach side cafes. As I wrote *One Bed*, I took inspiration from the picture of us pinned to the board next to my screen. It was taken on Red Beach, when we were young, tanned, slim and happy. And, possibly, tipsy. We're still happy, but not young, or tanned. Nor, sadly, slim! But writing *One Bed* was a lovely trip down memory lane.

My grateful thanks to my lovely editors Charlotte and Arsalan, who took what was initially a winding, throw-everything-at-it first draft, and helped me turn this manuscript from an ugly duckling into what I think is a swan. Writers are deeply introspective and often insecure, and I've felt Bea's angst often over my ten-plus year career, and writing this book was waaay cheaper than therapy! To

Katherine Gerbara, my writing partner (who got a blow-by-blow description of Golly's antics), thank you for being my sounding board and a happy, lovely presence on Whatsapp every weekday morning! She bears the brunt of me moaning about my characters going rogue, my plots not plotting and my words not wording.

I'm also grateful to Vaughan, my partner in life, and in travel. Although he's an intermittent reader (I know, I don't understand it either), he's an unfailing font of encouragement, and constantly reminds me that my wings are strong enough to keep me aloft and flying. To my kids Rourke and Tess, as you are both about to graduate from uni, remember that it's better to have a passport full of stamps than a house full of stuff.

The author and One More Chapter would like to thank everyone
who contributed to the publication of this story...

Analytics
James Brackin
Abigail Fryer

Audio
Fionnuala Barrett
Ciara Briggs

Contracts
Sasha Duszynska
Lewis

Design
Lucy Bennett
Fiona Greenway
Liane Payne
Dean Russell

Digital Sales
Lydia Grainge
Hannah Lismore
Emily Scorer

Editorial
Arsalan Isa
Charlotte Ledger
Laura McCallen
Ajebowale Roberts
Jennie Rothwell
Emily Thomas

Harper360
Emily Gerbner
Jean Marie Kelly
emma sullivan
Sophia Wilhelm

International Sales
Peter Borcsok
Ruth Burrow

Marketing & Publicity
Chloe Cummings
Emma Petfield

Operations
Melissa Okusanya
Hannah Stamp

Production
Denis Manson
Simon Moore
Francesca Tuzzeo

Rights
Helena Font Brillas
Ashton Mucha
Zoe Shine
Aisling Smythe

**The HarperCollins
Distribution Team**

**The HarperCollins
Finance & Royalties
Team**

**The HarperCollins
Legal Team**

**The HarperCollins
Technology Team**

Trade Marketing
Ben Hurd

UK Sales
Laura Carpenter
Isabel Coburn
Jay Cochrane
Sabina Lewis
Holly Martin
Harriet Williams
Leah Woods

**And every other
essential link in the
chain from delivery
drivers to booksellers
to librarians and
beyond!**

YOUR NUMBER ONE STOP

ONE MORE CHAPTER

FOR PAGETURNING BOOKS

One More Chapter is an
award-winning global
division of HarperCollins.

Sign up to our newsletter to get our
latest eBook deals and stay up to date
with our weekly Book Club!
<u>Subscribe here.</u>

Meet the team at
<u>www.onemorechapter.com</u>

Follow us!
🐦 <u>@OneMoreChapter_</u>
📘 <u>@OneMoreChapter</u>
📷 <u>@onemorechapterhc</u>

Do you write unputdownable fiction?
We love to hear from new voices.
Find out how to submit your novel at
<u>www.onemorechapter.com/submissions</u>